MIDDLE ENGLISH

HUMOROUS TALES IN

VERSE

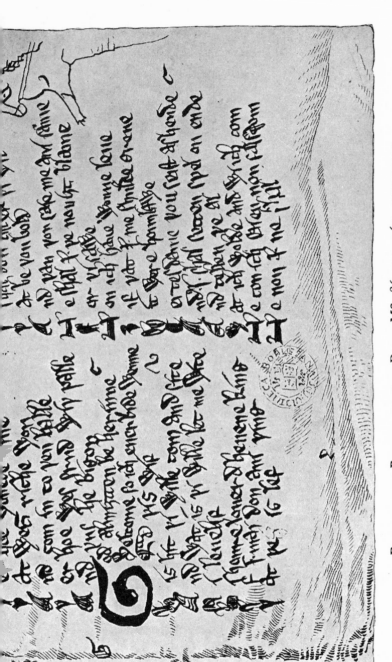

PHOTOGRAPHIC REPRODUCTION OF DIGBY MS. 86, FOL. 165, CONTAINING

THE BEGINNING OF THE FABLIAU, DAME SIRIZ

MIDDLE ENGLISH

HUMOROUS TALES IN

VERSE

Edited by
GEORGE H. McKNIGHT, Ph.D.

GORDIAN PRESS
NEW YORK
1971

Originally Published 1913
Reprinted 1971

Published by GORDIAN PRESS, INC.
Library of Congress Catalog Number 78-128190
SBN 87752-131-Y

Preface

I wish to offer due apology for the elaborate critical setting provided for three simple tales. It cannot be assumed that introduction, notes, and glossary will add to the entertainment afforded by these stories. The justification for the editor's work lies in the fact that these humorous tales have a serious interest. They are interesting not merely as affording specimens of the language of an earlier period, but as illustrating what may be called the comedy-relief element in the literature of an age that produced the *Cursor Mundi* and the *Ayenbite of Inwit,* and as affording an idea of the mode of diffusion of popular tales and the use made of them by literature.

I wish it were possible more fully to share the pleasures of the chase enjoyed in tracing the courses followed by these three stories. The hunt for sources and parallels has led, now into arid compilations like those by John of Bromyard and Vincent of Beauvais, again into the midst of the luxuriant oriental fictions of Nachshebi and Somadeva, again among the fresh folk-tales of Saxon, Breton, Finn, Berber, and American Negro. I realize that the pleasures of the hunt are not easily communicable, but it is my hope that some of the trophies of the hunt, mounted and arranged in the introduction to this volume, may have a scientific value.

In the texts of the present volume the capitalization and the punctuation are modern, except in the case of proper names, in which the manuscript form has been reproduced. Abbreviations also have been expanded. In other respects it has been my aim to reproduce the manuscript texts exactly. With this in view I have collated the proofs with rotographic copies of the manuscripts. The glossary aims to be exhaustive, including all the words and forms of words in the three texts. In the introduction the discussion of the language in each text has been made brief because of the full lists of forms collected in the glossary.

It is my pleasure to acknowledge courtesies shown me at the Harvard University Library, the Cornell University Library, and the British Museum Library, while I was making preliminary studies in the preparation of this book. I also wish to acknowledge suggestions for notes received from Professors J. M. Hart and W. Strunk, Jr., of Cornell University, and from Professor F. Tupper, Jr., of the University of Vermont, and helpful suggestions in the preparation of the manuscript as well as assistance in revising the proofs, from Professor Flügel, general editor of the series.

G. H. McK.

Contents

Introduction

Or me convient tel chose dire
Dont je vos puisse fere rire.
Quar je sai bien, ce est la pure,
Que de sarmun n'aves vos cure
Ne de cors seint oïr la vie.
De ce ne vos prent nule envie,
Mes de tel chose qui vose plese.

.   .   .   .   .

Roman de Renard, Prol. to Branch IV.

The Humorous Element in Middle English Narrative Literature

Narrative literature in English before the Norman
Conquest expresses the ideals of an aristocratic form of
society. It is rich in tales of heroic valor and saintly
fortitude, which are uniformly dignified in manner and
elevated in tone. There has recently been brought to
light evidence [1] of a taste less severe, in the form of
comic stories preserved from oblivion because they served
as material for experiments in Latin versification. But
there is no evidence that these more trivial tales formed
a part of the repertory of the dignified scop.

In the centuries immediately following the Norman
Conquest, literature in the English language can hardly
be said to have had an independent development. In the
main it reflects the fashions prevailing in the contempo-

---

1 W. P. Ker, *On the History of the Ballads*, 1100–1300, pp. 13, 14, and
footnote. (Repr. from *Proc. of Brit. Acad.* vol. IV.) London, 1910.

rary writings in French. Hence it is that one wishing
to find the source of literary tendencies in English during
this period, must look in French literature.

The literature in French in the period following the
Norman Conquest was much more broadly representative
of the different sides of human life than that in Anglo-
Saxon had been. If we narrow our attention to narrative, we find, corresponding to the dignified English epic
tales and legendary narratives, similarly dignified French
Chansons de geste, courtly romances, and saintly legends.
But along with the *Chanson de Roland* and its class and
the romances of Chrétien de Troyes and of his school,
there flourished tales less conventional in form and re-
flecting the gay and the humorous side of humanity.

These less serious tales seem to have owed their origin
in great part to a spirit of revolt [1] against the rigidity of the
ideals of chivalry and of religion and against the stiffness
and formality of prevailing literary conventions. This spirit
of revolt, which in lyric poetry produced the Goliardic
songs and in connection with the liturgical drama produced the Feast of Fools and the *Prose of the Ass*,
made itself distinctly felt in narrative literature. Already
in the *Pélerinage de Charlemagne*, of the last half of
the eleventh century, there is a spirit of burlesque, and
in the course of the twelfth and thirteenth centuries there
came into being a series of literary productions quite an-
tagonistic to the contemporary chivalrous productions.
The gallantry that informs the lyrics of the troubadours
and the romances of the Round Table has its counter-
part in the keen, often savage, ridicule of women that

---

[1] Cf. W. Pater, *The Renaissance*, pp. 1, 26.

forms the subject matter of an important body of French satirical writings. In a similar manner the reaction from the solemn piety of the saintly legends and devout tales leads to a series [1] of burlesque writings such as the *Martyre de saint Bacchus*, the *Miracles de saint Tortu et de saint Hareng*, or the *Fabliaus de Coquaigne*.

This gayer spirit manifests itself in another way in the attention paid to the more popular elements of contemporary story. The *trouvère*, no longer interested exclusively in the themes of court life or of the church, turned his attention also to situations in every day life and to the stories of contemporary folk-lore. The result was the production of two highly interesting sets of tales, the *fabliaux* and the branches of the *Roman de Renard*. The material of the *fabliaux* is derived in part from literary collections of stories used for conveying moral instruction, but much more often from tales in popular oral circulation, whether literary or oral in ultimate origin. The beast-epic tales also are derived sometimes, directly or indirectly, from the literary fable collections, but much more often from the animal tales of popular lore. The two sets of stories are alike, not only in a similar popular source of material, but in a similar manner of handling. Both in beast-tale and in *fabliau* there is manifest the inclination to emphasize the human or individual interest rather than the spiritual content, to tell the story for the story's sake. In the branches of the *Roman de Renard*, instead of the earlier literary type, the fable, which is little more than the concrete expression of an abstract idea, an animated proverb, we

1 Cf. J. Bédier, *Les Fabliaux*, p. 363.

have a new literary genre with distinctly individual characters; in the *fabliaux*, instead of stories like those of
the *Disciplina Clericalis*, or the *exempla* of Jacques de
Vitry or Étienne de Bourbon, used in literature princi-
pally to convey moral instruction, we have stories told
for their own intrinsic interest, edged with satire, and
embellished with much realistic and humorous detail.
The two extremes in the literary tendencies of the period,
so well represented in the two parts of the *Roman de la
Rose*, the idealism of Guillaume de Lorris contrasting
with the cynicism of Jean de Meun, finds further illus-
tration in the similar contrast between the excessive
idealism of the Round Table romances on the one hand
and, on the other, the realism combined with burlesque
in the *Roman de Renard* and the realism combined with
satire in the *fabliaux*.

If the tendencies of courtly French literature are reflected in English writings, it is to be expected that the
literature of reaction and revolt also should have its re-
presentatives in English. The number of such productions in English is not great but is fairly representative
of the several classes in French. Burlesque is represented
in English by *The Order of Fair-Ease*, an account of
an order of monks exhibiting all the characteristic monk-
ish vices, and by the *Land of Cokaygne*, a description of a
moral topsy-turvy land, or mock paradise,[1] in which —

> Al is dai nis þer no niȝte
> þer nis baret noþer strif
> Nis þer no deþ ac euer lif

. . . . .

[1] A similar theme is later handled in the seventeenth century in " An
Invitation to Lubberland, with an account of the great Plenty of that
fruitful country," repr. from the Roxburghe Ballads by John Ashton, *Hu-
mour, Wit, and Satire of the Seventeenth Century*, p. 34.

Nis þer flei, fle, no lowse
In cloþ, in toune, bed no house

.   .   .   .   .   .

þer beþ riuers grate and fine,
Of oile, melk, honi, and wine.
Water seruiþ þer to no þing
Bot to siȝt and to waussing.

Of the beast-epic tales English literature before
Chaucer can offer but one representative. England, if
we may believe Mr. Jacobs,[1] was the " home of the
Fable during the early Middle Age, and the centre of
dispersion whence the Mediaeval Æsop spread through
Europe." The contributions of the Englishmen, Odo
of Sherington and John of Sheppey, to medieval fable
literature are well known. It is equally well known that
Marie de France, in her famous collection of fables, and
Nicole Bozon, in the beast tales of his *Contes Moralisés*,
drew largely from English sources. Throughout the English literature of the thirteenth and fourteenth centuries,
for example in the *Ayenbite of Inwyt*, in *Piers Plowman*,
and in the *Gesta Romanorum*, fables appear not infrequently. Further, Lydgate is the author of a collection
of seven fables, and the Scotchman, Robert Henryson,
composed a collection consisting of a prologue and
thirteen fables, which in interest vie with the tales of
the beast-epic. In the light of these facts it seems strange
that we should have from the Middle English period,
before the *Noune Preestes Tale*, but the solitary specimen of the beast-epic tale in the story of *Vox and Wolf*
included in the present volume, and that the other
captivating tales of the French *Roman de Renard* should

---

1 J. W. Jacobs, *The Fables of Æsop*, I. pp. xvii., 181.

not appear in English until the end of the fifteenth century, when Caxton translated them from the Flemish.

That tales of the kind forming the subject-matter of the *fabliaux* circulated among the English population we have evidence in contemporary allusions. Oxford University in 1292 issued a warning against the "cantilenas sive fabulas de omasiis vel luxoriosis aut ad libidinem sonantibus." [1] In *Piers Plowman* and elsewhere there are frequent, usually disapproving, allusions [2] to tales of the kind. And have we not the evidence afforded by Chaucer in the kind of tales assigned by him to his characters of lower station? That many of the stories of French *fabliaux* not extant in English in *fabliau* form were well known among the English population, is further shown by the existence of English ballad versions of the French tales. For example,[3] the English ballad of *Queen Eleanor's Confession* tells the story of the French *fabliau*, *Du Chevalier qui fist sa femme confesse* (Montaiglon-Raynaud, I. 16); and the ballad, *The Boy and the Mantle*, handles the theme of the *fabliau*, *Le Mantel mautaillé* (III. 55). Many of the *fabliau* themes also appear in literature in various collections of stories in English. Within the framework of

1 Cited by Brandl, *Paul's Grundriss*, II. p. 629.

2 *Piers Plowman* (ed. Skeat), A 1. 48–50, B IV. 115, V. 413, XIII. 228 ff., 304 ff., 352 ff., CVII. 185–186, 194, CVIII. 22, 90–96, CIX. 49–50. Cf. also the allusions in Cursor Mundi, etc., quoted below, p. xviii.

3 Other English ballads with themes of the *fabliau* sort are : *Our Goodman* (Child, 274); *Get up and bar the Door* (275); *The Friar in the Well* (276), cf. the later English *fabliau*, *The Wright's Chaste Wife; The Wife wrapped in Wether's Skin* (277), cf. the later English *fabliau*, *The Wife in Morel's Skin; The Farmer's Curst Wife* (278); and *The Crafty Farmer* (283). The ruses employed in *The Lochmaben Harper* (192) and *Dick o' the Cow* (185) remind one of *fabliaux*.

the *Seven Sages* are included several such tales in verse, and in the Middle English *Disciplina Clericalis*, the philosopher makes use of several in the instruction of his son. The concrete methods of conveying moral instruction in use during the thirteenth and fourteenth centuries supplied a use for humorous tales, and the *Gesta Romanorum*, that compendium of tales ingeniously, often naïvely, applied to the conveyance [1] of moral doctrine, contains tales that serve as the subject matter for *fabliaux*. The *narrationes* that formed so conspicuous a feature of the sermons of the period were not always grave in tone, and books for moral instruction, such as Robert Mannyng's work of forbidding title, the *Handlyng Synne*, contain tales that are decidedly diverting in character.

To the superiority in vitality, then, of story collections over isolated stories and to the concrete methods of the medieval preacher we owe a number of Middle English humorous tales in verse. But of the single narrative interludes, if we may speak of the *fabliaux* as such, the comedy numbers in the minstrel repertory, we have few surviving specimens before Chaucer. Such productions were probably ephemeral, only occasionally regarded as worthy the parchment and the labor of writing. In fact the name *fabliau* seems to have stood for the transitory in literature. Henri d'Andeli,[2] in writing a serious tale, remarks, "Ce poème n'était pas un fabliau — il l'écrit sur du parchemin, et non sur des tablettes de cire." At all events, corresponding to about one hun-

1 For example the theme of the *Sir Cleges* appears in a tale of the *Gesta Romanorum*.

2 Bédier, *op. cit.* p. 38.

dred and fifty [1] French *fabliaux* of the period between
1159 and 1320, English [2] literature has but little to show.
Besides the *Dame Siriz,* included in the present volume, the only humorous tale in verse before the time
of Chaucer dealing exclusively with human beings is
the *Pennyworth of Wit.* Even this story, although it
handles a well known *fabliau* [3] motive, handles it in
such a way as to make classification uncertain. The emphasis is thrown on the lesson rather than on the incidents. The characters are not distinctly portrayed; they
are not even distinguished by personal names. Except
in somewhat greater fullness of detail there is little to
distinguish this story commonly classed as a *fabliau* from
a dry *exemplum* or a barren apologue.

Somewhat later in English literature, stories of the kind
that formed the subject matter of the *fabliaux* are more
frequent. A great deal of emphasis has been laid of late [4]
upon Chaucer's contribution to the development of the
fabliau in English and on the other hand to Chaucer's
indebtedness in narrative art to the earlier writers of
fabliaux. Besides producing his *fabliau* masterpieces,

1 Bédier, *op. cit.,* in his treatment of the subject includes 147.

2 Several of the French *fabliaux* were composed in England. Cf. Bédier,
op. cit. pp. 436–440.

3 It forms the subject of the French *fabliau, De la Bourse Pleine de Sens*
and of the German metrical tale of *Ehefrau und Bulerin* (*Gesammtaben-
teur,* no. xxxv.). In Middle English the story appears in two versions:
a longer version, *A Pennyworth of Wit* (printed by Kölbing, *Englische
Studien,* VII. III, and elsewhere), and a shorter version, *How a Mer-
chaunde dyd hys wyfe betray* (printed by Kölbing, *loc. cit.* and elsewhere).
The story was also popular in a later, chap-book version, of which numerous editions are to be found in the chap-book collections of the Harvard
University library and the British Museum library. The latest edition that
I have seen was in an Edinburgh bookstore. It was published by T. John-
son, Falkirk, 1815.

4 See the articles by H. S. Canby and W. M. Hart referred to in the
Bibliography.

Chaucer seems to have stimulated the production of English *fabliaux* by others. To Chaucer's influence must probably be referred Adam Cobsam's *The Wright's Chaste Wife*, *The Lady Prioress and her Suitors*, formerly attributed to Lydgate, the tale of *The Pardoner and the Tapster*, which served as an introduction to the pseudo-Chaucerian *Tale of Beryn*, and the *Freiris of Berwik*, attributed to Dunbar. Besides these tales with some degree of literary pretension, the fifteenth century was also familiar with certain more popular stories related in subject matter at least to the *fabliaux*. This class of ' bourdes,' as they were commonly called, includes the tale of *Sir Corneus*, or the *Cokewold's Dance*, the " god borde" of *The King and the Barker*, and the *Tale of the Basin*. Later on, also, the early printers, Wynkyn de Worde, William Copland, and others, catered to the taste of their time by publishing editions of humorous metrical tales in the form of booklets or tracts. To this means of preservation we owe the survival of a number of later tales of the *fabliau* order. These " Mery Iestes," as they were called, include the tales of *Dane Hewe of Leicestre*, the *Frere and the Boy*, the *Miller of Abyngton*, the *Vnluckie Firmentie*, the *Wyfe in Morrelles Skin*, and *How the Plowman lerned his Pater Noster*. In imitation of these stories the youthful Sir Thomas More composed his *Mery Iest how a Sergeaunt wold lerne to be a Frere*.

Besides the beast-epic tale, the *Vox and the Wolf*, and the *fabliau*, the *Dame Siriz*, the present volume contains a third humorous tale in verse, the *Sir Cleges*. This story is not easy to classify, consisting, as it does, of a humorous incident combined with a devout tale to make a Round Table romance. The story of the 'blows shared' is of the kind that form the themes of *fabliaux*, but the form of the story as a whole and the spirit in which it is told are not those of *fabliaux*. The story is a unique specimen in English, a humorous metrical romance.

A partial explanation of the smallness in the number of Middle English humorous tales is to be found no doubt in the opposition due to English puritanism. The evidence of Chaucer in this connection is well known. Chaucer's "gentils" object to tales of "ribaudye," and Chaucer himself apologizes for the "cherles tale" of the Miller and promises in compensation —

> . . . ynowe, grete and smale,
> Of storial thyng that toucheth gentilesse,
> And eek moralitee and hoolynesse.

The author of *Piers Plowman* also repeatedly [1] condemns "harlotries," as he calls the low stories, attributing them to the "deueles disours." Allusions of a condemnatory nature are not infrequent elsewhere. The author of *Cursor Mundi* says: [2] —

> As ȝeddyngis, japis, and folies
> And alle harlotries and ribaudies,
> Bot to here of Cristis Passioun
> To many a man it is ful laytsom.

In one of the lyrical [3] poems appears the reference: —

> þah told beon tales vntoun in toune.

1 See footnote to p. xiv above. For a description of the professional purveyors of such tales, see *Piers Plowman* (ed. Skeat) B XIII. 226, 237.
2 MS. Ashmole 60, f. 4, 5. Quoted by Halliwell, *Thornton Romances*, p. 261.
3 Harl. MS. 2253 (ed. Böddeker), W. L. IV. 37 (p. 153).

At the opening of the romance *Octavian* [1] appear the two following significant stanzas: —

> Bot fele men be of swyche manere,
> Goodnesse when hy scholden here,
> Hy nylled naght lesste with her ere,
>   To lerny wyt,
> But as a swyn with lowryng cher
>   All gronne he sytte.

> And fele of hem casted a cry
> Of thyng þat fallyd to rybaudy,
> That noon of hem, that sytte hym by,
>   May haue no lest.
> God schylde all thys company
>   Fram swych a gest.

Evidently the purveyor of reputable tales felt the competition. Ribald tales were plentiful enough, but they seem not to have appealed strongly to the class of people for whom literary versions were produced in English.

The gayety of *l'esprit gaulois* in the French *fabliaux*, and the tragic quality imparted to the Italian descendants of these tales, have often been commented upon. From the small number of examples it is hardly safe to draw any broad generalizations concerning the English *fabliaux*. It seems possible, however, to discover the influence of English puritanism affecting the quality as well as the number of English stories. M. Bédier [2] cites one of the French *fabliaux* which was composed by an Englishman. In this *fabliau* of English origin, the broad story of the French *Bourgeoise d' Orléans* is provided

---

[1] Octavian (ed. Sarazzin), South. version, stanzas 2, 3.
[2] *Op. cit.* p. 300.

with chivalrous setting and moral tone. We cannot say of the English of the thirteenth, fourteenth, and fifteenth centuries what Tacitus said of the early Teutons, that no one laughed at vice. But we can say that it was very unusual for them to laugh *with* vice. In all but one of the humorous stories mentioned above, before Chaucer and after Chaucer, the fun is at the expense of vice. The one exception is the *Dame Siriz*. In several of the other tales the fun is coarser, but in no other do we see a representation of vice triumphant. One of the greatest of Chaucer's literary contemporaries, in a masterpiece, *Sir Gawain and the Green Knight*, read morality into Arthurian romance. The same preoccupation with moral content did not work out as happily in some cases. In the *Sir Cleges*, a comic incident loses in humorous effect on account of the serious setting provided. In the *Pennyworth of Wit*, a tale which in French and particularly in German is enlivened by boisterous scenes and diverting details is quite stripped of these lighter elements. The tone is more that of Wulfstan than of Chaucer. The puritan spirit is obvious. The homelier ideals of the middle-class English-speaking element would not tolerate some of the liberties permitted in the more highly cultured French-speaking circles. Perhaps the inferior culture of the English-speaking class helps to explain why in these tales the moral is made so baldly prominent, why finer weapons were not used.

The three stories in the present volume will serve to illustrate the humorous element in Middle English narrative literature. The first two will illustrate what may be called the anti-chivalrous element in medieval literature, the kind of material to which Chaucer turned with profit in his later years when he was emancipated from the formal conventions of contemporary chivalry. A real appreciation of the work of Chaucer demands a knowledge of the cruder beginnings in a kind of writing at which he excelled.

DAME SIRIZ [1]

The story of Dame Siriz is perhaps one such as the world would very willingly let die. In fact the modern world has not found the story a congenial one. A story which, besides being known in several Latin versions, appeared also in the vernacular literatures of England, France, Spain, Italy, Germany, and Iceland, to say nothing of the oriental versions in Greek, Hebrew, Syriac, Arabic, Persian, and Sanskrit, a story which had a place in the stock of stories drawn upon by medieval preachers, and in the repertoire of medieval secular story tellers or minstrels, which was to be found in the fable collections of Germany, France, the Netherlands, Spain and England, and which supplied the story for dramatic productions in Denmark, Germany, France and England, is hardly known at the present day except to antiquarians. The theme of the story is in some respects repellent to the modern mind. Yet a tale once so widely known has an historic interest, and the history of the tale in its migrations is entertaining and instructive. Moreover, in the history of English literature the story

1 The form Siriz is preferred, because that is the form used in the title in the manuscript. That the pronunciation, however, was Sirith is proved by the rimes.

of Dame Siriz has a claim to attention because it is the earliest representative of its class, the *fabliau*, in fact the only English composition designated in the original title as a *fabliau*, and because its story is that of the earliest play with secular theme in English literature, — according to Creizenach,[1] "one of the best products of the medieval comic muse." Such considerations may serve as the apology for the appearance of the story in the present book.

There has been much controversy in recent years concerning the provenience of popular stories. In particular the theory of Benfey and his school that India was the great repository of popular stories, and that from India stories were distributed into other countries, has been sharply attacked.[2] In this connection the story of Dame Siriz is of interest and seems to be one instance in support of the theory of Indian, or at least oriental, origin.

It has long been recognized that this story is essentially oriental in character. Reduced to its more general terms, the story runs as follows: — A young man loves a lady. A procuress wins his suit for him by exhibiting to the lady a bitch, usually a weeping bitch. This bitch, the procuress asserts, was once a lady, but she has been thus transformed[3] because under circumstances similar to

---

[1] W. Creizenach, *Geschichte des neueren Dramas*, I. 454.

[2] Cf. J. Bédier, *Les Fabliaux*.

[3] A transformation of a woman into a bitch appears in an Arabic version of the story of the 'Three Wishes.' (Freytag, *Arabum proverbia*, I, 687, quoted by Liebrecht, *Orient and Occident*, III. 378.) A similar story is cited by R. Bassett (*Rev. des trad. pop.* XV. 150). In a Turkish story (*Plaisir après la Peine*, trad. J. A. Decourdemanche, Paris, 1896, pp. 113 ff.), a woman is converted into a mule by a man with the power of sorcery, because she rejected his love overtures.

those in which the lady addressed is placed, she refused
to yield to overtures of love. The idea of transformation [1] seems to be rooted in the oriental idea of me-
tempsychosis.

A priori evidence, then, seems to point to an orien-
al origin for this tale. Corroborative evidence is to be
found in an examination of the facts in the history of
the story. In Indian literature the story appears in two
versions. In the *Kathá Sarit Sagara*,[2] or " Ocean of
the Streams of Story," composed by Somadeva Bhatta
in the early part of the twelfth century A. D., the story
appears as a subordinate element in another story, which
itself appears in various versions in oriental and in occidental literature, the story of the man who has a talis-
man — in this particular case, a red lotus given by the
god, Siva — by which he may recognize any unfaith-
fulness on the part of his wife. In the story of Somadeva,
four merchants undertake to test the faithfulness of the
wife and have recourse to a female ascetic who makes
use of the ruse of the weeping bitch. In this case the
ruse is unsuccessful, and the suitors are subjected to indig-
nities. The fact must not be lost sight of that the weeping bitch incident here is a minor one in an independent story, and that relatively this version is not early.

Another Indian version [3] of the story is the one in

---

1 Transformations of human beings into beasts are, however, by no
means unknown to occidental literature. For instance, think of the story
of Circe, of the werwolves, of the Golden Ass of Apuleius, of the unfriendly
stepmothers of medieval story.

2 English translation by C. H. Tawney, Calcutta, 1880, vol. I. pp. 85–
91.

3 *Çukasaptati, Textus Simplicior*, transl. into German by R. Schmidt,
Kiel, 1894; *Textus Ornatior*, transl. into German by R. Schmidt, Stuttgart, 1899.

the *Çukasaptati,* or "Seventy Tales of a Parrot." It is
the second tale of the collection, and here appears independently. In this version of the story, a young man,
Vira by name, loves the princess Çaçiprabhā. His
mother, Yaçōdēvi, exhibits to Çaçiprabhā a dog which,
she asserts, in a former existence was a sister to herself
and to Çaçiprabhā, but has been born as a dog in the
present existence on account of her chastity. Moved
by her fears, the princess is induced to grant her love to
Vira.

From the *Çukasaptati*[1] this tale seems to have found
its way into the *Book of Sindibad,*[2] the oriental version
of the *Seven Sages.* In the *Book of Sindibad* the second
tale of the fourth vizier has affinity with two tales of
the *Çukasaptati.* It seems to be the result of a fusion
of the first and second tales of the Indian collection. In
the first of these tales a go-between has persuaded a
lady to accept the love of a suitor, but, unable to find
her client, by mistake she brings the lady's husband instead. The lady, with ready wit, lays the blame on her
husband and says she has tested him and proved him
unfaithful. Only after protracted supplication is the husband restored to grace. It will be noted that the first
part of this tale is like the second tale in the use of a go-
between, and it is not difficult to see how in this case
fusion might be the result of confusion.

Thus combined, the story of ' The Go-between and
the dog' and that of ' The Libertine Husband,' itself

1 Cf. D. Comparetti, *Researches respecting the Book of Sindibad,* transl.
by Coote, *Folk Lore Society,* London, 1882.
2 For a table showing the contents of the different versions of the *Book
of Sindibad,* see Bédier, *Les Fabliaux,* pp. 136, 137.

well known in occidental as well as in oriental literature, appear in all the oriental versions of the *Seven Sages* except the late [1] Persian *Sindibād Nāma*, in which the two tales are distinct. The various versions of the tale in the different oriental versions of the *Seven Sages* differ among themselves in details, but as a group tell a tale distinct from either Indian version. Perhaps the most striking point of difference between the Indian versions and those of the *Book of Sindibad* is in the cause of the transformation from woman to bitch. In both Indian versions a woman in one existence has been re-born as a bitch because she did not satisfy the elements of her nature. In all the versions of the *Book of Sindibad* the woman has been transformed within the present existence because: [1] — (Syriac version) the young man "cried unto God concerning her, and she was transformed"; (Greek version) the young man "cursed her and she was changed to a dog on the spot"; (Spanish version) the young man "cursed her, and straightway she became a she-dog"; (Hebrew version) the young man "called to his God concerning her, and she was turned into a bitch"; (Arabic version translated by Scott) the lover, a Jewish sorcerer, enraged, "by magic transformed her into a she-dog"; (Persian *Sindibād Nāma*, of the 14th century) the lady [2] had been changed into that form as a punishment for rejecting a lover's suit.

The tale of 'Go-between and Weeping-Bitch' which occurs in all the versions of the oriental *Seven Sages*,

1 Cf. Elsner, p. 7. See Bibliography.
2 An analysis of the *Syndibād Nāma* by Prof. Forbes Falconer is included by W. A. Clouston in his *Book of Sindibad*, pp. 5 ff.

the *Book of Sindibad,* seems to have been lost[1] in the migration of that collection of stories from orient to occident ; it does not appear in any of the extant occidental versions of the *Seven Sages.*[2] The oldest western version of the story is contained in the famous story collection by the converted Spanish Jew, Petrus Alphonsus, the *Disciplina Clericalis,* and it was usually by means of this well-known collection that the ' Weeping-Bitch ' story became known to the countries of Western Europe. Petrus himself says that he made use of Arabic writers (Elsner,[3] *op. cit.* p. 24) and his version shows a striking similarity to the original Arabic version, notably in the fact that in both the lover falls ill and the procuress comes to him instead of his seeking her out. The most important change made by Petrus in his handling of the tale seems to be due to his aim to adapt the story to a Christian public. For that reason he emphasizes the illness of the lover and represents the go-between as saying that the lady of her fictitious story sinned in that she caused the illness of a fellow man and that for this fault God punished her (Elsner,[3] *op. cit.* p. 26).

In the *Disciplina Clericalis,*[4] besides the significant modification in the cause of the transformation, there are

1 Comparetti assumes that the loss occurred in the course of oral transmission. There seems, however, to be evidence that versions of the *Seven Sages* containing the weeping-bitch story were not unknown in the West. Cf. the versions of the tale by Herolt, by J. de Vitry, also the *Dame Sirix* and the Italian version discussed below.

2 For a table showing the contents of the different versions of the occidental *Seven Sages,* see Bédier, *op. cit.* p. 136.

3 See Bibliography.

4 Two modern editions of the Latin version : (1) *Soc. des Bibliophiles,* Paris, 1825 ; (2) F. W. Val. Schmidt, Berlin, 1827. In these two editions, the content is the same, though there is difference in phraseology.

some minor modifications. To the invention of Petrus are to be attributed peculiarities, which are summarized by Elsner as follows:—(1) The husband, on his departure, trusts implicitly in the fidelity of his wife; (2) The lover, although ill, goes out, by which means he meets the go-between; (3) The lover is at first reluctant to reveal the cause of his trouble, and when he does so, does not ask for assistance; (4) The go-between keeps her bitch without food to make it ready to eat the mustard preparation; (5) The go-between, after giving the lady advice, craftily adds, " If I had known the love of the young man for my daughter, she should not have been transformed." Through these modifications the action of the story gains in verisimilitude and the characters in distinctness.

Upon this version by Petrus Alphonsus seem to be dependent, to some [1] extent at least, all the other occidental versions of the story. Elsner, in his dissertation, has compared the details in the different versions and has attempted to show the interrelations. His conclusions are not always convincing because he has laid too much stress upon differences in minor details, which are subject to change at the caprice of the individual writer and to modification to suit the purpose for which the story is used.

In the history of the occidental versions of this story it has seemed to the present writer more interesting and profitable to consider the different uses to which the story has been put and the various literary tendencies

[1] Direct influence of an oriental version is apparent in some cases. See below.

illustrated, than to make the attempt, necessarily vain, to show the exact interrelations between the score and more of different versions.

In addition to the Latin version, or versions,[1] of the *Disciplina* there are prose translations extant in the vernacular languages of France, of Spain, of Iceland, and of England. These translations are, in general, close, but with minor variations in detail. For example, the procuress is honorably received by the lady; in the Latin version, *pro magnae religionis specie;* in the French prose version, *pour sa simple conversation.* In the Spanish version the bitch is penned up during its foodless period, a feature that persists in the later Spanish fable version. In the Latin, French, Spanish, and Icelandic versions, the bitch is given to eat bread combined with mustard; in the English version the "old wif" gave to the "fastyng hound" "brode inowogh with anynoun froted." Such modifications in the story, however, are exceptional.

More significant in the history of the story are the modifications in the French metrical versions of the *Disciplina,* entitled *Le Chastoiement d'un Père à son Fils.* One of these versions is included in the Barbazan-Méon collection of *Fabliaux et Contes.* The 'Weeping-Bitch' story in this collection occupies 148 verses, and in general follows closely the Latin version. The most striking departure is the fact that the young man in the story of the go-between not only fell ill, but *died* from grief. The other French metrical version shows more

---

[1] The two versions extant differ in phraseology, but do not differ in the details of the story.

striking features of difference. In this version,[1] which
is nearly twice as long as the one just mentioned, the
young man at first, not content with messages, tries a
personal interview. As in the other metrical version the
period of the. dog's fast is three days, instead of two
as in the Latin version. But more important than
minor differences in detail is the difference in tone. In
this longer metrical version the young man in love is
made an exponent of *l'amour cortois*, and the extended
soliloquies of the young lover (vv. 57–119, 146–190)
as well as other details, are quite in the manner of the
school of Chrétien de Troyes.

The tales of the *Disciplina Clericalis* purport to be for
the purpose of conveying instruction to a young man.
This practical side to these stories led to their inclusion
in most of the medieval collections of *exempla* intended
for use in sermons. In consequence the tale of the
'weeping-bitch' found a place in several versions[2] of
the *Gesta Romanorum*. Of the version in this collection a
most interesting feature is the ingenious, not to say naïve,
way in which the author, from unpromising material,
has drawn a moralization. According to the allegorical
interpretation the chaste wife is the soul purified by bap-
tism. The soldier husband is Christ. The lover is worldly
vanity. The go-between is the devil. The bitch is the

---

1 Two modern editions : (1) *Soc. des Bibliophiles*, Paris, 1825; (2) Ed. by
M. Roesle, Munich, 1899. In edition (1) there are 388 verses in the ' weeping-bitch' story; in (2), a critical edition, there are 368.

2 This story does not appear in the Middle English *Gesta Romanorum.*
It appears, however, in the following continental versions : (1) Edition
publ. by Keller, Stuttgart, 1842; (2) Edition publ. by Oesterley, Berlin,
1871; (3) MS. Colmar Issenheim, 10, fol. 32. These references are from
Elsner, *op. cit.* p. 26. (4) *Le Violier des Histoires Romaines*, ed. by M. G
Brunet, Paris, 1858.

hope of long life and too much presuming on the mercy of God, because, just as that bitch was weeping from mustard, so hope frequently afflicts the soul.

Other *exempla* versions of this story are to be found in the *Preceptorium nouum et perutile* by Gotscaldus Hollen and the *Destructorium vitiorum* by Alexander de Hales. Both these somewhat condensed versions profess to be from Petrus,[1] and though containing some variant[2] details are probably drawn directly from the *Disciplina*. Still other versions used as *exempla* are the condensed ones in the *Scala Celi* by Johannes Gobii, in the *Promptuarium exemplorum* by Johannes Herolt, and in the *Speculum Morale* attributed to Vincentius Bellovacenses. These three versions Elsner concludes to be derived from the tale in the *Gesta Romanorum*, mainly on the ground that in the *Gesta Romanorum* the young man in the fictitious story of the go-between not only is ill but *dies* on account of love denied. The first and third, however, of these versions profess to be derived from Petrus Alphonsus, and the version by Herolt[3] agrees almost word for word with that of Vincentius, and there seems good reason for accepting the statements of the authors. The fact that the lover is represented as dying may be explained by the fact that these three authors of *exempla* drew not directly from the Latin *Disciplina* but from one of the doubtless more popularly known French metrical versions, in both of which the feature of the lover's death appears. These

1 " Alphigus " in the *Destructorium*.
2 See the end of the *Destructorium*.
3 The story of the ' weeping dog ' in Herolt's *Promptuarium* is credited to the *Seven Wise Masters*. Cf. T. F. Crane, *Exempla of Jacques de Vitry*, p. lxxvii.

three much condensed versions in their minor details correspond more closely to the metrical versions than to the one in the *Gesta Romanorum*, notably in the bitch's *three* days fast in the *Scala Celi* and in the personal wooing by the lover in Herolt and in the *Speculum Morale*.

In addition to the *exempla* versions thus far mentioned, all of which are related more or less directly to the version in the *Disciplina Clericalis*, there remain to be considered two others, in which the relationship is less close. The first one, by Jacques de Vitry (no. CCL.), is important because early.[1] The most striking peculiarities of this version, which is also included in Wright's *A Selection of Latin Stories* (no. xiii.), are as follows: — (1) The go-between at first fails in her attempts; (2) She bids the young man feign illness; (3) The bitch was once "a certain woman," not "daughter"; (4) The young man, when ill, by certain spells changed the woman into a bitch. This God permitted for her sin in letting a man die whom she might have saved. As Elsner has pointed out, here is a mingling of oriental and occidental characteristics. Oriental[2] are the repeated attempt of the go-between, the relationship of go-between to bitch, and the use of spells by the young man. Like the western versions based on the *Disciplina*, on the other hand, are the death of the lover in the story

1 " The first to regularly employ in sermons *exempla*, or narratives to instruct the people, as well as to keep up their attention when it was likely to flag, was Jacques de Vitry, who died at Rome in the year 1240." — W. A. Clouston, *Popular Tales and Fictions*, p. 11.

2 That the oriental version of this tale was known in western Europe seems to be indicated by the fact that in Herolt's *Promptuarium* the tale is attributed to the *Seven Wise Masters*.

of the go-between, the use of bread and *mustard*, and the fact that God permitted the transformation on account of the woman's sin. Peculiar to this version is the advice of the go-between to the young man to feign illness.

The other variant *exemplum* version is the one in the *Contes Moralisés* of Nicole Bozon (No. 138). The striking features of this version are as follows : — (1) The lady wooed is a *demoiselle*; [1] (2) The go-between is a *deablesse*; [2] (3) The lover is a clerk who had long wooed the *demoiselle* and who paid the go-between for her assistance; (4) In the story of the go-between, the lover, also a clerk, died of grief; (5) The bitch had been a daughter of the go-between; (6) God was angry and transformed the daughter into a bitch; (7) The go-between at the end remarks that death takes but one life, but *"par baudestrote"* are killed three at one time, *"sa alme e deus autres."* It will be noted that this version contains some [3] of the distinctive traits of the versions based upon the *Disciplina* version. It will be noted also that in several respects the version is independent. The distinctive peculiarities of this version, however, do not seem to be due to the influence of the oriental versions. Most interesting for the purpose of the present volume is the fact that the lover's part is played by a clerk who has

---

1 In this respect like the English *Interludium*.

2 In the play of Hansen, the go-between, before making use of the weeping-bitch device, has sent a devil to the lady in vain. At the end of the version in the *Destructorium*, allusion is made to the fact that the lady has successfully resisted a devil. In the " Metrical Tales of Adolfus," the go-between is referred to as " Daemonis adjutrix."

3 The death of the lover, and the transformation by God.

wooed the lady in vain, a feature which appears elsewhere only in the *Dame Siriz* and the related *Interludium* [1] and in the late Latin [2] version. It is well
known that Nicole Bozon in his collection of stories
drew freely from English popular sources, and it seems
not improbable that this feature of this eclectic version
may be related directly or indirectly to the English
fabliau version or to the English dramatic version upon
which the *fabliau* is based.

About the time of the invention of printing the stories of the *Disciplina Clericalis* were introduced into
the European book of Æsop. About 1480 Heinrich
Stainhöwel made a fable collection in German and
Latin including, besides fables proper collected from
various sources, also "*fabulae collectae*," comprising
the stories of the *Disciplina Clericalis* and the *Facetiae*
of Poggio. Versions of this fable collection appeared in
Italian, French, Spanish, Dutch, and English. In this
way the tale of the ' weeping-bitch ' found a place in
European fable collections, and the version of the story
in Caxton's ' *Fables of Æsop* ' is the earliest printed
version in English. The form of the story in the different fable versions does not differ save in minor details. It seems to have been derived from Petrus Alphonsus, but indirectly. In minor details it resembles
more the story as told in the expanded French metrical version, which no doubt was more popularly
known. For example, the young man makes direct suit

---

1 Bozon's version agrees with that of the *Interludium* in that the lover
is a clerk, the lady a maiden. Is it not probable that Bozon's tale offers
a condensed form of the tale of which the fragmentary *Interludium* gives
the first part?

2 Published by Tobler. See Bibliography.

to the lady, the period of the dog's fast is three days,
the young man in the story of the go-between dies.
In still another respect it resembles the *roman cortois* [1]
rather than the moral tale, in that instead of God it is
the gods that, from pity for the lover, turn the daughter of the go-between into a bitch. An interesting feature of Caxton's version is that the woman is converted
into a cat, probably due to one of Caxton's characteristic blunders in translation, the Latin *catella* being
mistaken for 'cat.'

This tale, which was included by Caxton in his
Æsop, did not find a permanent place in English fable
collections. It does not appear in the Wynkyn de
Worde collection of 1503. Nor does it appear in the
later collection by Bullokar in 1585, nor in the later
collections by Ogilby, by L'Estrange, and by Croxall.

The story of the 'weeping-bitch' appears in an
interesting guise in the *Metrical Tales of Adolfus*
(*Fabula* V.). Here again is evident the influence of
contemporary literary fashions. The story, in Latin
verse, though condensed, is told in an elaborate and
artificial style and is filled with classical allusions and
comparisons. In this version it is Venus,[2] "*alma Cy-
pris*," the protector of the true lover, that transforms
the daughter of the go-between.

That our story was in popular oral circulation seems
to be proved by a late Latin version recently published
by Tobler.[3] This Latin version,[4] according to Tobler,

---

1 Cf. p. xxix.
2 Similarly in the *Fastnachtspiel* of Hans Sachs it is the goddess Venus
that punishes the hard-hearted lady by transformation.
3 *Zt. f. rom. Phil.* x. 476–480.
4 This version in the manuscript follows a translation of the ' elegiac

seems to have been taken down from oral transmission, and the language seems to indicate a Venetian origin. This version has a number of interesting variations from the common forms of the story, variations such as one might expect in a popular tale. The bitch in this story is a " *kiçola*," which the go-between takes from her bosom and puts in her lap. No mention is made of the dog's tears. The lady asks the old woman where she got so fine a dog. The old woman bids her not to ask because it grieves her, but at length she is prevailed upon and weepingly tells that the *kiçola* was her daughter, transformed by a young man because she had spurned his love. In this story the lover is a clerk as in the *Dame Siriz* and the *exemplum* of Nicole Bozon.

Further proof, if further proof were needed, of the universal diffusion of this tale is afforded by the number of dramatic [1] handlings of the theme. In Denmark [2] a farce was made from this story; in France Gringoire used it in *Les Fantaisies de Mere Sotte;* [3] in Germany Hans Sachs used it as the theme of one of his *Fastnachtspiele;* finally in England it supplies the story for the fragmentary *Interludium de Clerico et Puella*.

This Middle English interlude is so closely related

comedy ' *Pamphilus*, and itself resembles another ' elegiac comedy ' by one Jacobus. Perhaps it retells the story of an Italian-Latin comedy.

[1] Tales of lovers and go-betweens are handled in the Latin elegiac comedies of the twelfth and thirteenth centuries. In one of these the lover is a priest and the lady a married woman. (C. F. Gayley, *Repr. Engl. Comedies*, N. Y., 1903, p. xvii.) But in none of these does the weeping-bitch appear. (Cf. W. Creizenach, *Gesch. des neueren Dramas*, I. 26–42.)

[2] See Bibliography, Christiern Hansen's *Komedier*.

[3] This version, which is cited by Elsner from a manuscript in the *Bibliothèque Nationale*, does not appear in the Elzevir edition of the works of Gringoire, and has not been seen by the present writer.

to the English *fabliau* that the two cannot conveniently be treated apart. Hence we proceed directly to the English *fabliau* of *Dame Siriz*. In one or two instances it has already been pointed out that there is evidence that the *Book of Sindibād* version of the weeping-bitch story was not entirely unknown in Western Europe. Very conclusive evidence to that effect is afforded by the English *Dame Siriz*. This story in its general outline follows the oriental versions of the *Book of Sindibād*. In the first place is to be noted the absence of all five traits mentioned above as distinctive of the version in the *Disciplina Clericalis*. So well known a tale as the one in the *Disciplina* can hardly have been unknown to the author of the *Dame Siriz*, and in certain minor details, for instance the use of mustard, the influence of the *Disciplina* version is evident. But the essential details of the *Dame Siriz* are like those of the oriental versions. A more close examination of the oriental versions shows that the version of the *Book of Sindibād* to which the *Dame Siriz* is most closely related is the Greek *Syntipas*. Elsner has shown the following points of agreement between the English tale and the one in the Greek *Syntipas* : —
(1) The lover woos personally; (2) The rejected lover does not become ill; (3) The lover calls on the go-between for assistance; (4) The go-between proceeds to work without delay; (5) The go-between gives the bitch pepper (in *Dame Siriz* both pepper and mustard); (6) The bitch is said to be the daughter of the go-between; (7) This daughter has been willing to love only her husband; (8) The rejected

lover has revenged himself. To these features, common to the English and the Greek versions, may be added the fact that in the English version the husband is a merchant, a feature that appears in the Hebrew and other oriental versions, though not explicitly mentioned in the *Syntipas*.

The English *Dame Siriz*, then, differs from most other western versions of the tale in that it is based directly on an oriental version of the story. Other peculiarities of this version are due to the literary genre to which it belongs. If in the expanded French metrical version the story is colored by the sentiment of courtly love, and if in the *Metrical Tales of Adolfus* the conventional and artificial form of Ovid's tales is given to the story, in this English version the story, as the title informs us, is told as a *fabliau*, characterized by humor and satire. The relation of this English tale to its *exempla* congeners is much that of a beast-epic tale to a fable version of the same story. Emphasis is laid on the living elements of the story. The *dramatis personae* are no longer merely a young man, a chaste wife and an old woman, but Wilekin, Margeri, and Dame Siriz, whose characters are revealed by means of realistic dialogue. In the longer French metrical version stress is laid on the love sensations of the young man; in the *fabliau*, stress is laid on the ruse by which the go-between accomplishes her purpose, and upon her dissembling, hypocritical character. Characteristic of the *fabliau* is the fact that the lover is a clerk, whom the medieval satirical writers of *fabliaux* are fond of introducing into such situations. The central figure in the English story is not the

lover, but Dame Siriz herself, and the gradual disclos-
ure of her character, from the dissimulation of her
first words to the hilarity of her language at the end,
is cleverly brought about. The character of the wife
Margeri is but dimly revealed. It may be remarked in
passing that in her character the author offers an enigma
not unlike that which Chaucer has left in the character
of Criseyde.

A feature of the *Dame Siriz* that cannot fail to at-
tract attention is the amount of dialogue. More than one
fourth of the whole poem is taken up with the dialogue
between the clerk, Wilekin, and the wife, Margeri,
an amount of space quite out of proportion to the importance of this preliminary dialogue to the action of the
story. Furthermore it has been pointed out[1] that in the
whole poem, apart from a narrative introduction of 24
verses, there are but 33 narrative verses to 403 verses in
dialogue. Within the individual scenes there are but 3
narrative lines. The transitions in the dialogue from one
speaker to another are not usually marked. For instance,
no explanation is given when Dame Siriz from speaking
to Wilekin turns to address the bitch. It is to be noted
further that the last six lines of the poem, spoken by
Dame Siriz, sound like an epilogue. From reasons such
as these, W. Heuser has concluded, correctly it seems,
that the fabliau is based upon an original interlude, to
which have been added a short introduction and a few
narrative interpolations scarcely more than stage di-
rections.[1]

This brings up the question concerning the relation-

---

1 W. Heuser, *Anglia*, xxx.'306-319.

ship of the *Dame Siriz* to the fragmentary *Interludium De Clerico et Puella*. It has long been recognized from similarity in phraseology amounting to identity between many verses,[1] that these two works are related, and it has usually been assumed that the interlude was based on the *fabliau*. Heuser comes to a quite contrary conclusion, which is doubtless correct. The *fabliau* is obviously based on a dramatic version. This original can hardly have been the extant interlude, because not only are the proper names different, but there is difference in certain important details. For example, the lady loved in the interlude, as in the version by Nicole Bozon, is a "damishel" and "mayden." The only conclusion left to be drawn is that these two works are related to a common original.

The unique manuscript in which the *Dame Siriz* is preserved, Digby MS. 86, the same one to which we owe the preservation of the unique text of the *Vox and Wolf*, is one of those displayed in the exhibition case of manuscripts in the Bodleian library. This manuscript, we are told, was probably written "at the priory at Worcester between 1272 and 1283." The *Dame Siriz* begins on folio 165 with the following heading in red ink, *Ci comēce le fablel & le cointise de dame siriz*.

On the subject of the dialect of the *Dame Siriz* different opinions have been expressed. Ten Brink assigns the original work to the Southeast, to Kent or Sussex. Brandl, on the other hand, assigns it to the Southwest

---

1 Vv. 82, 83 in *Dame Siriz* = v. 5 in the *Interludium*. Similarly 102 = 9, 112-114 = 25, 134 = 12, 135 = 30, 161 = 37, 167 = 38, 174 = 42, 175-177 = 43-47, 187, 188 = 53, 54, 191 = 62, 193 = 63, 196-199 = 65-69, 205 = 84, 207-209 = 69-71, 221, 222 = 57; cf. Heuser, *loc. cit.* 313.

Midland (in which dialect the MS. itself doubtless was written). A close examination of the existing form of the text reveals a mixture of forms from different dialects. The infinitive ends, now with, now without, final *-n*. The first personal pronoun appears as *ich, ihc,* and *I*. Other varying forms are: *ȝeue, geue ; muchele, michele, mikel ; senne, sunne.*

The most striking peculiarities, however, are those of Southern character. Very noticeable is the dropping or wrong application of initial *h-*, and the use of initial *w-* for older *hw-*, and the frequent use of the prefix *i-* before the verbal forms. Other Southern peculiarities are: *wes* for *was, cunnes* (O. E. *cynnes*), *ich, hoe* for *she, hye* for *þei,* the forms of the verb *be,* such spellings as *same* 'shame,' *srud* 'shroud,' *fles* 'flesh,' and the forms *haueþ* and *ledeþ* in the plural of the present indicative.

Along with these Southern forms appear a number of non-Southern features. The rimes *be* (infin.), *me ; eten, mete ; fare, kare,* indicate that in the original the final *-n* of the infinitive was dropped at least sometimes. The rimes *inne, wenne* (O. E. *wynn*) ; *inne, senne* (O.E. *synn*), indicate a non-Southern pronunciation of O.E. *y*. The rime *woldi, vilani* indicates the use of the form *i* for the pronoun of the first person. Heuser cites the rime *come, blome* as a sign of the East Midland dialect, and *iboen, noen* as specifically Lincolnshire. Besides these rimes we may cite the following non-Southern words or word-forms, some of them already cited by Heuser: *selk, ferli, mikel, til* (for 'to'), *allegate, witerli, gange* (infin.) *gar(en), godlec.*

From such dialectal peculiarities and the fact that the related interlude *De Clerico et Puella* is composed in the dialect of North Lincoln or South York, and from the allusion to the fair at Botolfston in Lincolnshire, Heuser concludes that the home of the interlude underlying the *fabliau* of *Dame Siriz* was Lincolnshire.

The *Dame Siriz*, then, in its present form is based on an East Midland original, and retains forms peculiar to that dialect. It was probably composed, however, by a resident of the South, and the manuscript, written at Worcester, was probably written by a scribe belonging to the Southwest.

The early date of the *Dame Siriz* is shown by the date of the manuscript, written between 1272 and 1283.

The versification is not uniform. The first 132 verses are in the tail-rime stanza with the rime scheme *a a b c c b*. Then follow 16 verses in couplets. During the remainder of the poem the tail-rime stanza and the couplet alternate irregularly, the change in the character of the verse seeming to correspond in no respect to the subject matter. Heuser supposes that the composer of the *fabliau* undertook to transform an original interlude in couplets, possibly from memory, into a poem with tail-rime stanzas, and that he was unequal to the task.

This tale, careless in its versification, is not more finished in other respects. It lacks in proportion, a characteristic which it shares with other Middle English tales. A more serious fault is a want of fitness of manner to matter, the stiffness of the tail-rime stanza ill suiting the trivial character of the story, unless indeed the effect of burlesque was consciously aimed at as in Chaucer's *Sir Thopas*. The situations, however, are presented with remarkable concreteness, and the characters, especially that of Dame Siriz, presented with a considerable degree of distinctness. The whole poem, too, is pervaded with sly irony, which only near the end breaks out in open hilarity.

The interlude *De Clerico et Puella*[1] is preserved in a unique manuscript, now Brit. Mus. Add. MS. 23986, of the first part of the fourteenth century. The interlude, which is in riming couplets, is incomplete, leaving off in the course of the dialogue between the lover and the go-between, so that the weeping-bitch does not appear. The theme[2] in this interlude is the same as that in the *fabliau*, as is proved conclusively by the verbal resemblances mentioned above, amounting even to identity between lines in the two works. There are, however, striking points of difference. The object of the clerk's love in the interlude is a "mayden" named Malkyn, and the go-between is named Mome Elwis. The dialogue, owing in part to the use of the couplet throughout, is more lively and natural than in the *fabliau*.

This interesting dramatic fragment is the sole[3] representative of a kind of composition once popular in England. According to Ward, interludes "from the Plantagenet times onwards seem to have not infrequently been produced to diversify or fill up the pauses of the banquet ensuing in great houses upon the more

---

1 " England hat nach dem Spiel von der Dame Siriz das ganze Mittelalter hindurch kein weiteres komisches Drama aufzuweisen." — W. Creizenach, *op. cit.* I. p. 454.

2 Cf. p. 13, note 4.

3 A second possible example is the *Dux Moraud*, cf. W. Heuser, *Anglia*, XXX. 180 ff.

substantial part of the repast." Evidence of the popu-
larity of such productions is afforded by the Wycliffite
protest[1] against clergy for taking part in representations
of interludes. This piece, according to Creizenach,
"seems to have been used by clerks." The marginal
notes in the manuscript are in Latin, and the subject
matter deals with a priest. This English interlude is
possibly related to a Latin dramatic composition, "perhaps Italian," referred to by Gayley,[2] "by one Jacobus," and dealing with the "intrigue, so dear to medieval satirists, between priest and labourer's wife."

THE VOX AND WOLF

To the same interesting manuscript which has preserved the unique copy of the *Dame Siriz* we owe also
the preservation of the entertaining tale of the *Vox and
Wolf*. This tale, aside from its own intrinsic interest,
has an importance in English literature, since it is the
sole representative in English before the time of Chaucer of the tales of the *Roman de Renard*. The medieval pseudo-natural history dealing with the habits and
qualities of beasts is well represented in English by the
early Middle English *Bestiary*, and, as has already been
pointed out above, England contributed its full share
toward the medieval culture of fables. It is somewhat
surprising, then, to find in Middle English but this solitary representative of the beast-epic tales so popular in
French.

---

[1] *Reliquiae Antiquae*, 2, 42 ff.; Mätzner, *Lesebuch*, 1, 2, 224 ff.; cf.
Creizenach, *op. cit.* I. 179, 180.
[2] *Op. cit.* p. xvii.

No exact original of the English *Vox and Wolf* is known, but the story in its main outline corresponds to Branch IV. of the French *Roman de Renard*. The story of Branch IV. in the ordinary version runs as follows: [1] — Renard arrives hungry one night before a monastery and finds an open gate. He devours two chickens and is about to proceed to a third when he is overcome with thirst. He finds a well in the courtyard, and at the bottom of this well he sees his own reflection, which he takes to be the face of his wife Hermeline. Renard calls down the well, "What are you doing?" An echo answers him. He calls a second time, and then, impatient, jumps into a bucket and descends, so rapidly that he nearly drowns. He is in despair of ever getting out, when Isengrim, the wolf, comes along. Isengrim sees his own reflection in the well beside Renard and thinks it to be his wife Hersent. For a time he heaps abuse upon the supposed Hersent. Renard allows him to proceed for a time; then he calms him by persuading him that he below is dead and in paradise. Isengrim wishes to go down. Renard points out the way, but advises him first to confess his sins. While Isengrim, with his face to the west, prays God to pardon his sins, Renard gets into a bucket. Isengrim, his prayer finished, gets into the other bucket, and descends, lifting the bucket with Renard. As the buckets pass, Isengrim asks Renard why he is going up. Renard replies, "I am going to paradise above; you are going to hell below. When one goes, the other comes . . ." Isengrim remains in the well all night. Next morning he is dis-

[1] The summary here follows that by Sudre. See Bibliography.

covered by servants of the monks, and is beaten with clubs and left for dead.

Besides this ordinary version of Branch IV. of the French *Roman*, there is preserved in a single manuscript [1] another distinct French version which is more simple in outline. In this unique version no mention is made of Renard mistaking his own reflection in the water for the face of Hermeline nor of the wolf's illusion concerning Hersent. [2] Isengrim's confession, which plays a conspicuous part in the ordinary version, in this simpler version is disposed of in a single sentence, and the paradise in this version is an earthly paradise. In minor details at the beginning and the end this version differs from the ordinary one, but the main outline of the story is the same. In both versions the story is told in a spirited manner, and it is not easy to say which affords the better entertainment.

Neither of these French versions corresponds exactly with the English tale; in the introductory part of the story the English version resembles more closely the simpler French story; in the latter part there is greater parallelism with the ordinary French version. It is clear, however, that the English tale, with its individual names, Sigrim and Reneuard, its lively narrative and realistic dialogue, and its human satire, is closely related to the versions in the *Roman de Renard*. [3]

1 *Bibl. de l'Arsenal*, 3334. Published by Chabaille in a supplement to the edition of Méon.

2 In the allusions to the well-story in branches VI. and IX. of the simpler version, Isengrim is represented as attracted solely by the opportunity offered to gourmandize.

3 The tales of the *Roman de Renard* are probably based on popular stories. These popular stories differ from the fables in that the didactic element is eliminated. To the popular tales the tales of the *Roman de Renard* add an anthropomorphic element.

To trace the exact relationship of this English tale of fox and wolf to the scores of other versions, written and oral, in the different countries of Europe, would be an impossible task. The inter-influences between written and oral versions are too complex ever to be exactly determined. There are, however, several related groups of versions which it is possible to distinguish.

In the first place the history of the version in the *Roman de Renard* deserves attention. This form of the story is retold, with minor modifications and with especial animus against the black monks, in the French *Renart le Contrefait*. It is not included in the Latin *Ysengrimus* composed at Ghent in 1148 by the scholar Nivard, nor in the *Reinardus Vulpes*, a later expanded version of the *Ysengrimus*. It does appear, however, in the German version of the *Roman de Renard*, the *Reinhart Fuchs* composed by Heinrich der Glichezâre about 1180. In this version appear the illusions caused by the reflections in the well in the case both of Reinhart and of Isengrim. The paradise in the well is alluringly described. Isengrim, seeing the eyes of Reinhart gleaming in the dark, asks what they are, and is told they are carbuncles. There is, however, no mention of the confession and absolution of Isengrim.

Derived from this early German version seems to be the one printed by J. von Lassberg in his *Lieder Saal*.[1] This story has two parts: — (1) The fox sees his own reflection in a well and mistakes it for his wife. Through love of her, he leaps in. (2) The wolf comes along and

---

[1] Vol. II. no. 93. Reprinted by Grimm, *Reinhart Fuchs*, pp. 356-8.

is led by the prospect of "manger süssen spise" to leap into the bucket. Corresponding with the two parts are two morals: — (1) One must not be made foolish by love; (2) One must not trust false friends.

Possibly remotely connected with the *Roman de Renard* version are two other tales: — (1) A fifteenth-century German version, printed by J. Baechtold (*Germania*, xxxiii. 257 ff.) in a collection of twenty-one tales which in the manuscript formed an appendix to Boner's Fables. No mention is made of a paradise in the well. The fox entices the wolf by saying, " dz mir all min tag nie so wol wz"; (2) The Italian fable in the *Novellette Esempi Morali e Apologhi di San Bernardino da Siena*, *Racconto* vi., in which the wolf is led to descend into the well by the prospect of a hen. Neither of these versions mentions the moon reflection.

The well story does not appear in the first part of the Flemish *Reynaert*, composed by a poet named William about 1250, but it appears in a somewhat modified form in a later anonymous second part, more than a century later. Here the she-wolf Hersinde, in bringing charges against Reynaert, brings up against him the well adventure. It is Hersinde that has heard Reynaert's cries in the well, and moved by his account of the fish below has entered the bucket, has suffered hunger and cold, and has escaped alive only after many blows. This Flemish version of the story is reproduced in the Low German *Reineke de Fos* and ultimately in Goethe's *Reinecke Fuchs*, in which Gieremund, the wife of Isegrim, complains concerning her adventure in the well.[1]

1 *Reinecke Fuchs*, xi. vv. 97–131.

Caxton's *Renard the Fox* [1] is a translation from the Flemish, and in Caxton's book it is Erswynde, the wife of Ysengrim, who tells how, attracted by the prospect of fish, she is beguiled by Renard.

Another version of the well-story which seems to be related [2] to the version in the Flemish *Reynaert* is the interesting fourteenth-century Italian [3] fable. In this version, in *terza rima*, which has been attributed to Boccaccio, but in the opinion of McKenzie is more likely by Antonio Pucci, the wolf is led, by the prospect of fish in the well, to leap into the bucket. Interesting is the distinctively Italian tragic ending, in which a dog avenges the wolf by killing the escaping fox.

M. Sudre believes that the well story is derived from popular tradition. In support of his belief he cites the fable version of the story by Odo of Sherington, who lived in the first half of the thirteenth century, and was the author of a number of fables which were before unknown to fable collections and which Odo is likely to have derived from popular sources. The simple version of the story as told by Odo agrees in its outline with the Flemish version just considered, and is not unlikely derived from a common popular source. The fox falls into a well by accident. The wolf is allured by the account of many fish and large ones. In the morning rustics club the wolf, Ysengrimus, nearly to death. It seems not at all improbable that this simple version may represent fairly closely the English form of the original popular

---

1 Cf. Caxton's *Reynart*, ed. Arber, p. 96. The adventure in the well is not included in the English eighteenth-century chap-book version, which seems to be an abridgment of Caxton.

2 Possibly derived from Odo of Sherington.

3 Printed by K. McKenzie. *Publ. M. L. A. of Amer.* xxi. 226 ff.

story, which was expanded in the French *Roman* by the anthropomorphic details of the illusions produced by the reflections in the water and of the paradise in the well, and by the burlesque account of the shriving of Isengrim. The fables of Odo were well known in different countries. It is quite probable that Odo's fable supplied the matter for the first part of the Italian fable mentioned above, and Fable no. 14 in the Spanish *Libro de los Gatos* is a close translation from Odo. Practically the same story is told in no. 59 of the Latin fables by John of Sheppey, who lived in the fourteenth century.

A second family of versions of the story of the fox in the well seems to have a common parentage in the tale as told by Petrus Alphonsus in his *Disciplina Clericalis*. The tale by Petrus runs as follows:—A peasant vexed at his oxen exclaims, "May the wolves eat you!" A wolf hears, and at the end of the day claims the oxen. The peasant demurs. They set out to seek a judge and meet a fox, who undertakes to settle the case out of court. To the peasant he promises to award the oxen if he is given a chicken for himself and one for his wife; to the wolf he promises that the peasant will give a cheese the size of the moon if the wolf will quit his claim on the oxen. The fox then conducts the wolf to a well in which the moon is shining. He points out the moon's reflection in the well, and tells the wolf this is his cheese. The wolf asks the fox to bring up the cheese. The fox descends in a bucket, but pretends the cheese is too heavy for him alone. The wolf descends to help. The two pass on the way, and the wolf is left to his own devices at the bottom of the well.

In this version there will be recognized two new and quite independent elements: — (1) The introduction concerning the peasant, the oxen, and the wolf; (2) The moon mistaken for cheese. Of these elements the first forms the material for Branch IX. of the French *Roman de Renart*, with a different conclusion, however, and with Bruin the bear playing the part taken by the wolf in the *Disciplina* story. It also forms the first part of a genuinely Indo-European popular tale known in Finland, Lapland, Sweden, Norway, Denmark, Germany, France, Spain, Lithuania, Russia, Greece, Syria and India. K. Krohn,[1] who has made an exhaustive study of the various forms of this tale, refers to the version in the *Disciplina* as "die unvollständige und corrumpirte form des Petrus Alfonsi." The moon element in the tale also is the subject of a widely known popular story. According to Krohn (p. 41), "it enters not only the beast-epic but fable literature in general through the translation of the story in the *Disciplina Clericalis* and thus has spread here and there among the folk."

The exact source of this combination of the story of the fox in the well with that of the moon reflection it is impossible to determine. It is interesting, however, to note that practically the same story as told by Petrus, though with a different introduction, was told by the Jewish Rabbi Raschi in the preceding century. Since Petrus derived his tales from Hebrew and oriental sources, one is at first inclined to attribute this story combination to Hebrew origin. The fact, however, that the story does not appear elsewhere[2] in Hebrew

1 See Bibliography.
2 It is not told by Hai Gaon (969–1038), who professes to tell the same

fable collections, and that Raschi was born about 1040 in Troyes, in the part of France where beast tales at that particular time were being actively propagated, leads one to conclude that Raschi made use of a current popular tale which through some channel, Hebrew or other, later supplied Petrus with his version of the story.

The tale as told by Petrus Alphonsus appeared in the various vernacular versions of his story collection. Of these the most interesting is the expanded courtly French metrical version of the *C(h)astoiement*. Here the influence of the *Roman de Renard* is apparent. The Fox and Wolf bear the names respectively of *Regnart* and *Ysengrims*, and the burlesque element is prominent, particularly in the passage where Regnart proposing himself as judge says,

> " Car j'ai esté à bone escole
> Et a Boloigne et a Paris
> Ou j'ai des lois asses apris
> Que loial jugement ferai
> De vos contes, quant jes orrai."
>
> ed. Roesle, vv. 81–85.

The tale by Petrus, like the *Dame Siriz*, found its way into the fable collection of Stainhöwel and thence into the fable collections of the Netherlands, Spain, France, and England, besides that of Germany. In Caxton's edition it stands as number ix. of " The Fables of Alfonce." It is cited by N. S. Guillon as appearing

tale from Rabbi Meir as is told by Raschi. (See *Publ. M. L. A. Amer.* XXIII. pp. 497 ff.) Further, it is not included in the Syriac *Fables of Sophos* (J. Landsberger, *Die Fabeln des Sophos*, Posen, 1859), nor in the Hebrew *Parabolae Vulpium* of Barachia Nikdan, which contains several kindred tales, notably the story of the wolf fishing with his tail through the ice.

in the *Fables* of Marie de France from the MS. *de la Bibl. de Saint-Germain-des-Pres*, no. 1830. It is not included, however, in the Warnke edition of the *Fables* by Marie.

An interesting version of this form of the story is the one included in the *Contes Moralisés* of Nicole Bozon, no. 128, under the moralization, *De Mala societate fugienda*, and in the Latin translation from Bozon (Hervieux, *Fabulistes Latins*, III. no. 10). In this version it is a sheep that is led by the fox to mistake the reflection of the moon in the well for a cheese and to descend in the bucket. That Bozon in this fable was drawing from English popular tradition seems certain from the fact that the sheep lamenting his condition at the bottom of the well is made to say, *in English*, "For was hyt never myn kynd chese in welle to fynd." It is possible that the English popular story corresponding to the popular stories used by Petrus and by Raschi had the sheep as a principal character.[1] In this connection it is worthy of note that in another fable in the collection by Bozon (no. 46) the fox and the wolf see the reflection of the moon in the water, and the wolf is led to fish with his tail for the supposed cheese, a quite different combination of the moon reflection incident with a story even more widely known than that of the fox in the well.

The *Disciplina* version of the story is admirably handled by Robert Henryson in his collection of fables. This Scotch fable in seven-line stanzas, on account of

---

[1] Perhaps the substitution of sheep for wolf is due to Bozon's desire to differentiate this story from the story of the fox and the wolf fishing with his tail, which, as told by Bozon, is also associated with the moon reflection story.

its concreteness of detail and liveliness of manner and interesting Scotch phrases, deserves to be classed among the very best versions of the story. The *Disciplina* form of the story is also used by Hans Sachs in his "Fabel mit dem Pauer, Fuchs und Wolff" and, with another story replacing that of the peasant and his oxen, in the sixteenth-century German fable collection by Burkhard Waldis (Book 4, Fable 8). It is also the form used by La Fontaine, who elaborates in details, notably in the appearance of the moon reflection, which is *échancré* in appearance like cheese, and in Renard's enticing description of the quality of the cheese. Moland, in his edition of La Fontaine, cites as a source for La Fontaine's fable, the *Apologii Phædrii*, 100 fables by Jacques Regnier, Pars 1, p. 24, published in 1643, which the present writer has been unable to examine. Another version possibly belonging to the *Disciplina* family is the Italian fable *della Volpe e 'l Lupo*, one of a collection of one hundred fables by Verdizotti, published at Venice in 1570. The La Fontaine version, in turn, seems to be the source of a later Latin version in the *Fabulae Aesopiae*, Book 8, Fable 24, by F. J. Desbillons, 5th ed. Paris, 1769. In later English versions the fable in the *Disciplina* version is not frequent.[1] It does appear, however, in a very much condensed form, as number 3 in a collection of fables in *The Principles of Grammar, or Youth's English Directory*, by G. Wright, London, 1794.

---

[1] It does not appear in Bullokar's collection, 1585, nor among Gay's *Fables*, nor in the *Aesop at Tunbridge*, London, 1628, nor in *Fables for Ladies* by E. Moore, about 1750, nor in *Fables of Flora* by Langhorne, nor in the large collection, *Fables and Satires*, by Sir G. Boothby, Edinb., 1809, nor in *Aesops Fables*, by T. James, Philadelphia, 1851.

The bucket trick played on the wolf by the fox certainly forms the subject of an amusing tale. The practical lesson, however, to be derived from this tale is not
so obvious as in most fables. Perhaps this fact helps[1]
to explain why the story was not more generally adopted
in later fable collections, where a very much inferior
tale of the fox in the well makes frequent appearance.
This inferior version, possibly not related in origin to
the story in the present book, appears as number 15 in
the *Hecatomithion secundum*, an Italian collection of
Latin fables by L. Abstemius, published at Venice in
1499. The very simple narrative is as follows : — A
fox falls into a well. He calls on a wolf for assistance.
The wolf, instead of assisting, proceeds to ask questions.
The fox rebukes him, bidding him first to render aid,
then to ask questions. From an Italian collection this
fable was adopted into a Turkish collection (*Fables
Turques*, transl. by J. A. Decourdemanche, no. 31).
It appears in the collection of *Centum Fabulae* by the
Italian Gabriele Faerno.[2] It also appears in the principal English fable collections of the last three centuries.
From Abstemius it was adopted by L'Estrange and, like
other fables in his expanded collection, supplied with
a " Moral " and a " Reflexion." It appears also in the
collection by S. Croxall, the leading English collection
of the eighteenth century, and in the collection by T.
Bewick,[3] who derives his version from Croxall. It

1 The main reason, doubtless, is the fact that the tale never formed a
part of the earlier canonical collections, the *Phaedrus*, the *Avian*, and the
Romulus from which the later collections were put together.
2 The edition consulted by the present writer was that of London, 1672,
p. 79.
3 First published in 1818. In the edition of London, 1885, this fable appears on page 311.

appears on the continent in the *Esope-Esopus* (French
and German in parallel columns) by Carl Mouton,
Hamburg, 1750, and a similar tale with the position of
fox and wolf reversed is told by Lenoble (*Œuvres*, t.
xiv. p. 515). The ultimate source of this version is not
known to the present writer. A similar tale of Hare and
Fox, however, appears in the Syriac *Sophos* [1] (cf. Bibliography) of the eleventh century, which in turn was
probably translated from the Greek. [2]

Was the story of the fox and wolf in the well derived ultimately from the orient? This must remain
an open question. Sudre [3] has pointed out that the tale
in the French *Roman* did not reach France through the
Aesopian or Phaedrian collections, and as early as 1855
Weber [4] pointed out that in Indian literature there is
nothing analogous to the buckets in the well. Professor
Fleischer [5] of Leipzig is authority for the statement that
this fable of fox and wolf does not appear in any Ara-
bian book. The oriental fable of fox and goat in the
well, which has persisted in fable collections to the present day and which is perhaps the closest oriental ana-
logue, is an independent tale. Its resemblance to Branch
xviii. of the *Roman de Renard* is more close than to
Branch iv. On the other hand, in support of the theory
of oriental origin, there may be cited certain other oriental analogues. In the *Pantchatantra* [6] appears a tale

1 The tale of hare and fox in the *Sophos* has a moral different from that
in the later tale. Fable no. 24 in the *Sophos*, dealing with a drowning boy
and a man on the shore, has the moral of the later tale of fox and wolf.
2 Cf. J. Jacobs, *Fables of Aesop*, I. 154, 155.
3 L. Sudre, *op. cit.* p. 226.
4 *Indische Studien*, III. 368.
5 Gelbhaus, *Ueber Stoffe Altdeutscher Poesie*, p. 39, Berlin, 1887.
6 Transl. by Lancereau, p. 216. Cf. also Kirchhof's *Wendunmuth*, 7, 26.

in which a hare conducts a lion to a deep well where
the lion sees his own reflection, and led by the hare to
take the reflection for an enemy, leaps in and loses his
life. A modern Indian form of this tale with jackals
taking the place of the hare, is recorded in *Old Deccan
Days* by M. Frere, in a tale entitled "Singh Rajah
and the Cunning Little Jackals." This tale, in its main
outline and in certain details reminds of the incident in
the fox and the wolf story where Isengrim mistakes his
reflection in the well for his wife Hersent. Another tale,
in which the elephant is conducted by a hare to the edge
of a lake, where he mistakes the shadow of the moon for
the king of the hares, is also recorded in the *Pantchatantra.*[1] These analogues, however, are not remarkably
close, and we must conclude that if the story of fox and
wolf in the well came from the East, it did not, as Sudre
has pointed out, follow the literary route followed by
other fables. If it came from the East by an oral route,
the buckets element seems to be a western [2] addition.

There remains to be mentioned an Arabic tale *Le
renard et la hyène* (Meidani, *Proverbes* (6), t. ii. p.
7, and *Ech cherichi ap. cheikho, Madjani'l adab* (7),
t. i. p. 89) cited by R. Basset (*Rev. des trad. pop.*
xxi., 300). A parallel to the conception of the earthly
paradise in the well is to be found in the Arabic tale [3]
of "Le Paradis Souterrain," in which a man goes to

---

1 Translation by Lancereau, p. 216.

2 In an elegiac poem composed by Riparius in the fourteenth century
(cited by Creizenach, i. 28) a trick like that played by the fox on the wolf
is played by a peasant on a clerk. Can the beast tale have been an adapta-
tion of a tale originally dealing with human beings?

3 *Contes et Légendes Arabes*, by R. Basset, no. 481 (*Rev. des trad.
pop.* xv. p. 667).

a well to draw water. The bucket falls to the bottom. The man descends to get the bucket and finds a door opening into a paradise.

It seems probable that the tale of fox and wolf as told in Branch IV. of the *Roman de Renard* is derived for the most part from popular tradition. This view is confirmed by the fact that the tale is a familiar one in modern folk story. It persists in popular story in Spain [1] and in Portugal.[2] A Breton popular version is cited by L. F. Sauvé.[3] A fox on the point of being eaten by a wolf points out the reflection of the moon in the water, saying that it is a young girl bathing. The wolf leaps in to devour her and is drowned. A similar tale, in which, however, the fox pushes the wolf into the well, appears in a cycle of beast tales of La Bresse.[4]

Another popular tale told in Southern France is effectively reproduced by P. Redonnel.[5] A fox is in a tree eating cheese. A wolf asks what he is eating. The fox replies, "The moon." The fox as he eats drops a crumb to the wolf from time to time. Both are thirsty, and they set out for a drink. On the way the fox explains that he found the moon trembling at the bottom of a well and carried it off. The two come to a well with two buckets. The fox descends first and drinks ; then signals for the wolf to get into the other bucket. The wolf is left in the well. It will be noted that this entertainingly told story has its inconsistencies. The fox in

---

1 Antonio de Trueba, *Narraciones populares*, Leipzig, 1875, pp. 91 ff.
2 Coelho, *Contos populares portuguexes*, Lisbon, 1879, pp. 13-15.
3 *Rev. des trad. pop.* I. 363-4.
4 Sébillot, *Contes des Provinces de France. Le Renard de Bassieu et la loup d'Hotonnes.*
5 *Rev. des trad. pop.* II. 611-12.

the tree is not easy to conceive of, and the relation of the moon story to the trick on the wolf is not made clear.

In Northern France the tale is one of an epic cycle of tales concerning the relations of fox and wolf. In this collection the wolf, angry at the fox for a trick played on him, pursues him. The fox, about to be caught, comes to a well, leaps into a bucket and goes to the bottom. He cries for assistance. The wolf, still in angry pursuit, gets into the other bucket and is mocked by the fox as the two buckets pass.

In this connection it is worthy of note that the notion of another world at the bottom of a deep well is not unknown to modern folk-lore. In France, we are told,[1] certain wells are so deep that they are supposed to reach a subterranean world.

Other cycles of popular beast tales are told in parts of Germany and are recorded by J. Haltrich.[2] One group of tales deals with the wolf alone, another with the fox alone, a third, a cycle of ten stories, with the relations of fox and wolf. In this cycle the well story follows the tale in which the fox, by feigning death, gets fish from a peasant. The wolf eats the fish and then, thirsty, is conducted by the fox to a well, where the buckets adventure occurs.

What is the relation of these popular tales to the literary versions? In some cases probably we have to do with popular survivals of the oral sources of the beast-epic tales. In other cases the modern popular tales are probably derived from a literary source. It is probable

1 P. Sébillot, *Le Folk-lore de France*, II. 323.
2 J. Haltrich, *Zur Volkskunde der Siebenbürger*.

that in modern popular story oral and literary streams of tradition meet. In the case of the German cycles of popular tales mentioned above, Wolf, the later editor of the collection by Haltrich, concludes that the tales are probably not derived from the earlier beast-epic, because: (1) the central incident of the beast-epic, the illness and healing of the lion and the trial of the fox, is absent, and the lion does not appear at all; (2) the beasts do not have proper names. Wolf concludes that these German popular tales probably have their source in the well-known German fable collections of the sixteenth century, by Burkhard Waldis in 1548 and by Erasmus Alberus in 1580.

The well adventure has not been recorded among the popular beast tales collected in Africa.[1] Among the American negroes,[2] however, a similar tale is told in which it is the rabbit that outwits the fox, an oriental characteristic, since in oriental beast tales the jackal and hare, and occasionally the tortoise, divide the honors in the tales of trickery.

The English tale of *The Vox and the Wolf* has been much admired and praised. It, perhaps more than any other English humorous poem before Chaucer, shows the buoyancy of spirit and lightness of touch that characterize some of the contemporary productions in French. Yet the English poem offers little that is new. It is probably based on a French original, and in certain cases it has not reproduced its original very dis-

---

1 Cf. A. Seidel, *Geschichten der Afrikaner*, Berlin, 1896; Callaway, *Nursery Tales of the Zulus*, London, 1868; W. H. I. Bleek, *Reineke Fuchs in Afrika*, Weimar, 1870.
2 J. C. Harris, *Uncle Remus : his songs and sayings*, no. 16.

tinctly. This is evident particularly in the relation
of the incident of the henyard with the well story.
From references here and there (vv. 34, 40, 54, 55,
98) throughout the tale, one must infer that Reneuard
has devoured some, possibly three, of the hens, yet no
mention is made of this fact. The most distinctive addition in subject matter in the English version is the
dialogue between cock and fox near the beginning. In
the emphasis that he has given to this preliminary incident, the English writer resembles the author of the
Dame Siriz and Chaucer in his *Nonne Preestes Tale*.
The episode has little organic connection with the main
incident and in a way mars the proportion of the narrative, yet it does contribute to the verisimilitude and
the living interest of the story. In manner the English
version lacks some of the very effective descriptive
touches which make the movements and attitudes of fox
and wolf, particularly in the simpler version of the
French *Roman de Renard*, so lifelike. Perhaps the most
distinctive quality of the English version is not wit, but
the humorous realization of the naïveté in the characters
of the beasts, shown where it is said of the fox,

> Him were leuere meten one hen
> Than half an oundred wimmen.

and when the author remarks concerning the fox caught
in the well,

> Hit miȝte han iben his wille
> To lete þat boket hongi stille.

and in the cringing manner of the hungry wolf, when
he says,

> "Ich wende, al so oþre doþ
> þat ich Iseie were soþ."

The poem is composed throughout in tetrameter
couplets. The style is simple and in keeping with the
subject matter, more so than in the *Dame Siriz*. The
dialogue, particularly, is simple and natural. An interesting feature of the style is the use here and there of
popular proverbial expressions, such as : 'þat ne can
meþ to his mete,' 97; ' Him is wo in euche londe, þat is
þef mid his honde,' 101, 102.

The date of composition was not far from 1275, as
is shown by the age of the manuscript as well as by the
character of the language.

The dialect is Southern, as is evident by the spelling
of the very title. Other indications are the frequent
dropping or misplacing of initial *h-*, the use of initial
w- for earlier *hw-*, the forms *awecche, recche*, the plural
forms *hennen*, etc., the ending *-eþ* in the third plural
of the present indicative, the preservation of the prefix
i- in verb forms. The West-Southern scribe betrays
himself by the representation of O.E. *y* by *u*. The real
pronunciation of this sound it is difficult to determine,
since the rimes are not consistent. A Southeastern pronunciation seems to be indicated by such rimes as ;
aquenche, drunche, 13, 14, and *sugge, abugge; putte,
mette*. On the other hand such rimes as : *kun, him;
sitte, putte*, indicate a Midland pronunciation.

Sir Cleges

The third story of the present collection, that of Sir
Cleges, is somewhat more than a century younger than
the other two. The time of composition was not far

from that of the Canterbury Tales. If there had been a
minstrel in the famous company of pilgrims, this tale
might with fitness have been attributed to him. Not
only is the tail-rime stanza employed in the tale the favorite one in later minstrel stories, but the hero is particularly a minstrel hero. The generosity of Sir Cleges is
displayed particularly toward minstrels. At the Christmas feasts provided by Sir Cleges, the minstrels figure
conspicuously, and the gifts of

> Hors and robys and rych thynges,
> Gold and syluer and oþer thynges

make it easy to believe in the sincerity of the words of
the minstrel in the Edinburgh manuscript,

> " We mynstrellys mysse hym sekyrly,
> Seth he went out of cuntre."   (vv. 496, 497.)

The animus[1] against porters and their kind is appropriate to minstrels and appears not infrequently in minstrel
tales. Furthermore in the Edinburgh text the minstrel
is actually represented as singing before King Uther a
"gest" concerning the virtues of Cleges. The tale,
then, may be regarded as a minstrel tale, exemplifying
many of the qualities of style that Chaucer so gleefully
burlesqued in his tale of Sir Thopas.

The story of Sir Cleges seems to have been a minstrel's Christmas story, for it will be noticed that the
idea of Christmas is everywhere prominent. The lavish
hospitality of Cleges was particularly displayed in the
annual Christmas feasts, the loss of his property is particularly due to Christmas generosity, and the miracle
through which he was restored to prosperity was a

---

1 Cf. *King Horn*, *Sir Tristrem*, and the ballad of *Hind Etin*.

Christmas miracle. Doubtless the story was one which
the minstrel loved to tell to encourage liberality at Yule-
tide feasts, and we can readily understand why to the
listeners at Christmas entertainments this tale might be
a favorite one in the minstrel repertory.

The story is one with an evident moral. This moral
is enforced by a narrative of dual character. Probably
what was intended to be the main theme, was the generosity of Cleges rewarded in this life by divine interposition; what was possibly not intended as the principal element, but which nevertheless most catches the
attention and clings longest to the memory, is the re-
verse of this, the greed of the king's servants punished
with logical justice. The unity in the story is to be found
only in the presentation of the opposite rewards of
generosity and of greed. If we look at the story in this
way, we see a logical appropriateness in the inclusion
of the humorous anecdote of the strokes shared within
the pious tale of generosity divinely rewarded.

The man who has spent all his goods in generosity is
by no means a unique character in romantic story. The
close resemblance between the beginning of *Sir Cleges*
and that of *Sir Amadace* [1] has often been remarked.
In the fifteenth-century tale of *The Knyght and his
Wyfe* [2] also, the knight

> . . . eche ȝere was wont to mak
> A gret fest for oure lady sake.
> But he spendyt so largely
> That in poverte he fel in hye.

[1] *Three Early English Metrical Romances* (ed. Robson), Camden Society, London, 1842.
[2] Remains of the Early Popular Poetry of England, by W. C. Hazlitt,
London, 1866, vol. II.

In the late ballad, *A True Tale of Robin Hood* (Child, no. 154), we learn how Robin Hood, Earl of Huntington, consumed his wealth in 'wine and costly cheere.' In the versions of the Launfal story also, in the *Launfal*[1] by Thomas Chestre and the later version, *Sir Lambewell*,[2] we meet a similar character. In the *Launfal* we read how,

> He gaf gyftys largelyche,
> Gold, and sylver, and clodes ryche,
> To squyer and to knyght.

The manner, however, in which the knight is restored to prosperity is widely different in these different tales. In the *Sir Amadace*, the account of the generous knight serves as an introduction to an interesting version of the well known folk tale of the 'grateful dead.' In *The Knyght and his Wyfe*, it introduces a story of the direct interposition of the Virgin Mary, one of the Mary legends which were so popular in contemporary French literature. In the *True Tale of Robin Hood*, it introduces the well known ballad story of outlawry. In the Launfal stories, it introduces a tale of aid through the fairy mistress Trieamour. The tale of *Sir Cleges* is unlike any of these others. If classified according to its first element, it would be classed as a *dit* or *conte dévot*, or perhaps better, as a legend, if Sir Cleges may be regarded as one of Saint Julian's devotees, a martyr to hospitality.

The means of relief in the case of Sir Cleges, the miracle of the cherries at Christmas time, is as pleasing

---

1 *Launfal* (ed. Ritson), reprinted, Edinburgh, 1891.
2 Bishop Percy's Folio Manuscript (ed. Hales and Furnivall), London, 1867, vol. I.

as in any of the similar stories mentioned. Similar miracles figure not infrequently in romantic and legendary
story. In the legend of St. Dorothy [1] we read how in
response to the prayer of the chaste maiden, a fair child
appears with a basket of roses and apples, which Dorothy sends to Theophilus. In the *Decameron*,[2] Ansaldo,
the lover of Dianara, successfully accomplishes the supposedly impossible task imposed upon him, and on the
first of January made to spring up a beautiful garden
from which he picked the fairest fruits and flowers and
sent as an unwelcome gift to the surprised lady. In the
Ludus Coventriae [3] (xv), in the play on "The Birth
of Christ," when Joseph and Mary are on the way to
Bethlehem in the winter time, a cherry-tree, at first
bare, successively blooms, bears ripe cherries, and finally
bends down to Joseph whom Mary wishes to pluck
cherries for her.[4] Ability to exhibit fruit out of season
was also one of the accomplishments of the popular heroes of magic, Friar Bacon and Doctor Faustus.[5] None

1 Caxton, *Golden Legend*, *Life of St. Dorothy*.
2 Tenth day, Novella 5.
3 Ed. Halliwell, Shakspeare Soc. London, 1841. Halliwell points out
that " this fable of the cherry tree is the subject of a well known Christmas
carol,which has been printed by Hone, *Ancient Mysteries Described*," p.90.
4 That similar stories circulate in modern folk-tales is shown by H. Finck
in the *New York Evening Post* (quoted by the *Literary Digest*, Jan. 7,
1911). He cites a French folk-tale of the Department of Ille-et-Vilaine, of
an apple-tree. Mary wished to taste the fruit, and Joseph refused to gather
the apples for her, saying it was a shame to touch the apple-tree at Christmas time. Whereupon the branches, of their own accord, bent down, and
Mary plucked the fruit. Joseph then tried to pick some of the apples for
himself, but the branches suddenly returned on high.
5 W. C. Hazlitt, *National Tales and Legends*, London, 1899, p. 75.
Hazlitt cites other parallels, among them " Another story of this kind in
Painter's 'Palace of Pleasure.' " E. K. Chambers (*The Mediaeval Stage*,
I. 252, 253) cites the thirteenth-century *Vita* of St. Hadwigis, in which
appears the story of trees in bloom in mid-winter, and gives reference to a
number of parallel stories. The miracle of the Glastonbury thorn might
also be cited in this connection.

of these stories, however, is more pleasing than that of
Sir Cleges, who after kneeling in prayer "underneth a
chery-tre," in rising takes a branch in his hand, and—

> Gren leuys þer-on he fond
> And ronde beryes in fere.

The cherries have an appropriateness in English story.
They have always been a favorite fruit among the English. In *Piers Plowman* (A 7,281) poor people are
represented as eating "ripe chiries monye," [1] and one
of the English popular institutions was the *cherry fair* [2]
held in cherry orchards. But the presentation of a gift
to the king seems not so appropriate to English story.
It is hazardous to form a judgment concerning the origin
of a winged tale like the present one, but the presentation of gifts to a king, although not infrequent in European folk-tales, seems like an oriental feature and
is especially frequent in oriental story. According to
Clouston,[3] "All great men in the East expect a present
from a visitor, and look upon themselves as affronted,
and even defrauded, when the compliment is omitted.
See 1 *Samuel*, ix, 7, and *Isaiah*, lvii, 9." The same custom persists to-day among African tribes, one is told.

Combined with the tale of generosity divinely re-
compensed is another story, of greed requited. As has
been said, it is not easy to determine whether the author of *Sir Cleges* intended this second story as an episode in the story of the generous knight or if he intended
the first part of the story to serve as a setting for the
widely known story of the blows shared. If we judge
by the structure of such a story as Chaucer's *Nonne*

1 Version C. "chiries sam-rede."
2 Brand, *Popular Antiquities*, II. 457.
3 *Popular Tales and Fictions*, Edinburgh, 1887, II. 467.

Preestes Tale we may conclude that the second part was intended as the *pièce de résistance*. In any case the author has devoted nearly half of his narrative to the second element, and it is this part of the story which provides the greater amount of entertainment whether to the modern reader or to the medieval listener.

The story of the man who is made to promise a share of an expected reward to one or more greedy servants and who, therefore, chooses blows for his reward, is one of the most wide-spread of tales. The universality of its theme makes it appropriate to any nation and to any time, and for that reason it is not possible to assign it to any nationality. The nature of the tale is such that it would be vain to attempt to discover the exact inter-relations between the score and more of different extant versions.

The definiteness of the underlying idea in this story rendered it especially suitable for oral transmission. Hence it is not surprising to find it circulating widely as a folk-tale. Among the Arabs it was well known. M. René Basset [1] cites the following version. A eunuch promises El Mo'tadhib, the Prince of the Faithful, to bring him a man to make him laugh. He introduces a street story-teller named Ibn el Maghâzik, but exacts from him a promise of half the expected reward. Ibn fails, and is ordered to be given ten strokes. He asks that the ten be made twenty. When he has received ten, he explains that the other half of the reward is to go to the eunuch. The king laughs.

[1] René Basset, *Contes et Légendes Arabes*, no. 57, *Rev. des trad. pop.* XII. 675-7   M. Basset cites several other Arabic versions of this story, besides two Italian folk-tales.

Another [1] Arabic version passed over among the Berbers. A chief bids his servant find a man to make him laugh. If the chief is made to laugh, he will pay a hundred *réaux ;* if not, a hundred blows. The servant brings El' Askolani, but demands half of the *réaux* in case of success. El' Askolani fails, and the chief orders that one hundred strokes be given. When the story-teller has received fifty, he bids give the remaining fifty to the servant, at the same time explaining the servant's stipulation. The chief doubles up with laughter and gives El' Askolani one hundred *réaux.*

An Italian popular tale, in which a stupid boy presents a fine fish to the king, but is made to promise shares of the expected reward to three servants, is told by Marc. Monnier. [2] A Greek popular story with a similar beginning but with the conclusion rendered ineffective, is told by E. Legrand. [3] From Italy John G. Saxe supposedly derived the version that he tells under the title, "The Nobleman, the Fisherman, and the Porter, An Italian Legend." In Italy the story is also told by Sacchetti [4] and by Straparola. [5] In Spain it appears in the *Cuentos de Juan Aragones,* [6] no. 3. In Sweden it is produced by Bäckstrom in his *Svenske Voksbocker* (2,

1 R. Basset, *Nouveaux Contes Berbères*, Paris, 1897, no. 119, "*Part à deux.*" In this volume M. Basset discusses numerous other versions, in Arabic, Italian, German, and French.

2 *Les Contes Populaires en Italie*, pp. 236, 237. An Italian version, Nerucci, *Sessanta Novelle Populari Montalesi*, Florence, 1880, Nov 27, *La Novella di Sonno*, pp. 233-7.

3 *Recueil de Contes Populaires Grecs*, Paris, 1881, pp. 53-55.

4 *Novelle*, Milano, 1815, vol. III. p. 169.

5 *Notti Piacevoli*, Notta 7, Favola 3.

6 Another Spanish version cited by Oesterley (in his edition of *Schimpf und Ernst*) is that in the *Margerita Facetiarum*, Alfonsi Aragon, Reg. Vafredicti, etc., Argent. 1508, p. 4b.

p. 78, n. 30). In Germany it appears in Pauli's
Schimpf und Ernst (no. 614), in Grimm's *Kinder
und Hausmärchen* (no. 7), and in a poem by C. F.
G. Hahn,[1] organist at Dargun, entitled "Wallenstein
und der kühne Pferdehirte aus der Umgegend von Güst-
row."

In the world's noodle literature the story is one frequently occurring. The adventure is attributed to the
famous Turkish court-fool, Nasureddin Chodscha,[2] who
presented early cucumbers to Tamburlane. In German
jest-books it was one of the best-known adventures of
the celebrated Pfarrer von Kalenberg.[3] In England a
similar story appears in "The Pleasant Conceites of
Old Hobson the Merry Londoner."[4]

The same story appears in the form of anecdotes
connected with various persons. The anecdote is told
of the Italian actor Mezzetin[5] (fl. 1688–97). Mezzetin had dedicated a piece to the Duke of Saint Aignan,
who paid liberally for dedications. He called on the
Duke. The Swiss guard, suspecting the purpose of his
visit, was unwilling to admit him. Mezzetin offered
him a third of the expected gift. On the stairway he
was obliged to make the same promise to the first
lackey, and in the ante-chamber a like one to the *valet
de chambre*. When he came into the presence of the

1 Mecklenburg's *Volks-Sagen*, col. & ed. by A. Niederhöffer, Leipzig,
1859, III. 196–199.
2 Flögel, *Geschichte der Hofnarren*, 176–178.
3 F. W. Ebeling, *Die Kahlenberger*, Berlin, 1890; F. Bobertag, *Narrenbuch*, Berlin, 1885, pp. 7–86; F. H. von der Hagen, *Narrenbuch*, Halle,
1811, pp. 271–352; *Lyrum Larum Lyrissimum*, 1700, no. 184; Henrici Bebelii, *Facetiarum*, Tübingen, 1544, Lib. II. (The last two references are
from Liebrecht-Dunlop, *History of Fiction*, II. 153 note.)
4 W. C. Hazlitt, *Shakespeare's Jest Books*, p. 40, no. 24.
5 L. Moland, *Molière et la Comédie Italienne*, pp. 375–6.

Duke, Mezzetin said, "Here is a theatrical piece which I take the liberty of presenting to you and for which I ask that you give me a hundred *coups de bâton*." On hearing Mezzetin's explanation, the Duke gave the servants a severe reprimand and sent 100 louis to Mezzetin's wife, who had promised nothing to the servants. Tallemant des Réaux [1] tells the same anecdote concerning the actor Jodelet. In this case the actor asked his patron, the Chancellor Séquier, to distribute a hundred *coups de bâton* among four *valets de chambre* who had successively exacted promises.

This story, appearing so frequently in folk-tale, in jest-book, and in biographical anecdote, has a very obvious moral. This moral element made the story a useful one to the medieval preacher, and it appears in books of *exempla*. In the *Summa Praedicantium* of John [2] of Bromyard it appears (fol. C xiii. b) under the heading *Invidia*. This *exemplum*, which is reprinted in Wright's "Latin Stories," [3] runs as follows : 'A certain man coming to the Emperor Frederick with fruits of which the Emperor was very fond, was unable to gain admittance unless he should pay to the door keeper half his gain. The emperor, delighted with the fruits, bade the bearer ask for something in return. The man asked that the emperor command that a hundred blows be given him. When the emperor learned the cause, he ordered the blows of the bearer of the fruits, to be paid lightly, those of the door keeper, heavily.' Another interesting *exemplum* version of the story is that in the

1 Tallemant des Réaux, *Memoirs of Chancellor Séquier.*
2 See Bibliography.
3 Percy Society Publications, VIII. 122.

English *Gesta Romanorum*,[1] no. XC. This version,
like the one in the *Sir Cleges*, has an elaborate introduction. In certain essential details also it closely resembles the *Sir Cleges* version. A king had two sons. To
one he gave his kingdom; to the other, a prodigal, he
gave the choice between two caskets. The chosen
casket contained twenty shillings; to these the king
added a penny. Thus provided, the prince met a man
with a pannier containing a wonderful fish with gold
head, silver body and green tail. He bought the fish
for twenty shillings and paid the remaining penny for
the pannier. He bore the pannier with the fish to the
manor house of a great lord. The porter demanded the
head of the fish, and instead of it the prince promised
him half the expected reward. The usher of the hall
demanded the body and was promised half of the remaining reward. The chamberlain, who demanded the
tail, was promised half the remaining part. The noble
lord, upon receipt of the gift, bade the prince ask a boon.
The servants advised various requests, but the prince
asked twelve buffets. The lord granted the request regarding the buffets to be divided, but threw in for good
measure his daughter and his kingdom for the prince
alone.

The great variety [2] in the forms of this popular tale
will have been noticed. The one who asks for the blows

---

1 E. E. T. S. Extra series, XXXIII. 413–416, no. XC.

2 There are in circulation many similar tales, such as the *Tale of the
Three Wishes* (cf. Bédier, pp. 220, 221), the *Dit du Buffet* (cf. Montaiglon et Raynaud, Notes) the *Envious and the Avaricious* (cf. J. W. Jacobs,
op. cit., Notes), besides scattering folk-tales and adventures like those of
Til Eulenspiegel. Most like of all, and closely associated with the story of
the blows shared, is the one called " Luckily they are not Peaches " (Cf.
W. A. Clouston, *Pop. Tales & Fictions*, II. 467 ff.)

is in one story a groom, in another a prince; in one a
stupid peasant boy, in another a witty actor. The number of greedy servants varies from one to four, of the
blows, from two to five hundred. The variety of gifts
offered in the different versions includes cucumbers, apples, berries, cherries, a falcon, and a fish, or the offering is a good story or a good play. The tale is told merely
to excite a laugh, or to point a moral. The people who
tell it are Berbers in Africa, Arabs in Asia, Germans,
Swedes, Spaniards, Greeks, Italians, and English in
Europe. But in all its migrations and with all the vari-
ation in detail, the essential idea remains constant.

None of the versions of this protean tale known to
the present writer could have served as the exact original
for the English *Sir Cleges*. Nor is it known who was
the author or whether the English story is a translation
from the French or an original English composition. But
though singularly neglected[1] by earlier literary historians,
it is a highly interesting composition. Its faults are evident. It is a mongrel composition consisting of a *fabliau*
tale forming an episode in a *conte dévot* and the whole
provided with an Arthurian setting. The scenes of the
story in general lack the distinctness which usually char-
acterizes the scenes in Chaucer's works. The characters
lack the many-sidedness of reality; they are little more
than types. For instance there is little attempt to distinguish between the porter, the usher, and the steward.
Each represents the same type, that of the greedy servant. The description of Sir Cleges is like that burlesqued

---

[1] The story of *Sir Cleges* is not mentioned by Körting, nor by Ten
Brink; Jusserand mentions it only in a footnote.

in *Sir Thopas*. The manner too is stiff; the humorous
anecdote is not presented in correspondingly humorous
style. But with all these faults, the story is a pleasing one.
Besides the interest it affords as a narrative, the story,
while not offering clear pictures, does give interesting
details of minstrel customs, of life in the hall, of domestic relations and of Christmas cheer. There is a sweet
domesticity in the scene where, after Cleges has been
comforted by his loyal wife, ' they wash and go to meat '
and then ' drive the time away with mirth ' in playing
with their children, and a prettiness of detail in the scene
where Cleges, kneeling in prayer under the tree, finds
the branch in his hand covered with green leaves and
' beryes ' in clusters. The last part of the story makes
up in comedy of situation what it lacks in appropriateness
to the main theme. It is this part of the story which is
told with greatest gusto. The truculent manners of the
king's attendants are brought out with great distinctness
by the minstrel who doubtless had himself experienced
treatment similar to that experienced by Sir Cleges and
been obliged to sit in the ' beggars row.' The minstrel
lingers with evident satisfaction over the details of the
blows paid to the servants.

> The fyrst stroke he leyd hym onne,
> He brake a-two hys schulder bone,
> And hys ryȝht arme also.

There are no fine shades of humor here, but doubtless
the details were relished by a gleeman's audience, and
they are not entirely unpalatable to the modern reader,
it must be confessed.

The *Sir Cleges* is preserved in two paper manuscripts,

both belonging to the end of the fifteenth century; one MS. Jac. v. 7, 27, in the Advocates' Library at Edinburgh, the other, Ashmole MS. 61, in the Bodleian Library at Oxford. The text of the Edinburgh manuscript was printed by Henry Weber, in his *Metrical Romances*, Edinburgh, 1810, 1. 329 ff. The two texts have been printed in parallel columns by A. Treichel, *Englische Studien*, xxii. 374 ff. The Oxford text is printed in the present volume.

Between the texts in these two manuscripts there are many points of difference [1] in detail. As has been said, the story is a minstrel story, and it has evidently been written down twice independently, from oral recitation or from memory. The differences are such as one would expect to originate in oral transmission. Neither manuscript is derived from the other; both texts go back to a common original, and in each appear variations originating in the independent line of transmission. The two manuscripts complement each other admirably. When single lines, or more frequently, three lines, of a stanza, are missing in one, they can be supplied from the other. In some important details the Edinburgh text is the better one, but in the present volume the Oxford text has been printed because the Edinburgh lacks some stanzas at the end. The Edinburgh text has, however, been used to supply lines missing in the Oxford text. The most important variations are indicated in the notes.

The verse form used in the *Sir Cleges* is the twelve-line

---

1 Treichel, *op. cit.* pp. 359 ff., gives a careful discussion of the differences between the two manuscripts. The Edinburgh MS. has 531 verses, the Oxford 570. Only 180 lines, about one third, are exactly alike. Of the remainder, 108 differ in one word, so that nearly half the verses are unlike in several words, or entirely unlike.

tail-rime stanza. The regular rime scheme is *a a b c c b d d b e e b*. Variations from this scheme are found in the Oxford manuscript only in stanzas 16, 17, 19, 33, 41, 46 and 47. Assonance appears in a few instances. There are also a few instances of impure rime, but several of the apparent instances are due to the scribe. Alliteration is not an organic feature of the verse, but occurs occasionally, either through the survival of old formulae or through the use of two words with the same root. For a detailed discussion of the metrical features, see Treichel, *op. cit.* 364 ff.

The dialect of the original work is somewhat disguised on account of scribal peculiarities. In the Oxford manuscript appear frequent Scottish features. From the evidence, however, of the rimes common to the two versions and of the inflectional forms, Treichel (*op. cit.* 371 ff.) concludes that the original work was composed in the northern part of the Midland of England. In the present volume the different inflectional forms will be found registered in the glossary.

From the evidence of the rimes *iȝt, yte* and *ee, y,* Treichel (*op. cit.* 374) sets the date of composition at not earlier than the beginning of the fifteenth century.

Dame Siriz

Ci comence le fablel *et* la cointise de dame siriz.

As I com bi an waie,
Hof on ich herde saie,
    Ful modi mon and proud;
Wis he wes of lore,
And gouþlich vnder gore,   5
    And cloþed in fair sroud.

To louien he bigon
On wedded wimmon,
    þer-of he heuede wrong;
His herte hire wes alon,   10
þat reste neuede he non,
    þe loue wes so strong.

Wel ȝerne he him biþoute
Hou he hire gete moute
    In ani cunnes wise.   15

In the variant readings, W. = Wright, M. = Mätzner. Besides
the variants indicated W. & M. have regularly *th* for þ and *v* for
consonantal *u*. In the text of the present volume the punctuation
is supplied by the editor.
Title. MS. comēce, W. fables, MS. fablel. — 7 W. & M. be-
gon. — 9 W. & M. Therof. — 13 W. & M. bi-thoute.

Þat befel on an day
Þe louerd wend away
  Hon his marchaundise.

He wente him to þen inne
Þer hoe wonede inne,   20
  Þat wes riche won;
And com in to þen halle,
Þer hoe wes srud wiþ palle,
  And þus he bigon : —

"God almiȝtten be her-inne!"   25
 " Welcome, so ich euer bide wenne,"
  Quod þis wif.
" His hit þi wille, com and site,
And wat is þi wille let me wite,
  Mi leuelif.   30

Bi houre louerd, heuene-king,
If I mai don ani þing
  Þat þe is lef,
Þou miȝtt finden me ful fre.
Fol bleþeli willi don for þe,   35
  Wiþ-houten gref."

22 W. & M. into, M. them. — 25 MS. her inne. — 27 W &
M. Quod.—28 W. & M. comme. — 30 W. & M. leve lif.—36
MS. Wiþ houten, W. & M. Withhouten.

" Dame, god þe forȝelde,
Bote on þat þou me nout bimelde,
   Ne make þe wroþ,
Min hernde willi to þe bede ;   40
Bote wraþþen þe for ani dede
   Were me loþ."

" Nai I-wis, wilekin,
For no-þing þat euer is min,
   Þau þou hit ȝirne,   45
Houncurteis ne willi be;
Ne con I nout on vilte,
   Ne nout I nelle lerne.

Þou mait saien al þine wille,
And I shal herknen and sitten stille,   50
   Þat þou haue told.
And if þat þou me tellest skil,
I shal don after þi wil,
   Þat be þou bold.

And þau þou saie me ani same,   55
Ne shal I þe nouiȝt blame
   For þi sawe."
" Nou ich haue wonne leue,
Ȝif þat I me shulde greue,
   Hit were hounlawe.   60

37 W. & M. for-ȝelde. — 38 W. & M. bi-melde. — 43 W. &
M. i-wis. — 44 MS. no þing. — 49 M. alle. — 60 W. & M.
hounlaw.

Certes, dame, þou seist as hende,
And I shal setten spel on ende,
    And tellen þe al,
Wat ich wolde, and wi ich com;
Ne con ich saien non falsdom,   65
    Ne non I ne shal.

Ich habbe I-loued þe moni ȝer,
Þau ich nabbe nout ben her
    Mi loue to schowe.
Wile þi louerd is in toune,   70
Ne mai no mon wiþ þe holden roune
    Wiþ no þewe.

Ȝurstendai ich herde saie,
As ich wende bi þe waie,
    Of oure sire;   75
Me tolde me þat he was gon
To þe feire of botolfston
    In lincolne-schire.

And for ich weste þat he ves houte,
Þarfore ich am I-gon aboute   80
    To speken wiþ þe.
Him burþ to liken wel his lif,
Þat miȝtte welde secc a vif
    In priuite.

64 W. & M. What. — 67 W. & M. i-loved. — 73 W. & M.
ȝursten-dai. — 78 W. & M. Lincolneschire, MS. lincolne schire.
— 80 W. & M. i-gon. — 83 W. sett, M. selc.

Dame, if hit is þi wille,   85
Boþ dernelike and stille,
   Ich wille þe loue."
"Þat woldi don for non þin[g],
Bi houre louerd, heuene-king,
   Þat ous is boue!   90

Ich habe mi louerd þat is mi spouse,
Þat maiden broute me to house
   Mid menske I-nou;
He loueþ me and ich him wel,
Oure loue is also trewe as stel,   95
   Wiþ-houten wou.

Þau he be from hom on his hernde,
Ich were ounseli, if ich lernede
   To ben on hore.
Þat ne shal neuere be,   100
Þat I shal don selk falsete,
   On bedde ne on flore.

Neuer more his lif-wile,
Thau he were on hondred mile
   Bi-ȝende rome,   105
For no þing ne shuldi take
Mon on erþe to ben mi make,
   Ar his hom-come."

88 MS. þin. — 92 M. meiden. — 93 W. & M. i-nou. MS. I
nou. — 96 W. & M. With houten, MS. Wiþ houten. — 101 W.
& M. falseté. — 105 MS. Bi ȝende rome. — 106 W. & M. shuld I

"Dame, dame, torn þi mod;
    þi curteisi was euer god,   110
      And ȝet shal be;
For þe louerd þat ous haueþ wrout,
Amend þi mod, and torn þi þout,
      And rew on me."

"We, we! oldest þou me a fol?   115
So ich euer mote biden ȝol,
    þou art ounwis.
Mi þout ne shalt þou newer wende;
Mi louerd is curteis mon and hende,
    And mon of pris;   120

And ich am wif boþe god and trewe;
Trewer womon ne mai no mon cnowe
    þen ich am.
þilke time ne shal neuer bitide
þat mon for wouing ne þoru prude   125
    Shal do me scham."

"Swete leumon, merci!
Same ne vilani
    Ne bede I þe non;
Bote derne loue I þe bede,   130
As mon þat wolde of loue spede,
    And fi[n]de won."

124 W. & M. bi-tide. — 127 W. & M. lemmon, MS. lenmon,
or leumon (?). — 132 MS. & W. fide.

" So bide Ich euere mete oþer drinke,
   Her þou lesest al þi swinke;
   Þou miȝt gon hom, leue broþer,   135
   For [ne] wille ich þe loue, ne non oþer,
   Bote mi wedde houssebonde;
   To tellen hit þe ne wille ich wonde."
" Certes, dame, þat me forþinkeþ;
   An[d] wo is þe mon þa[t] muchel swinkeþ, 140
   And at þe laste leseþ his sped!
   To maken menis his him ned.
   Bi me I saie ful I-wis,
   Þat loue þe loue þat I shal mis.
   An[d], dame, haue nou godnedai!   145
   And þilke louerd, þat al welde mai,
   Leue þat þi þout so tourne,
   Þat ihc for þe no leng ne mourne."

Dreri-mod he wente awai,
   And þoute boþe niȝt and dai   150
      Hire al for to wende.
   A frend him radde for to fare,
   And leuen al his muchele kare,
      To dame siriz þe hende.

---

133 W. & M. ich. — 136 MS. om. ' ne.' — 139 W. & M.
for-thinketh. — 140 MS. An, W. & M. And, MS. þa. — 143
W. & M. i-wis. MS. I. wis. — 145 MS. An. W. & M. godne dai. —
149 M. Dreri-mod. — 154 MS. siriz, as usually.

Þider he wente him anon,   155
So suiþe so he miȝtte gon,
   No mon he ni mette.
Ful he wes of tene and treie;
Mid wordes milde and eke sleie
   Faire he hire grette.   160

" God þe I-blessi, dame siriz!
Ich am I-com to speken þe wiz,
   For ful muchele nede.
And ich mai haue help of þe
Þou shalt haue, þat þou shalt se,   165
   Ful riche mede."

" Welcomen art þou, leue sone;
And if ich mai oþer cone
   In eni wise for þe do,
I shal strengþen me þer-to.
For-þi, leue sone, tel þou me   170
Wat þou woldest I dude for þe."
" Bote, leue nelde, ful euele I fare;
I lede mi lif wiþ tene and kare;

Wiþ muchel hounsele ich lede mi lif,
And þat is for on suete wif   175
   Þat heiȝtte margeri.

---

161 W. & M. i-blessi. MS. I. blessi. — 162 W. & M. i-com.
MS. I-com. — 170 W. & M. ther-to. — 171 W. & M. For-thi.
— 173 W. & M. Nelde.

Ich haue I-loued hire moni dai,
And of hire loue hoe seiz me nai;
   Hider ich com for-þi.   180

Bote if hoe wende hire mod,
For serewe mon ich wakese wod,
   Oþer mi selue quelle.
Ich heuede I-þout miself to slo;
For-þen radde a frend me go   185
   To þe mi sereue telle.

He saide me, wiþ-houten faille,
Þat þou me couþest helpe and uaile,
   And bringen me of wo
Þoru þine crafftes and þine dedes;   190
And ich wile ȝeue þe riche mede,
   Wiþ þat hit be so."

" Benedicite be herinne!
Her hauest þou, sone, mikel senne.
Louerd, for his suete nome,   195
Lete þe þerfore hauen no shome!
Þou seruest affter godes grome,
Wen þou seist on me silk blame.
For ich am old, and sek and lame;
Seknesse haueþ maked me ful tame.   200

178 W. & M. i-loved. MS. I. loued. — 179 W. & M. seith.
— 180 W. & M. for-thi. — 183 W. & M. miselve. — 184 W.
& M. i-thout. — 187 W. & M. withhouten. — 188 W. & M. vaile.

Blesse þe, blesse þe, leue knaue !
Leste þou mes-auenter haue,
For þis lesing þat is founden
Opp-on me, þat am harde I-bonden.
Ich am on holi wimon,   205
On wicchecrafft nout I ne con,
Bote wiþ gode men almesdede.
Ilke dai mi lif I fede,
And bidde mi pater noster and mi crede,
Þat goed hem helpe at hore nede,   210
Þat helpen me mi lif to lede,
And leue þat hem mote wel spede.
His lif and his soule worþe I-shend,
Þat þe to me þis hernde haueþ send ;
And leue me to ben I-wreken   215
On him þis shome me haueþ spek*en*."

"Leue nelde, bilef al þis ;
    Me þinkeþ þa[t] þou art onwis.
    Þe mon þat me to þe taute,
He weste þat þou hous couþest saute.   220
Help, dame siriþ, if þou maut,
To make me wiþ þe sueting saut,

201 W. & M. bless. — 202 W. & M. mesaventer, MS. mes
auenter. — 204 W. & M. Oppon, i-bonden, MS. I bonden. —
207 W. & M. witchecrafft. — 209 W. & M. pater-noster. —
213 W. & M. i-shend. — 215 W. & M. i-wreken. — 216 W.
& M. speken. — 217 W. & M. Nelde. bi-lef. — 218 MS. þa ;
W. & M. that. — 220 W. touhest, MS. couþest or touþest(?).

And ich wille geue þe gift ful stark,
Moni a pound and moni a marke,
Warme pilche and warme shon,   225
Wiþ þat min hernde be wel don.
Of muchel godlec miȝt þou ȝelpe,
If hit be so þat þou me helpe."
" Liȝ me nout, wilekin, bi þi leute
Is hit þin hernest þou tekest me ?   230
Louest þou wel dame margeri ? "
" Ȝe, nelde, witerli ;
Ich hire loue, hit mot me spille,
Bote ich gete hire to mi wille."
" Wat, god wilekin, me reweþ þi scaþe,   235
Houre louerd sende þe help raþe !

Weste hic hit miȝtte ben forholen,
Me wolde þunche wel solen
   þi wille for to fullen.
Make me siker wiþ word on honde,   240
Þat þou wolt helen, and I wile fonde
   If ich mai hire tellen.

For al þe world ne woldi nout
Þat ich were to chapitre I-brout
   For none selke werkes.   245

---

224 MS. apound, amarke. — 230 W. tehest, M. techest. —
232 W. & M. Nelde. — 235 MS. wilekin. — 236 MS. louerd.
— 237 W. & M. for-holen. — 244 W. & M. i-brout.

Mi iugement were sone I-giuen
To ben wiþ shome somer driuen
   Wiþ prestes and with clarkes."

"I-wis, nelde, ne woldi   **250**
þat þou heuedest uilani
   Ne shame for mi goed.
Her I þe mi trouþe pliȝtte,
Ich shal helen bi mi miȝtte,
   Bi þe holi roed!"
                            255

"Welcome, wilekin, hiderward;
Her hauest I-maked a foreward
   þat þe mai ful wel like.
þou maiȝt blesse þilke siþ,
For þou maiȝt make þe ful bliþ;   **260**
   Dar þou namore sike.

To goder-hele euer come þou hider,
For sone willi gange þider,
   And maken hire hounderstonde.
I shal kenne hire sulke a lore;   **265**
þat hoe shal louien þe mikel more
   þen ani mon In londe."

246 W. & M. jugement, i-given. — 249 W. & M. I-wis, Nelde.
— 250 W. & M. vilani. — 255 MS. wilekin. 256 W. & M.
i-maked. — 261 W. To geder hele, M. To goder hele. W. & M.
hide[r]. — 264 MS. alore. — 266 W. & M. in.

"Al so haui godes griþ,
  Wel hauest þou said, dame siriþ,
    And goder-hele shal ben þin.
  Haue her twenti shiling,   270
  Þis ich ȝeue þe to meding,
    To buggen þe sep and swin."

"So ich euere brouke hous oþer flet,
  Neren neuer penes beter biset
    Þen þes shulen ben.   275
  For I shal don a iuperti,
  And a ferli maistri,
    Þat þou shalt ful wel sen.

Pepir nou shalt þou eten,
  Þis mustart shal ben þi mete,   280
    And gar þin eien to rene;
  I shal make a lesing
  Of þin heie-renning,
    Ich wot wel wer and wenne."

"Wat! nou const þou no god?   285
  Me þinkeþ þat þou art wod:
    Ȝeuest þo þe welpe mustard?"
"Be stille, boinard!

---

270 W. Have, M. Hawe. — 276 W. & M. juperti, MS.
aiuperti. — 279 MS. Pepis. — 282 MS. alesing. — 287 W. tho,
M. thou.

I shal mit þis ilke gin
Gar hire loue to ben al þin.　　　　　　　　290
Ne shal ich neuer haue reste ne ro
Til ich haue told hou þou shalt do.
Abid me her til min hom-come."
" ʒus, bi þe somer blome,
Heþen nulli ben binomen,　　　　　　　　295
Til þou be aʒein comen "
Dame siriþ bigon to go,
As a wrecche þat is wo,
Þat hoe come hire to þen inne
Þer þis gode wif wes inne.　　　　　　　　300
Þo hoe to þe dore com,
Swiþe reuliche hoe bigon :
" Louerd," hoe seiþ, "wo is holde wiues,
Þat in pouerte ledeþ ay liues ;
Not no mon so muchel of pine　　　　　　305
As poure wif þat falleþ in ansine.
Þat mai ilke mon bi me wite
For mai I nouþer gange ne site.
Ded woldi ben ful fain.
Hounger and þurst me haueþ nei slain ;　　310
Ich ne mai mine limes on-wold,
For mikel hounger and þurst and cold.
War-to liueth selke a wrecche ?
Wi nul goed mi soule fecche ? "

291 MS. nero. — 293 MS. hom come. — 294 W. & M. binomen. — 310 W. & M. Hounger. — 311 W. & MS. on wold.
— 313 W. & M. War-to. MS. awrecche.

"Seli wif, god þe hounbinde!   315
  To dai wille I þe mete finde
    For loue of goed.
  Ich haue reuþe of þi wo,
  For euele I-cloþed I se þe go,
    And euele I-shoed.   320

  Com her-in, ich wile þe fede,"
" Goed almiȝtten do þe mede,
  And þe louerd þat wes on rode I-don,
  And faste fourti daus to non,
  And heuene and erþe haueþ to welde. 325
  As þilke louerd þe forȝelde.
  Haue her fles and eke bred,
  And make þe glad, hit is mi red;
  And haue her þe coppe wiþ þe drinke;
  Goed do þe mede for þi swinke."   330
Þenne spac þat holde wif,
Crist awarie hire lif!
" Alas! Alas! þat euer I liue!
  Al þe sunne ich wolde forgiue
  Þe mon þat smite of min heued!   335
  Ich wolde mi lif me were bireued!"

---

319 W. & M. i-clothed, MS. I. cloþed. — 320 W. & M.
i-shoed, MS. I shoed. — 321 W. & M. herin. — 323 W. & M.
loverd, i-don. — 326 W. & M. for-ȝelde. — 329 W. & M. drinke.
— 330 W. & M. Goed mede the for. — 331 W. & M. olde.—
334 W. & M. for-give. — 335 W. & M. off. — 336 W. & M.
bi-reved.

" Seli wif, what eilleþ þe ? "
" Bote eþe mai I sori be :
Ich heuede a douter feir and fre,
Feiror ne miȝtte no mon se.   340
Hoe heuede a curteis hossebonde ;
Freour mon miȝtte no mon fonde.
Mi douter louede him al to wel;
For þi maki sori del.
Oppon a dai he was out wend,   345
And þar-þoru wes mi douter shend.
He hede on ernde out of toune ;
And com a modi clarc wiþ croune,
To mi douter his loue beed,
And hoe nolde nout folewe his red.   350
He ne miȝtte his wille haue,
For no þing he miȝtte craue.
Þenne bigon þe clerc to wiche,
And shop mi douter til a biche.
Þis is mi douter þat ich of speke;   355
For del of hire min herte breke.
Loke hou hire heien greten,
On hire cheken þe teres meten.

339 W. & M. douter. MS. adouter. — 340 W. & M. Feirer.
— 342 MS. nomon. — 343 W. & M. douter. — 344 W. & M.
For-thi mak I. — 345 MS. adai, W. & M. oute. — 346 W. &
M. thar- forn, douter. — 348 MS. amodi. — 349 W. & M. douter.
— 352 W. & M. nothing. — 353 W. & M. bi-gon. — 354 MS.
abiche. 355 W. & M. douter.

For þi, dame, were hit no wonder,
Þau min herte burste assunder.   360
A[nd] wose euer is ȝong houssewif,
Ha loueþ ful luitel hire lif,
And eni clerc of loue hire bede,
Bote hoe grante and lete him spede."
" A ! louerd crist, wat mai þenne do !   365
Þis enderdai com a clarc me to,
And bed me loue on his manere,
And ich him nolde nout I-here.
Ich trouue he wolle me forsape.
Hou troustu, nelde, ich moue ascape ? "   370
" God almiȝtten be þin help
Þat þou ne be nouþer bicche ne welp !
Leue dame, if eni clerc
Bedeþ þe þat loue-werc,
Ich rede þat þou grante his bone,   375
And bicom his lefmon sone.
And if þat þou so ne dost,
A worse red þou ounderfost."

" Louerd crist, þat me is wo,
Þat þe clarc me hede fro,   380
Ar he me heuede biwonne.

359 W. & M. For-thi, wonder. — 360 W. & M. thah.—
361 MS. A, W. & M. hever. — 362 M. Hoe.—363 W. &
M. An. — 364 W. & M. graunte. — 365 M. inserts *I* after mai.
— 368 W. & M. i-here. — 369 W. & M. for-sape. — 370 W. &
M. Nelde. — 375 W. & M. graunte.— 376 W. & M. bi-com.

Me were leuere þen ani fe
That he heuede enes leien bi me,
  And efft-sones bigunne.

Euer-more, nelde, ich wille be þin,   385
Wiþ þat þou feche me willekin,
  þe clarc of wam I telle,
Giftes willi geue þe
þat þou maiȝt euer þe betere be,
  Bi godes houne belle!"   390

" Soþliche, mi swete dame,
And if I mai wiþ-houte blame,
  Fain ich wille ffonde;
And if ich mai wiþ him mete,
Bi eni wei oþer bi strete,   395
  Nout ne willi wonde.

Haue goddai, dame! forþ willi go."
" Allegate loke þat þou do so
  As ich þe bad;
Bote þat þou me wilekin bringe,   400
Ne mai neuer lawe ne singe,
  Ne be glad."

384 MS. efft sones, W. & M. bi-gunne. — 385 W. & M.
Evermore, Nelde. — 388 W. & M. give. — 392 W. & M.
withhoute. — 393 W. & M. fonde. — 397 W. & M. god dai.
— 401 M. inserts *I* after mai.

" I wis, dame, if I mai,
Ich wille bringen him ӡet to-dai,
  Bi mine miӡtte."   405
Hoe wente hire to hire inne,
Her hoe founde wilekinne,
  Bi houre driӡtte!

" Swete wilekin, be þou nout dred,
For of þin her[n]de ich haue wel sped. 410
Swiþe com for þider wiþ me,
For hoe haueþ send affter þe.
I-wis nou maiӡt þou ben aboue,
For þou hauest grantise of hire loue."
" God þe for-ӡelde, leue nelde,   415
Þat heuene and erþe haueþ to welde!"

Þis modi mon bigon to gon
Wiþ Siriz to his leuemon
  In þilke stounde.
Dame Siriz bigon to telle,   420
And swor bi godes ouene belle,
  Hoe heuede him founde.

" Dame, so haue ich wilekin sout,
For nou haue ich him I-brout."
" Welcome, wilekin, swete þing, 425
Þou art welcomore þen þe king.

403 W. & M. I-wis. — 410 MS. herde. — 411 M. for*th*
thider. — 412 W. & M. affter. — 413 W. & M I-wis. —
414 W. & M. grauntise. — 415 MS. for ӡelde. W. & M. Nelde.
— 424 W. & M. i-brout.

Wilekin þe swete,
Mi loue I þe bihete,
   To don al þine wille.
Turnd ich haue mi þout,   430
For I ne wolde nout
   Þat þou þe shuldest spille."

" Dame, so ich euere bide noen,
And ich am redi and I-boen
   To don al þat þou saie.   435
Nelde, par ma fai!
Þou most gange awai,
   Wile ich and hoe shulen plaie."

" Goddot so I wille:
And loke þat þou hire tille,   440
   And strek out hire þes.
God ȝeue þe muchel kare,
Ȝeif þat þou hire spare,
   Þe wile þou mid hire bes.

And wose is onwis,   445
And for non *pris*
   Ne con geten his leuemon,
I shal, for mi mede,
Garen him to spede,
   For ful wel I con."   450

428 W. & M. bi-hete. — 434 W. & M. i-boen. — 444 M.
here. — 446 W. & M. pris.

Appendix to Dame Siriz

Hic Incipt Interludium de clerico et puella.

Clericus ait,   Clericus
" Damishel, reste wel ! "   Clericus
" Sir, welcum, by saynt michel! "   Puella
" Wer esty sire, wer esty dame ? "   Clericus
" By gode, es noyer her at hame."   Puella   5
" Wel wor suilc a man to life   Clericus
   Yat suilc a may mithe haue to wyfe."
" Do way, by crist and leonard,   Puella
   No wily lufe na clerc fayllard,
   Na kepi herbherg, clerc, in huse, no y flore   10
   Bot his hers ly wit uten dore.
   Go forth yi way, god sire,
   ffor her hastu losye al yi wile."
" Nu, nu, by crist and by sant ihon;   Clericus
   In al yis land ne wis hi none,   15
   Mayden, yat hi luf mor yan ye,
   Hif me micht euer ye bether be.
   ffor ye hy sory nicht and day,
   Y may say, hay wayleuay ! "
   Y luf ye mar yan mi lif,   20
   Yu hates me mar yan yayt dos chnief.
   Yat es nouct for mys-gilt,
   Certhes, for yi luf ham hi spilt.
   A, suythe mayden, reu of me,
   Yat es ty luf hand ay salbe,   25

ffor ye luf of y[e] mod[er] of efne,
Yu mend yi mode and her my steuene!"
"By crist of heuene and sant ione, *Puella*
Clerc of scole ne kepi non,
ffor many god wymman haf yai don scam — 30
By crist, yu michtis haf ben at hame!"
"Synt it noyir gat may be, *Clericus*
Ihesu crist by-te[c]hy ye,
And send neulic bot yar inne,
Yat yi be lesit of al my pyne." 35
"Go nu, truan, go nu, go, *Puella*
ffor mikel yu canstu of sory and wo!"

"God te blis, mome helwis!" *Clericus*
"Son, welcum, by san dinis!" *Mome-Elwis*
"Hic am comin to ye, mome, *Clericus* 40
Yu hel me noth, yu say me sone.
Hic am a clerc yat hauntes scole,
Y lydy my lif wyt mikel dole.
Me wor leuer to be dedh,
Yan led ye lif yat hyc ledh 45
ffor ay mayden with and schen,
ffayrer ho lond hawy non syen.
Yo hat mayden malkyn, y wene.
Nu yu wost quam y mene.
Yo wonys at the tounes ende, 50
Yat suyt lif so fayr and hende.
Bot if yo wil hir mod amende,

Neuly crist my ded me send!
Men send me hyder, vyt-vten fayle,
To haf yi help anty cunsayle; 55
Yar for amy cummen here,
Yat yu salt be my herand-bere,
To mac me and yat mayden sayct,
And hi sal gef ye of my nayct,
So yat heuer al yy lyf 60
Saltu be ye better wyf.
So help me crist, and hy may spede,
Riche saltu haf yi mede."

" A, son, vat saystu? Benedicite! Mome Ellwis
Lift hup yi hand and blis ye! 65
ffor it es boyt syn and scam,
Yat yu on me hafs layt thys blam.
ffor hic am anald quyne and a lam,
Y led my lyf wit godis loue,
Wit my roc y me fede, 70
Cani do non oyir dede,
Bot my pater noster and my crede,
To say crist for missedede,
And myn auy mary —
ffor my scynnes hic am sory — 75
And my deprofundis
ffor al yat y sin lys;
ffor cani me non oyir yink —
Yat wot crist, of heuene kync.
Ihesu crist of heuene hey, 80

Gef yat hay may heng hey,
And gef yat hy may se,
Yat yay be heng' on a tre,
Yat yis ley as leyit onne me.
ffor aly wymam ami on."   85

The Fox and Wolf in the Well

Of þe vox and of þe wolf

A vox gon out of þe wode go,
Afingret so, þat him wes wo;
He nes neuere in none wise
Afingret erour half so swiþe.
He ne hoeld nouþer wey ne strete,   5
For him wes loþ men to mete;
Him were leuere meten one hen,
þen half anoundred wimmen.
He strok swiþe ouer-al,
So þat he ofsei ane wal;   10
Wiþinne þe walle wes on hous,
The wox wes þider swiþe wous;
For he þohute his hounger aquenche,
Oþer mid mete, oþer mid drunche.
Abouten he biheld wel ȝerne;   15
þo eroust bigon þe vox to erne.
Al fort he come to one walle,
And som þer-of wes afalle,

W. = Wright and Halliwell, *Reliquiae Antiquae*; M. =
Mätzner, *Altenglische sprachproben.* In W. and in H. throughout
þ appears as *th* and consonantal *u* as *v*.
    8 W. & M. Than half an oundred. — 9 W. & M. all. — 13 W.
& M. aquenche. — 18 W. & M. therof wes a-falle.

And wes þe wal ouer-al to-broke,
And on ȝat þer wes I-loke;   20
At þe furmeste bruche þat he fond,
He lep in, and ouer he wond.
Þo he wes inne, smere he lou,
And þer-of he hadde gome I-nou;
For he com in wiþ-outen leue   25
Boþen of haiward and of reue.

On hous þer wes, þe dore wes ope,
Hennen weren þerinne I-crope,
Fiue, þat makeþ anne flok,
And mid hem sat on kok.   30
Þe kok him wes flowen on hey,
And two hennen him seten ney.
" Wox," quod þe kok, " wat dest þou þare?
Go hom, crist þe ȝeue kare!
Houre hennen þou dest ofte shome."   35
" Be stille, ich hote, a godes nome!"
Quaþ þe wox, " sire chauntecler,
Þou fle adoun, and com me ner.
I nabbe don her nout bote goed,
I have leten þine hennen blod;   40
Hy weren seke ounder þe ribe,
Þat hy ne miȝtte non lengour libe.

19 MS. to breke. — 20 W. & M. i-loke. — 24 W. & M.
i-nou. — 28 W. & M. i-crope, MS. I crope. — 36 MS. agodes.

Bote here heddre were I-take;
Þat I do for almes sake.
Ich haue hem letten eddre blod,   45
And þe, chauntecler, hit wolde don goed.
Þou hauest þat ilke ounder þe splen,
Þou nestes neuere daies ten;
For þine lif-dayes beþ al ago,
Bote þou bi mine rede do;   50
I do þe lete blod ounder þe brest,
Oþer sone axe after þe prest."
" Go wei," quod þe kok, " wo þe bi-go!
Þou hauest don oure kunne wo.
Go mid þan þat þou hauest nouþe;   55
Acoursed be þou of godes mouþe!
For were I adoun bi godes nome!
Ich miȝte ben siker of oþre shome
Ac weste hit houre cellerer,
Þat þou were I-comen her.   60
He wolde sone after þe ȝonge,
Mid pikes and stones and staues stronge;
Alle þine bones he wolde to-breke;
Þene we weren wel awreke."

H E wes stille, ne spak namore,   65
    Ac he werþ aþurst wel sore;

43 W. & M. i-take, MS. I take. — 49 W. & M. a-go. — 58
W. & M. owre. — 59 M. wiste. — 60 W. & M. i-comen, MS.
I comen. — 63 MS. to breke.

þe þurst him dede more wo,
þen heuede raþer his hounger do.
Ouer-al he ede and sohvte;
On auenture his wiit him brohute,   70
To one putte wes water inne
þat wes I-maked mid grete ginne.
Tuo boketes þer he founde,
þat oþer wende to þe grounde,
þat wen me shulde þat on opwinde,   75
þat oþer wolde adoun winde.
He ne hounderstod nout of þe ginne,
He nom þat boket, and lep þerinne;
For he hopede I-nou to drinke.
þis boket biginneþ to sinke;   80
To late þe vox wes biþout,
þo he wes in þe ginne I-brout.
I-nou he gon him bi-þenche,
Ac hit ne halp mid none wrenche;
Adoun he moste, he wes þerinne;   85
I-kaut he wes mid swikele ginne.
Hit miȝte han iben wel his wille
To lete þat boket hongi stille.
Wat mid serewe and mid drede,

---

72 W. & M. i-maked, MS. I maked. — 75 W. & M. opwinde, M. omits on. — 76 W. & M. a-doun. — 79 W. & M.
i-nou, MS. I nou. — 80 W. & M. beginneth. — 81 W. & M.
bi-þout. — 82 W. & M. i-brout, MS. I brout. — 83 MS. bi
þenche. — 85 W. & M. A-doun. — 86 W. & M i-kaut. —
87 W. & M. i-ben, MS. hani ben.

Al his þurst him ouer-hede.   90
Al þus he com to þe grounde,
And water I-nou þer he founde.
Þo he fond water, ӡerne he dronk,
Him þoute þat water þere stonk,
For hit wes to-ӡeines his wille.   95
" Wo worþe," quaþ þe vox, " lust and wille,
Þat ne can meþ to his mete !
Ӡef ich neuede to muchel I-ete,
Þis ilke shome neddi nouþe;
Nedde lust I-ben of mine mouþe.   100
Him is wo in euche londe,
Þat is þef mid his honde.
Ich am I-kaut mid swikele ginne,
Oþer soum deuel me broute her-inne.
I was woned to ben wiis,   105
Ac nou of me I-don hit hiis."

Þ E vox wep, and reuliche bigan.
Þer com a wolf gon after þan
Out of þe depe wode bliue,
For he wes afingret swiþe.   110
Noþing he ne founde in al þe niӡte,
Wer-mide his honger aquenche miӡtte.

90 W. & M. over-hede, MS. ouer hede. — 91 W. & M. come.
— 92 W. & M. i-nou. — 95 MS. to ӡeines. — 96 W. & M.
quath. — 97 M. con. — 98 W. & M. i-ete, MS. I ete. — 100
W. & M. i-ben, MS. I ben. — 103 W. & M. i-kaut, MS. I kaut.
— 106 W. & M. i-don, MS. I don. — 112 W., MS. Wer mide,
W. & M. aquenche, M. Wer-mid e.

He com to þe putte, þene vox I-herde;
He him kneu wel bi his rerde,
For hit wes his neiȝebore,   115
And his gossip, of children bore.
A-doun bi þe putte he sat.
Quod þe wolf, "Wat may ben þat
þat ich in þe putte I-here?
Hertou cristine, oþer mi fere?   120
Say me soþ, ne gabbe þou me nout,
Wo haueþ þe in þe putte, I-brout?"
þe vox hine I-kneu wel for his kun,
And þo eroust kom wiit to him;
For he þoute mid soumme ginne,   125
Him-self houpbringe, þene wolf þerinne.
Quod þe vox, "Wo is nou þere?
Ich wene hit is sigrim þat ich here."
"þat is soþ," þe wolf sede,
"Ac wat art þou, so god þe rede?"   130

"A," quod þe vox, "ich wille þe telle;
On alpi word ich lie nelle.
Ich am reneuard, þi frend,
And ȝif ich þine come heuede I-wend,
Ich hedde so I-bede for þe,   135
þat þou sholdest comen to me."

113 W. & M. i-herde. — 114 W. & M. by. — 118 M. What.
— 119 W. & M. i-here. — 122 W. & M. i-brout. — 123 W.
& M. i-kneu, MS. I kneu. — 128 W. & M. Sigrim. — 134 W.
& M. i-wend. — 135 W. & M. i-bade.

" Mid þe ? " quod þe wolf, " War to ?
 Wat shulde ich ine þe putte do ? "
Quod þe vox, " Þou art ounwiis,
Her is þe blisse of paradiis ;   140
Her ich mai euere wel fare,
Wiþ-outen pine, wiþouten kare ;
Her is mete, her is drinke,
Her is blisse wiþouten swinke ;
Her nis hounger neuermo,   145
Ne non oþer kunnes wo ;
Of alle gode her is I-nou."
Mid þilke wordes þe volf lou.

" Art þou ded, so god þe rede,
      Oþer of þe worlde ? " þe wolf sede.   150
Quod þe wolf, " Wenne storue þou,
And wat dest þou þere nou ?
Ne beþ nout ʒet þre daies ago,
Þat þou and þi wif also,
And þine children, smale and grete,   155
Alle to-gedere mid me hete."
" Þat is soþ," quod þe vox,
" Gode þonk, nou hit is þus,
 Þat ihc am to criste vend.
Not hit non of mine frend.   160
 I nolde, for al þe worldes goed,
 Ben ine þe worlde, þer ich hem fond.

137 W. & M. war-to. — 147 W. & M. i-nou. — 153 W. &
M. a-go.

Wat shuldich ine þe worlde go,
þer nis bote kare and wo,
And liuie in fulþe and in sunne?   165
Ac her beþ ioies fele cunne;
Her beþ boþe shep and get."
þe wolf haueþ hounger swiþe gret,
For he nedde ȝare I-ete;
And þo he herde speken of mete,   170
He wolde bleþeliche ben þare.
" A ! " quod þe wolf, " gode I-fere,
Moni goed mel þou hauest me binome;
Let me adoun to þe kome.
And al ich wole þe for-ȝeue."   175
" Ȝe," quod þe vox, " were þou I-sriue,
And sunnen heuedest al forsake,
And to klene lif I-take,
Ich wolde so bidde for þe,
þat þou sholdest comen to me."   180

TO wom shuldich," þe wolfe seīde,
    Ben I-knowe of mine misdede?
Her nis noþing aliue,
þat me kouþe her nou sriue.

---

156 MS. to gedere. — 166 W. & M. joies. — 169 W. & M.
i-ete, MS. I ete. — 171 W. & M. i-fere, MS. I fere. — 174 W.
& M. a-doun. — 175 MS. for ȝeue. — 176 W. & M. i-srive,
MS. I sriue. — 178 W. & M. i take, MS. I take. — 182 W. &
M. i-knowe, MS. I knowe.

Þou hauest ben ofte min I-fere,   185
Woltou nou mi srift I-here,
And al mi liif I shal þe telle ? "
" Nay," quod þe vox, " I nelle."
" Neltou," quod þe wolf, " þin ore,
Ich am afingret swiþe sore;   190
Ich wot to niȝt ich worþe ded,
Bote þou do me somne reed.
For cristes loue be mi prest."
Þe wolf bey adoun his brest,
And gon to siken harde and stronge.   195
" Woltou," quod þe vox, "srift ounderfonge,
Tel þine sunnen on and on,
Þat þer bileue neuer on."

" Sone," quod þe wolf, " wel I-faie,
       Ich habbe ben qued al mi lifdaie;   200
Ich habbe widewene kors,
Þerfore ich fare þe wors.
A þousent shep ich habbe abiten,
And mo, ȝef hy weren I-writen.
Ac hit me of-þinkeþ sore.   205
Maister, shal I tellen more ? "

---

185 W. & M. i-fere, MS. I fere. — 186 W. & M. i-here,
WS. I here. — 191 W. & M. to-niȝt. — 194 W. & H. a-doun.
— 196 W. & M. ounderfonge. — 199 W. & M. quad, MS. I fare,
W. & M. i-faie. — 200 W. & M. lif-daie. — 204 W. & M.
i-writen, MS. I writen. — 205 MS. of þinkeþ.

"Ȝe," quod þe vox, " al þou most sugge,
Oþer elles-wer þou most abugge."
" Gossip," quod þe wolf, " forȝef hit me,
Ich habbe ofte sehid qued bi þe,   210
Men seide þat þou on þine liue
Misferdest mid mine wiue ;
Ich þe aperseiuede one stounde,
And in bedde togedere ou founde.
Ich wes ofte ou ful ney,   215
And in bedde to-gedere ou sey.
Ich wende, al-so oþre doþ,
Þat ich I-seie were soþ,
And þerfore þou were me loþ ;
Gode gossip, ne be þou nohut wroþ."   220

" Vuolf," quod þe vox him þo,
    " Al þat þou hauest her bifore I-do,
In þohut, in speche, and in dede,
In euche oþeres kunnes quede,
Ich þe forȝeue at þisse nede."   225
" Crist þe forȝelde ! " þe wolf seide.
" Nou ich am in clene liue,
Ne recche ich of childe ne of wiue.
Ac sei me wat I shal do,
And ou ich may comen þe to."   230

207 W. & M. quad. — 208 MS. elles wer. — 213 W. & M.
aperseivede. — 214 W. & M. to-gedere. — 216 MS. to gedere ou
ley, M. sey. — 218 W. & M. i-seie, MS. I seie. — 221 W. &
M. quad. — 222 W. & M. i-do, MS. I do.

"Do?" quod þe vox. "Ich wille þe lere.
I-siist þou a boket hongi þere?
Þere is a bruche of heuene blisse,
Lep þerinne, mid I-wisse,
And þou shalt comen to me sone."   235
Quod the wolf, "þat is liȝt to done."
He lep in, and way sumdel;
Þat weste þe vox ful wel.
Þe wolf gon sinke, þe vox arise;
Þo gon þe wolf sore agrise.   240
Þo he com amidde þe putte,
Þe wolfe þene vox opward mette.
"Gossip," quod þe wolf, "Wat nou?
Wat hauest þou I-munt? weder wolt þou?"
"Weder, Ich wille?" þe vox sede.   245
"Ich wille oup, so god me rede!
And nou go doun, wiþ þi meel,
Þi biȝete worþ wel smal.
Ac ich am þerof glad and bliþe,
Þat þou art nomen in clene liue.   250
Þi soule-cnul ich wille do ringe,
And masse for þine soule singe."
Þe wrecche bineþe noþing ne vind,
Bote cold water, and hounger him bind;
To colde gistninge he wes I-bede,   255
Wroggen haueþ his dou I-knede.

232 MS. I siist. — 234 W. & M. i-wisse, MS. I wisse. —
240 W. & M. agrise. — 244 W. & M. i-munt, MS. I munt.
— 251 W. & M. soul-cnul. — 255 W. & M. i-bede, MS. I bede.
— 256 W. & M. i-knede, MS. I knede.

Þe wolf in þe putte stod,
    Afingret so þat he ves wod.
    Inou he cursede þat þider him broute;
    Þe vox þer of luitel route.   260
Þe put him wes þe house ney,
Þer freren woneden swiþe sley.
Þo þat hit com to þe time,
Þat hoe shulden arisen Ine,
For to suggen here houssong,   265
O frere þere wes among,
Of here slep hem shulde awecche,
Wen hoe shulden þidere recche.
He seide, " Ariseþ on and on,
And komeþ to houssong heuereuchon."   270
Þis ilke frere heyte ailmer;
He wes hoere maister curtiler.
He wes hofþurst swiþe stronge;
Riȝt amidward here houssonge
Al-hone to þe putte he hede;   275
For he wende bete his nede.
He com to þe putte, and drou,
And þe wolf wes heui I-nou.
Þe frere mid al his maine tey
So longe þat he þene wolf I-sey!   280
For he sei þene wolf þer sitte,
He gradde, " Þe deuel is in þe putte! "

259 MS. I nou.— 264 W. & M. ime. — 270 M. hevere uchon.
— 275 W. & M. Alhone, MS. Al hone. — 278 W. & M. i-nou,
MS. I nou.— 280 W. & M. i-sey, MS. I sey.

To þe putte hy gounnen gon,
  Alle mid pikes and staues and ston,
Euch mon mid þat he hedde; 285
Wo wes him þat wepne nedde.
Hy comen to þe putte þene wolf opdrowe;
Þo hede þe wreche fomen I-nowe,
Þat weren egre him to slete
Mid grete houndes, and to bete. 290
Wel and wroþe he wes I-swonge,
Mid staues and speres he wes I-stounge.
Þe wox bicharde him, mid Iwisse,
For he ne fond nones kunnes blisse,
Ne hof duntes forȝeuenesse. explicit. 295

287 W. & M. op-drowe. — 288 W. & M. i-nowe, MS. I nowe.
— 291 W. & M. i-swonge, MS. I swonge. — 292 W. & M.
i-stounge, MS. I stounge. — 293 W. & M. i-wisse, MS. I wisse.

Sir Cleges

[L]ystyns, lordynges, *and* ʒe schall here Ashmole MS. 61.
Off ansytourres, þat be-fore vs were,
   Bothe herdy *and* wyght,
Yn tyme of vt*er and* pendragonn,
Kyng artour fad*er* of grete renoune,   5
   A sembly man of syght.
He had a knyʒht, hyʒt s*ir* clegys;
A douʒtyer man was non at nedys
   Of þe ronde-tabull ryʒht.
He was man of hy statour   10
And þer-to feyre of all fetour,
   A man of mekyll myʒht.

Mour curtas knyʒht þan he was one
Yn all þis werld was þer non.
   He was so gentyll *and* fre,   15
To squyres þat tr*a*ueyled *i*n lond of werre
And w*er* fallyn in pou*er*te bare,
   He gaff þem gold *and* fe.
Hys tenant*es* feyr he wold rehete;
No man he wold buske ne bete;   20
   Meke as meyd was he.
Hys mete was redy to eu*er*y man
That wold com *and* vyset hy*m* than;
   He was full of plente.

The knyght had a gentyll wyffe,   25
A better myȝht non be of lyfe,
    Ne non semblyer in syght.
Dame clarys hyght þat lady ;
Off all godnes sche had treuly
    Glad chere boþe dey *and* nyȝht.   30
Grete almus-folke boþe þei were
Both to pore man *and* to frere ;
    They cheryd many a wyȝht.
ffor þem had no man ouȝht lore
Wheþer þei wer ryche or pore,   35
    Of hym þei schuld haue ryȝht.

Euery ȝere sir clegys wold
In crystyn-mes a fest hold
    Yn þe worschype of þat **dey**,
[As Ryall in all thynge   40
As he hade ben A kynge,
    For-soth as I you saye.]
Ryche *and* pore in þat contre
At þat fest þei schuld be ;
    Ther wold no man sey nay.   45
Mynstrellus wold not be be-hynd,
Myrthys wer þei may ffynd,
    That is most to þer pay.

Mynstrellus when þe fest was don,
Schuld not with-outyn gyftes gon   50
    That wer both rych *and* gode,

Verses 40–42 are supplied from the Edinburgh MS.

Hors *and* robys *and* rych thyng*es*,
Gold *and* sylu*er and* oþer thyng*es*,
   To mend *with* þer mode
X ȝere *our* xii sych fest*es* þei held   55
Yn worschype of hy*m*, þat all weld
   And for vs dyȝed vpon þe rode.
Be than his gode be-gan to schake,
Sych fest*es* he gan make,
   The knyght of jentyll blode.   60

To hold hys feste he wold not lete;
   Hys rych man*er*s to wede he sete;
   He thouȝt hy*m*-selue oute to quyte.
Thus he festyd many a ȝere
Both gentyll men *and* comener   65
   Yn þe name of god all-myȝht.
So at þe last, soth to sey,
All hys gode was spendyd a-way;
   Than he had bot a lyte.
Thoff hys god were ne-hond leste,   70
Yn þe wyrschyp he made a feste;
   He hopyd god wold hy*m* quyte.

Hys ryalty he forder*yd* ay,
To hys man*er*s *wer* sold a-wey,
   That hy*m* was left bot one;   75
And þ*at* was of lytell valew,
That he *and* hys wyfe so trew
   Oneth myȝht lyfe þer-one.

Hys men, þat wer so mych of pride,
Wente a-wey onne euery syde;   80
  With hym þer left not one.
To duell with hym þer left no mo
Bot hys wyfe and his chylder two;
  Than made he mekyll mone.

Yt fell on a crystenmes eue;   85
Syr clegys and his wyfe,
  They duellyd by cardyff syde.
When it drew to-werd þe none,
Syr clegys fell in swownyng sone;
  Wo be-thought hym þat tyde,   90
What myrth he was wonte to hold,
And he, he had hys maners solde,
  Tenandrys and landes wyde.
Mekyll sorow made he þer;
He wrong hys hondes and wepyd sore,   95
  ffor fallyd was hys pride.

And as he walkyd vppe and done,
Sore syȝeng, he herd a sowne
  Off dyuerse mynstralsy,
Off trumpers, pypers, and nakerners,   100
Off herpers, notys and gytherners.
  Off sytall and of sautrey.
Many carrals and grete dansyng
Yn euery syde herd he syng,
  In euery place, treuly.   105

He wrong hys hond*es* *and* wepyd **sore** ;
Mekyll mon he made þer,
   Syʒeng full pytewysly.

" A Ih*e*su, heue*n*-kyng,
Off nouʒht þ*o*u madyst all thyng ;   110
   Y thanke þe of thy sonde.
The myrth þ*a*t I was won to **make**
Yn þ*is* tyme for þ*i* sake.
   Y fede both fre *and* bond,
And all þ*a*t eu*er* com *in* þ*i* name,   115
They wantyd noþ*er* wylde ne tame,
   That was in any lond,
Off rych metys *and* drynk*es* gode
That long*es* for any man*us* fode,
   Off cost I wold not wonde."   120

Als he stode in mo*u*rny*n*g so,
And hys wyfe com hy*m* to,
   Yn armys sche hy*m* hente.
Sche kyssed hy*m* w*ith* glad chere,
And seyd : " My trew wedyd fere,   125
   Y herd wele what ʒe ment.
Ʒe se wele, s*ir*, it helpys nouʒht,
To take sorow in ʒour thouʒht ;
   Ther-for I rede ʒe stynte.
[Let your*e* sorowe A-waye gon   130
And thanke God of hys lone
   Of all þ*a*t he hath sent.]

Be crystes sake, I rede ȝe lyne
Of all þe sorow þat ȝe be Ine
   A-ȝene þis holy dey.   135
Now euery man schuld be mery *and* glad
With sych godes as þei had;
   Be ȝe so, I ȝou pray.
Go we to ouer mete be-lyue
And make vs both merry *and* blythe,   140
   Als wele as euer we may.
I hold it for þe best, trewly;
Y haue made owre mete treuly,
   Y hope, vnto ȝour pay."

"Now I assent," quoþ cleges tho.   145
   Yn with hyr he gan go
   Som-what with better chere.
When he fell in thouȝt *and* care,
Sche comforth hym euer mour,
   Hys sorow for-to stere.   150
After he gan to wex blyth
And wyped hys terys blyue,
   That hang on hys lyre.
Than þei wesch *and* went to mete,
With sych god as þei myȝht gete,   155
   And made mery chere.

Verses 130–132 are supplied from the Edinburgh MS.
145 MS. the.

When þei had ete, þe soth to sey,
With myrth þei drofe þe dey a-wey,
    The best wey þat they myȝht.
With þer chylder pley þei dyde   160
And after euensong went to bede
    At serteyn of þe nyght.
The sclepyd, to it rong at þe chyrche,
Godes seruys forto wyrche,
    As it was skyll *and* ryght.   165
Vp þei ros *and* went þeþer,
They *and* þer chylder togeþer,
    When þei were redy dyȝht.

Syr cleges knelyd on hys kne,
To Ih[es]u cryst prayd he   170
    Be chesyn of hys wyfe :
" Grasyos lord," he seyd tho,
" My wyfe *and* my chylder two,
    Kepe vs out of stryffe."
The lady prayd hym ageyn ;
Sche seyd : " god kepe my lord fro peyn
    Yn-to euer-lastyng lyffe."   175
Seruys was don *and* hom þey wente ;
The thankyd god omnipotent
    They went home so ryfe.

When he to hys palys com,   180
He thouȝt his sorow was ouer-gon ;

Hys sorow he gan stynt.
He made hys wyfe be-for hy*m* gon
And hy[s]chyld*er* eu*er*ychon;
 Hy*m*-selue a-lone he wente
Yn-to a garthyn þ*er* be-syde.   185
He knelyd a-don in þ*at* tyde
 And pr*a*yd to god v*er*ament.
He thankyd god w*ith* all hys hert
Of all desesyd in pou*er*te
 That eu*er* to hy*m* he sente.   190

As he knelyd on*ne* hys kne
Vnd*er*-neth a chery tre,
 Makying hys pr*a*ere,
He raw3ht a bow3e i*n* hys hond,   195
To ryse þ*er*-by *and* vp-stond;
 No leng*er* knelyd he þ*er*.
When þe bow3he was in hys hond,
Gren leuys þ*er-o*n he fond
 And ronde beryes in fere.   200
He seyd: " Dere god in tr*i*nyte,
What man*er* beryes may þ*is* be,
 That grow þ*is* tyme of 3ere ? "

" Y haue not se þ*is* tyme of 3ere,
 That treys any fruyt schuld bere,   205
Als ferre as I haue sought."
 He thou3t to tayst it, yff he couthe;

One of þem he put in hys mouthe;
  Spare wold he nouȝht.   210
After a chery it relesyd clene,
The best þat euer he had sene,
  Seth he was man wrouȝht.
A lytell bow he gan of-slyfe;
And thouȝht he wold schew it hys wyfe; 215
  Yn hys hond he it brouȝht.

" Lo, dame, here is a nowylte;
  In ouer garthyn vpon a tre
    Y found it, sykerly.   220
Y ame a-ferd, it is tokenyng
Be-cause of ouer grete plenyng,
  That mour greuans is ny."
His wyfe seyd: " It is tokenyng
Off mour godnes þat is comyng; 225
  We shall haue mour plente.
Haue we les our haue we mour,
All-wey thanke we god þer-fore;
  Yt is þe best treulye."

The lady seyd with gode cher: 230
" Late vs fyll a panyer
  Off þe frute þat god hath sente.
To-morow, when þe dey do spryng,
Ȝe schall to cardyff to þe kyng,
  ffull feyre hym to presente.

Sych a gyft ȝe may hafe þer,   235
That a[ll] we schall ye beter fare;
   I tell ȝou, verament."
Sir clegys grantyd sone þer-to:
"To-morow to cardyff I wyll go
   After ȝour entent."   240

The morne, when it was dey-lyght,
   The lady had þe pannyer dyght;
   To hyr eldyst son seyd sche:
"Take vp þis pannyer gladly
And bere it at thy bake esyly   245
   After þi fader so fre."
Syr clegys þan a staff he toke;
He had no hors, so seyth þe boke,
   To ryde hys jorneye,
Neþer sted ne palferey,   250
Bot a staff was his hakney,
   As maner in pouerte.

Syr cleges and hys son gent
The ryght wey to cardyfe went
   On crystenmes dey.   255
To þe castell-ȝate þei com full ryȝht,
As þei wer to mete dyght,
   At none, þe soth to sey.
As sir cleges wold in go,
Yn pore clothyng was he tho,   260
   In a symple aray.

The port*er* seyd full spytously :
" Thow schall w*ith*-draw þe smertly,
   Y rede, w*ith*-oute deley.

Els, be god *and* seynt mary,   265
Y schall breke þi hede smertly,
   To stond in begers route.
Yff þou draw any mo*ur* in-werd,
Thow schall rew it aft*er*werd;
   Y schall þe so cloute."   270
" Gode s*ir*," seyd s*ir* cleges tho,
" Y pr*ay* ȝou, late me in go ;
   Thys is w*ith*-outen doute.
The kyng I haue a pr*e*sent browȝt
ffro hy*m*, þ*at* made all thinge of nouȝt ;   275
   Be-hold *and* loke a-boute ! "

The po*ur*ter to þe pa*n*nyer wente ;
Sone þe lyde vp he hente ;
   The cherys he gan be-hold.
Wele he wyst, for his co*m*my*n*g,   280
ffor hys pr*e*sent to þe kyng,
   Grete gyft*es* haue he schuld.
He seyd : " Be hym þ*at* me dere bouȝht,
Yn at þis ȝate co*m*mys þou nouȝht,
   Be hy*m* þ*at* made þis mold,   285
The thyrd p*ar*te bot þou gr*a*unte me
Off þ*at* the kyng wyll gyff þe,
   Whe þ*er* it be sylu*er* o*ur* gold."

Syr cleges seyd: " þer-to I sente."
He ȝaue hym leue, *and* in he wente   290
   With-outen mo*ur* lettyng.
Yn he went a grete pas;
The offycers at þe dore was
   With a staff standyng.
Yn com *sir* cleges so wyght;   295
He seyd : " Go, chorle, out of my syght,
   With-out any mo*ur* lettyng.
Y schall þe bete eu*er*y lythe,
Hede *and* body, with-outyn grythe,
   And þou make mo*ur* pr*e*syng."   300

" Gode *sir*," seyd *sir* cleges than,
" For hys loue, þ*at* made man,
   Sese ȝo*ur* angry mode !
ffor I haue a pr*e*sante brouȝt
ffro hym þ*at* made all thyng of nowȝht   305
   And dyed vpon þe rode.
Thys nyght þ*is* fruyt grew;
Be-hold, wheþ*er* I be fals o*ur* trew;
   They be gentyll *and* gode."
The vsscher lyfte vp þe lyde smertly;   310
The feyrest cherys þ*at* eu*er* he sey;
   He m*er*uyllyd in his mode."

The vsscher seyd: " Be mary suete,
Thou comyst not i*n* þ*is* halle o*n* fete,
   Y tell þe, sykerly,   315

Bot þou graunte me, with-out wernyng,
The thyrd parte of þi wyneng,
 When þou comyst a-geyn to me."
Syr cleges sey non oþer wone,
Bot þer he grantyd hym a-non;   320
 Yt wold non oþer-weys be.
Than sir cleges with heuy chere
Toke his son and his pannyer;
 In-to þe hall went he.

The stewerd stert fast in þe hall,   325
Among þe lordes in þe halle,
 That weryd ryche wede.
He went to sir cleges boldly
And seyd : " Who made þe so herdy,
 To come heþer, our þou were bede ? 330
Cherle," he seyd, " þou arte to bolde.
With-draw þe with þe clothes olde,
 Smertly, I þe rede."
He seyd : " Sir, I haue a present brouȝt
ffro þat lord þat vs dere bouȝht   335
 And on þe rode gan bled."

The stewerd stert forth wele sone
And plukyd vp þe lyde a-non,
 Als smertly as he mouȝht.
The stewerd seyd : " Be mary dere, 340
Thys saw I neuer þis tyme of ȝere,
 Seth I was man I-wrouȝht.

Thow schall cum no nere þe kyng,
Bot if þou grante me myn askyng,
   Be hym þat me dere bouȝt.   345
The thyrd parte of þe kynges gyfte
Y wyll haue, be my thryfte,
   Or els go truse þe oute ! ''

Syr cleges stode and be-thouȝt hym þan :
'' And I schuld parte be-twyx thre men,   350
   My-selue schuld haue no-thyng.
ffor my traueyll schall I not gete,
Bot if it be a melys mete.''
   Thus thouȝht hym sore syȝeng.
He seyd : '' Herlot, has þou no tong ?   355
Speke to me and tary not long
   And grante me myn askyng,
Or with a staff I schall þe twake
And bete þi ragges to þi bake
   And schofe þe out hedlyng ! ''   360

Syr cleges saw non oþer bote,
Hys askyng grante hym he mote,
   And seyd with syȝhyng sore :
'' What þat euer þe kyng rewerd,
Ȝe schall haue þe thyrd parte,   365
   Wheþer it be lesse our more.''
When sir cleges had seyd þat word,
The stewerd and he wer a-corde
   And seyd to hym no more.

Vp to þe kyng sone he went;   370
  ffull feyn he proferd hys presente,
Knelyng onne hys kne hym be-fore.

Syr cleges vn-coueryd þe pannyer
And schewyd þe kyng þe cherys clere,
  Vpon þe ground knelyng.   375
He seyd : " Ihesu, ouer sauyoure,
Sente ȝou þis fruyt with grete honour
  Thys dey onne erth growyng."
The kyng saw þe cherys fressch and new,
And seyd : " I thanke þe, swete Ihesu,   380
  Here is a feyre newyng."
He comandyd sir cleges to mete,
A word after with hym to speke,
  With [out] any feylyng.

The kyng þer-for made a presente   385
And send vn-to a lady gente,
  Was born in corne-weyle.
Sche was a lady bryght and schen;
After sche was hys awne quen,
  With-outen any feyle.   390
The cherys wer serued throuȝhe þe hall.
Than seyd þe kyng, a lord ryall :
  " Be mery, be my conseyle!
And he þat brouȝt me þis present,
Y schall make hym so content,   390
  It schall hym wele a-vayle."

When all men wer merye *and* glad,
Anon þe kyng a squyre bade:
  " Bryng hym me be-forne,
The pore man þat þe cherys brouȝt."   400
Anon he went *and* taryd nouȝht,
  With-outen any scorne.
He brouȝht cleges be-for þe kyng;
Anon he fell in knelyng,
He wend hys gyft had be lorn.   405
He spake to þe kyng with wordes felle.
He seyd: " Lege lord, what is ȝour wylle?
  Y ame ȝour man fre-borne."

I thanke þe hertely," seyd þe kyng,
  " Off þi grete presentyng.   410
  That þou hast to me do.
Thow hast honouryd all my feste
With þi deyntes, moste *and* leste,
  And worschyped me all-so.
What þat euer thou wyll haue,   15
Y wyll þe grante, so god me saue,
  That þin hert stondes to,
Wheþer it be lond our lede,
Or oþer gode, so god me spede,
  How-þat- euer it go."   420

He seyd: " Garemersy, lege kyng!
Thys is to me a hye thing.
  ffor sych one as I be.

fforto grante me lond our lede
Or any gode, so god me spede,   425
 Thys is to myche for me.
Bot seth þat I schall ches my-selue,
I aske no-thyng bot strokes XII
 ffrely now grante ȝe me,
With my staff to pay þem all,   430
Myn aduersarys in þis hall,
 ffor seynt charyte."

Than ansuerd vter, þe kyng;
 He seyd : " I repent my grantyng,
 The couenand þat I made."   435
He seyd : " Be hym þat made me and the,
Thou had be better take gold our fe ;
 Mour nede þer-to þou hade."
Syr cleges seyd with-outen warryng :
" Lord, it is ȝour awne grante[yng] ;   440
 Yt may not be deleyd."
The kyng was angary and greuyd sore ;
Neuer-þe-les he grante hym thore,
 The dyntes schuld be payd.

Syr cleges went in-to þe hall   445
Among þe grete lordes all,
 With-outen any mour.
He souȝht after þe stewerd ;
He thouȝt, to pay hym his rewerd,
 ffor he had greuyd hym sore.   450

He gafe þe stewerd sych a stroke,
That he fell doune lyke a bloke
     Among all þat ther were.
And after he gaff hym strokes thre, —
He seyd : " Sir, for þi curtasse,   455
     Stryke þou me no mour ! "

Out of þe hall sir cleges wente ;
To pay mo strokes he had mente,
     With-owtyn any lette.
To þe vsscher he gan go ;   460
Sore strokes ȝaffe he tho,
     When þei to-geder mette,
That after-werd many a dey
He wold wern no man þe wey ;
     So grymly he hym grete.   465
Syr [cleges] seyd : " Be my thryfte,
Thou hast the thyrd parte of my gyfte,
     Ryght euyn as I þe hyȝht."

To þe porter com he ȝare ;
ffoure strokes payd he thare ;   470
     His parte had he tho.
Aftyr-werd many a dey
He wold wern no man þe wey,
     Neþer to ryde ne go.
The fyrst stroke he leyd hym onne,   475
He brake a-two hys schulder bone
     And hys ryȝht arme also.

Syr cleges seyd : " Be my thryfte,
Thow hast þe thyrd parte of my gyfte ;
 Couenant made we so."   480

The kyng was sett in hys parlere,
Myrth *and* reuell forto here ;
 Syr cleges theder wente.
An harper had a geyst I-seyd,
That made þe kyng full wele apayd, 485
 As to hys entente.
Than seyd þe kyng to þis herper ;
" Mykyll þou may ofte-tyme here,
 ffor thou hast ferre wente.
Tell me trew, if þou can ;   490
Knowyst þou thys pore man
 That þis dey me presente ? "

He seyd : " My lege, with-outen les,
Som-tyme men callyd hym cleges ;
 He was a knyght of ȝoure. 495
Y may thinke, when þat he was
ffull of fortone *and* of grace,
 A man of hye stature."
The kyng seyd : " Þis is not he in-dede ;
Yt is long gon þat he was dede 500
 That I louyd paramour.
Wold god þat he wer wyth me ;
Y had hym leuer than knyghtes thre,
 That knyght was styff in stoure."

Syr cleges knelyd be-for þe kyng ;   505
ffor he had grantyd hym hys askyng,
    He thankyd hym curtasly.
Spesyally þe kyng hym prayd,
The thre men, þat he strokes payd,
    Where-for it was and why.   510
He seyd : " I myght not com in-werd,
To I grantyd Iche of þem þe thyrd parte
    Off þat ȝe wold gyff me.
Be þat I schuld haue noȝht my-selue ;
To dele among theym strokys xii   515
    Me thouȝt it best, trewly."

The lordes lewȝe, both old and ȝenge,
And all þat ther wer wyth þe kyng,
    They made solas I-nowȝe.
They lewȝe, so þei myȝt not sytte ;   520
They seyd : " It was a nobull wytte,
    Be cryst we make a vow."
The kyng send after hys stewerd
And seyd : "And he grante þe any rewerd,
    Askyth it be þe law."   525
The stewerd seyd and lukyd grym ;
" Y thynke neuer to haue a-do with hym ;
    Y wold I had neuer hym knaw."

The kyng seyd : " With-outen blame,
Tell me, gode man, what is þi name,   530
    Befor me anon-ryght ! "

" My lege," he seyd, " þis man ȝou tellys,
Som-tyme men callyd me *sir* cleges;
   Y was ȝo*ur* awne knyght."
" Arte þou my knyght, þat s*er*uyd me,   535
That was so gentyll *and* so fre,
   Both strong, herdy *and* wyght ? "
" Ȝe, lord," he seyd, " so mote I the,
Tyll god all-myȝht hath vyset me;
   Thus pou*er*te hath me dyȝht."   540

The kyng gaffe hy*m* ano*n*-ryȝht
All þ*at* long*es* to a knyght,
   To a-ray hys body w*ith*.
The castell of cardyff also
W*ith* all þe pou*r*tena*n*s þer-to,   545
   To hold w*ith* pes *and* grythe.
Than he made hym hys stuerd
Of all hys londys aft*er*-werd,
   Off wat*er*, lond, *and* frythe,
A cowpe of gold he gafe hy*m* blythe,   550
To bere to dam clarys, hy*s* wyfe,
   Tokeny*n*g of Ioy *and* myrthe.

The kyng made hys son squyre
And gafe hy*m* a coler forte were
   W*ith* a hu*n*dryth pownd of rente.   555
When þ*ei* com home i*n* þis maner,
Dame clarys, þ*at* lady clere,
   Sche thankyd god verame*n*t.

Sche thanked god of all man*er*,
For sche had both knyght *and* squyre   560
    Som-what to þer entente.
Vpon þe dettys þ*at* they hyght,
They payd als fast as þei myght,
    To eu*er*y man w*er* content.

A gentyll stewerd he was hold;   565
All men hym knew, ʒong *and* hold,
    Yn lond w*er* þ*at* he wente.
Ther fell to hym so grete ryches,
He vansyd hys kynne, mo*ur* *and* les,
    The knyght c*ur*tas *and* hend.   570
Hys lady *and* he lyued many ʒere
W*ith* Ioy and m*er*y chere,
    Tyll god dyde for them send.
ffor þer godnes þ*at* þei dyd here,
Ther saulys went to heue*n* clere,   575
    Ther is Ioy w*ith*-outen ende.
                     Amen.

Notes

Notes

DAME SIRIZ

1. As I com by an waie. The opening lines are significant. In the first place, there is no direct address to the audience such as is usual in metrical romance. In the second place, the reference to source is not to a written source but to a wayside tale. Several of the popular ballads open in a similar way; cf. nos. 26, 38, 108, 180, 188, etc., in Child's collection.

5. vnder gore. Cf. ' glad under gore,' Böddeker, *Altenglische Dichtungen*, W. L. 1, 16 ; ' geynest vnder gore,' ib. W. L. 2, 37. ' And slepe under my gore,' Chaucer's *Sir Thopas*, 78. For other references, see Bradley-Stratmann, *M. E. Dict.* and *N. E. D.* The idea of the line is the same as that expressed at greater length by Host Bailly in speaking of the monk and of the Nun's Priest in the prologue and epilogue, respectively, to the *Nonne Preestes Tale.*

10. alon. The rime seems to demand *alone*, a M. E. compound from O. E. *eall* + *ana*. The line would then read, ' to her alone belonged his heart.' Against this interpretation (favored by Professor Flügel) may be cited the unusual use of *hire* with dative force and the early use of *alone* as a single word, not elsewhere cited as early as this. See *N. E. D.* A second possible interpretation of *alon* would be ' all on,' since the manuscript does not make it clear whether one word is intended or two. This explanation has to assume imperfect rime. Cf. ' On hir was al my love leyd,' *Boke of the Duchesse*, 1146. A third explanation, advanced by Mätzner, is that offered in the glossary to the present volume. This explanation involves imperfect rime, and lacks the support of perfect parallels, *along*, in this sense, being usually accompanied by the preposition *on*, as in ' Mi lif is al on þe ylong,' Böddeker, *op. cit.* G. L. VIII, 154. For other instances, cf. Böddeker, glossary.

13. ȝerne he him bi-þoute, ' earnestly he reflected.' Cf. ' Godess þeoww himm ȝeorne birrþ biþennkenn,' *Orm.* 2916 (Mätzner).

14. moute. Mätzner explains this form as an analogical one influenced by the infinitive form *mugan*, and cites from Rich. R. of Hampole the form *mught*.

19. wente him. The verb preserves its earlier meaning 'turn' and hence takes an object. Cf. v. 155, etc.

þen. O. E. *þæm*, dat. Cf. 22, 299. Cf. also Layamon, 14289, ' to þan inne ' (cited by Mätzner).

22. þen halle. The old gender distinction has been lost, since O. E. *heal(l)* was feminine.

23. palle. Cf. *Sir Launfal* (ed. Ritson), 944, ' The lady was clad yn purpere palle.' Mätzner cites also *Orm*. 8171, Layamon, 1, 55, L. Minot, p. 30, *Towneley Plays*, p. 186.

25. Notice the form of greeting in keeping with clerkly dignity.

26. so ich euer bide wenne. A frequent form of asseveration, ' as sure as I expect happiness.' Cf. vv. 113, 116, 273, 433. Cf. also Chaucer's *Nonne Preestes Tale*, 246, ' So haue I Ioye or blis.' Mätzner compares, ' swa ich abide are,' Lay. 1, 129, ' Swa ich æuere ibiden are,' Lay. 1, 141.

wenne. The spelling is Kentish, but the rime is Midland.

34. fre, ' ready to give and act for you.' Cf. Chaucer's *fredom*, also the similar development of meaning in ' liberal.'

37. Notice how the clerk maintains the sanctimonious manner shown in v. 25. Cf. also 112, 146, 161.

38. Bote on þat, ' only provided that.'

43. Wilekin. This diminutive form was probably not uncommon, since it has survived in the surname Wilkin. It is a Low German diminutive form. In the German tale *Rittertreue* (*Gesammtabenteuer*, 1, 6) appears the character ' gràve Willekin von Muntaburc.'

47. vilté. The context seems to indicate a meaning like that of *houncurteis* in the preceding line. It looks as if the word has been influenced in meaning by the independent word of the same root form, *vilani*, and meant something like ' boorishness ' or ' churlishness.' The French word *viltet* means, according to Godefroy, ' bassesse,' ' état misérable,' ' chose misérable,' ' méprisable,' and in the *Chanson de Roland* it is coupled with *hunte*, ' hunte e à viltet,' 437. The word *vilani*, on the other hand, in lines 128 and 250, is coupled with ' shame ' and has a meaning more properly belonging to *vilté*.

con. This word, like the modern French *savoir*, expresses the two meanings of ' know ' and ' be able.' Here it means ' know.'

54. þat be þou bolde, ' of that be assured.' Cf. *Ywain and Gawain* (ed. Schleich), 169, ' þat be ȝe balde,' 1285, ' þat be þou balde,' 2781, þat be ȝe balde.' Cf. also *Townl. Myst.* (ed. *Surt. Soc.*), p. 78 (Mätzner).

56. nouiȝt, ' not at all.' O. E. *nā + wiht*.

62. setten spel on ende, ' say my speech to the end ' (Mätzner). According to *N. E. D.* the phrase in M. E. means ' begin a discourse.'

75. oure sire, ' your husband.' The *oure* probably means ' your,' though, as Mätzner has pointed out, the singular forms of the second person are used. But cf. *ou* ' you ' in Vox and Wolf, 214, 215, 216.

77. feire of botolfston. Boston takes its name from St. Botolph, the patron saint of sailors. According to the Anglo-Saxon Chronicle (Parker MS. 654), *Botulf ongon mynster timbran æt Icanho*. Around this monastery, which was destroyed by the Danes in 870, grew up a town. After the Norman Conquest Boston, or Botolfston, was a port of importance. In 1204, when the *quinzième* tax was imposed on the ports of England, that of Boston was second in amount only to that of London. At this period a great annual fair was held at Boston, a great market held by special license from the king, a place that would naturally be visited by the merchant husband of dame Margeri. (Cf. Thom. of Walsingham, *Hist. Angl.* p. 54.) For reference to fairs and some of the customs connected with them, see *P. Plowman*, A iv, 43, v, 119, 171, and Brand's *Popular Antiquities* (ed. Ellis), ii, 453–470. The etymology of ' fair,' Lat. *feriae*, later *feria*, suggests that these yearly markets were held at times of church festivals (Mätzner).

In Chaucer's *Shipman's Tale* the deceived husband is absent at a fair in Bruges (v. 325).

81, 82. Cf. *Interludium*, 5, 6.

83. Cf. *Sir Eglamour* (ed. Halliwell), 1088, ' Wele were hym that hur myght welde.' Cf. also *Floris and Blauncheflur*, 251–4C.

Wel were þat ilke mon
þat miȝte winne wiþ þat on ;
Ne þorte he neure, ful iwis,
Wilne more of paradis.

secc. Mätzner's emendation to *selc* seems right. Cf. 101, 198, 245, 264, 313.

102. on flore. Cf. *Interludium*, 9.

116. So ich euer biden 3ol. Similar expressions occur in lines 26, 133, 273. The modern equivalent is ' as sure as Christmas.' See 26 note.

119. curteis mon and hende. A frequently occurring formula in metrical romance. Cf. *Sir Isumbras*, (Naples MS.) 15. ' Curteis and hynde he was.' (Quoted by Halliwell, *Thornton Romances*, p. 269, etc.)

140. þa, scribal error for *þat*.

143. Bi me I saie, ' concerning myself I am speaking.' ' That is my situation.'

146. Cf. 25 note, 37 note. Cf. also 112, 161.

149–160. The quickness of the transition from the first dialogue to the second is noteworthy as indicating that the underlying form of the story is a dramatic version. It is also worthy of note that Wilekin is not merely a love-sick character needing to be coaxed by the go-between, but is active in every way in prosecuting his suit. He is not a hero of courtly romance.

152. A frend him radde. That the advice of the friend and the method of wooing subsequently adopted, were not strange to English life of the fourteenth century must be inferred from *Piers Plowman* (C VII. 185, 186) where Luxuria confesses that he—

... sende out olde baudes
For to wynne to my wil · wommen with gyle ;
By sorcerye som tyme · and some tyme by maistrye.

154. Siriz. This name does not appear in English outside the present poem. The variant spelling *Siriþ* indicates the true pronunciation, as is proved by the rimes (161–2, 267–8), the ȝ replacing þ, as in *wiȝ* 162 (for *wiþ*), *seiȝ* 179. The name cannot be French, as is indicated by the non-French ending -þ. It is more likely from the Norse *Sigriðr*, a name which is not surprising if, as Heuser (*Anglia*, xxx, 318) believes, the work was originally composed in the Danish East of England. The name may, however, be derived from the O. E. *Sigehreð*, analogous with the O. E. *Sigebryht*.

156. suiþe, ' quickly.' The development in meaning is the same as in the German *geschwind*, which comes from the same root, meaning ' strong.'

159. wordes milde. A frequent expression in metrical romance. Cf. *Sir Eglamour* (ed. Halliwell), 85, 607.

161, 162. Siriz, wiz. The rime indicates the pronunciation as *Sirith*.

173. nelde. This word is usually printed as a proper noun. The word, which is always used vocatively, probably means ' old lady ' and is, as Heuser has pointed out (*op. cit.* p. 319) parallel with *mome* in the *Interludium*. The initial *n* certainly comes from a preceding indefinite article, and is the result of wrong division between words. Such wrong division is frequent. For instance, in *A Pennyworth of Wit* appear *anice* for *a nice* 34, *a neld* for *an eld* 79, *no noþer* for *nonoþer* 194, *þinold* for *þin old* 341, *þeldman* 157.

173 ff. Some of the phrases in this love complaint are similar to those in contemporary love lyrics. For example, with line 182 compare ' On molde y waxe mad,' Böddeker, *Altengl. Dichtungen*, W. L. III, 2, or with line 189, ' broht icham in wo,' *op. cit.* 13. On the whole, however, the language, in spite of the stiffness of the versification, is appropriately prosaic.

179. seiz, for *seiþ*. Cf. *wiz* for *wiþ* 162, *Siriz* for *Siriþ*.

194. senne, see note to v. 26.

201. Blesse þe. The earliest use of this phrase in exclamation cited in *N. E. D.* is 1590.

204. harde I-bonden. Cf. *Ludus Coventriae* (ed. Halliwell, p. 345) where Anima Christi says of the devil, " fful harde I xal hym bynde."

212. hem mote wel spede, ' for them [things] may speed well ' (or ' prosper ').

216. On him þis. Elliptical expression. ' That ' must be supplied in translation.

233. Cf. *Interludium*, 22.

240. word on honde. Mätzner conjectures that *on* is for *an*, which appears not infrequently for *and*. It would be less arbitrary, in my opinion, to assume here a reference to the raising of the right hand in taking oath. Cf. —

> King Arthur then held up his hand
> According there as was the law.

The Marriage of Sir Gawain, stanza 5; Child, *Ballads*, no. 31.

Cf. also the discussion of an analogous O. E. phrase, *hand ofer heafod*, by F. Tupper, Jr., *Journ. of Engl. and Germ. Phil.* xi. 97 ff.

247. somer driuen. Mätzner assumes either *sumer-driuen*, 'sumpter-driven,' (O. E. *sēamere*), or [*on*] *sumer*, 'in summer,' or a corrupt line. The first assumption seems most plausible. For an account of the custom of punishing women by making them ride on an ass, see Grimm, *Rechtsalt*, 4th ed. II, p. 318. In the *Chanson de Roland*, Ganelon, in announcing to Marsilies the punishment in store for him, says, —

> " Getez serez sur un malvais sumier
> par jugement iloec perdrez le chief : " [481–2].

Cf. also 701, 1828. In these instances *sumier* means 'mule' or 'ass.' This same word in England had a developed meaning, and in the dialects sum(m)er is used as the name of supporting beams of various kinds. It seems possible, then, that the custom alluded to in the text is that of *charivari*. Cf. Wright, *Dialect Dictionary* under *summer*.

261. Togoder hele. Mätzner's reading *To goder hele* is right. The phrase '*goder hele*' is not infrequent. Mätzner cites Lay. I. 153, Rob. of Gl. 368, *Townl. Myst.* p. 89. Cf. also *goder hiie*, 268 below. *Wroper-hele* is not infrequent. Cf. *P. Plowman*, B XIV, 120, Böddeker, *op. cit.* p. 451.

273. So ich euere. See 26 note.

277. maistri, 'artifice,' 'trick.' Perhaps influenced in its meaning by the independent word *mystery*.

279. The transition from addressing Wilekin to addressing the dog is very abrupt and is good evidence in support of Heuser's contention that the *Dame Siriz* is based upon a dramatic original.

Pepis. Mätzner reads *Pepir* and seems certainly to be right in his emendation. The use of pepper is one of the oriental traits in the *Dame Siriz*. Cf. *Introduction*.

315. Seli wif, 'good woman.' Cf. 337.
hounbinde. Cf. *harde I-bonden*, 204.

324. daus = the more frequent 'dawes.' O. E. dagas.
to non. This expression remains a crux. Mätzner suggests ' at noon,' and it is worth remembering that anchorites and hermits took but one meal a day, and that meal came at 12 instead of 9 on fast-days. Cf. *P. Plowman* (ed. Skeat), B VI, 146 note. Can the author's conception have been that Christ merely kept forty successive fast days ? Cf. *Sir Cleges*, 324 note.

340. Feiror, etc.: A stereotyped form of expression. Cf.
Sir Isumbras (ed. Halliwell), 25, 26.

> Als fayre a lady to wyefe had he
> Als any erthly mane thurte see.

353. clerc to wiche. The medieval idea of the command
of clerks over the powers of magic is illustrated in the popular stories
that grew up about Roger Bacon. Upon this command depends the
well known medieval popular tale, appearing in various forms as
Le Pauvre Clerc, *Der arme Schuler*, *The Freiris of Berwik*, etc.
Threats of transformation were used by others besides clerks. Ralph
Roister Doister (IV, 3), wooing Christian Custance, threatens

> "Yes, in faith, Kitte, I shall thee and thine so charme
> That all women incarnate by thee may beware."

390, 421. belle. Mätzner translates as 'belly' and cites the
analogy of other oaths referring to parts of God's body, blood, bones,
etc. It must be noted, however, that the M. E. word for 'belly'
without exception elsewhere has a final -*i* or -*y* or -*u* or -*w* to
correspond with the final -*g* of O. E. *belg, bælg*. Another possible
interpretation, cited by Mätzner from Wright's *Prov. Dictionary*,
is 'mantle.' Bradley-Stratmann cites *belle*, meaning 'tunic,' and
the allusion in the oath may be to a garment familiar through
representations of God in liturgical plays or mystery plays. A more
likely interpretation, however, is 'bell,' referring to the bell used in
the mass. 'By bell and book,' or 'book and bell,' was a frequent
form of asseveration in the Middle Ages (cf. *N. E. D.*). Cf. also
"by seint Poules belle," one of the oaths of Host Bailly (*Prol. to
Nonnes Preestes Tale*, 14). Cf. also: 'by buke and by belle'
(*Awntyrs of Arthure*, 30); 'Than he hym cursyd with boke and
belle' (Harleian *Morte Arthur*, 3018).

> "But þat ich wille, þat þou swere
> On auter and on messegere,
> On þe belles þat men ringes,
> On messeboke þe prest on singes."
>
> *Havelok.* (Emerson, *M. E. Reader*, p. 76, vv. 23–26.)

406. wente hire, cf. 19 note.
411. for þider, for *forþ þider*.

THE VOX AND WOLF

1. vox, a characteristic Southern form. The corresponding feminine form persists in modern English, as ' vixen.'

9. strok. One would like to take this as the preterit of *strecchen*, suggesting the stretching involved in peering. Mätzner's interpretation, however, is probably the correct one ; 'went,' 'passed,' O. E. *strīcan*. The furtive movements of the fox are well expressed by this word. Notice the opposite developments in meaning in mod. Engl. *strike* and *swing*.

12. wous. The *w-* replaces *v-* as it does in *wox* 12, 33 (for *vox*). *Vous* would be the Southern M. E. form for O. E. *fūs*, ' ready,' ' prepared.'

21. bruche. Mätzner explains as ' opportunity ' from O. E. *brȳce*, ' use,' ' profit.' Is it not more probably from O. E. *brece*, *brice*, ' breaking,' ' breach ?' The Southern character of the text is sufficient to explain the *u* for the O. E. *i*. Cf. the rime, ' *kun, him*, 123-4 ; *sugge, abugge*, 207-8 ; *sitte, putte*, 281-2.

22. wond, ' got,' ' passed ' (Mätzner). Perhaps the original meaning of the word was still felt, and it may be translated by ' twisted ' or ' wriggled.'

26. haiward, ' hedge-ward,' an officer whose duty it was to protect the growing crops in the enclosed fields. Cf. *Piers Plowman*, C VI, 16, and C XIV, 45, and the notes by Skeat, who cites from the romance of *Alisander* (ed. Weber, l. 5754) :

> In tyme of heruest mery it is ynough,
> Peres and apples hongeth on bough ;
> The hayward bloweth mery his horne,
> In eueryche felde ripe is corne.

The second passage cited reads as follows :

> Thauh the messager make hus wey · a-mydde the whete,
> Wole nowys man wroth be · ne hus wed take ;
> Ys non haiwarde yhote · hus wed for to take ;
> > *Necessitas non habet legem.*
> Ac yf the marchaunt make hus way · ouere menne corne,
> And the haywarde happe · with hym for to mete,
> Other hus hatt other hus hode · othere elles hus gloues
> The marchaunt mot for-go · other moneye of hus porse.

That the hayward's police duties were somewhat more general in character than the etymology of his name would indicate, is shown by the following passages cited by Mätzner.

> "The hayward heteth us harm to habben of his ;
> The bailif bockneth us bale."
>
> Wright, *Political Songs*, p. 149.

and
> "Canstow . . . have an horne and be hay-warde,
> And liggen out a nyghtes,
> And kepe my corn in my croft
> From pykers and theeves."

Cf. the haywart's part in the poem on the ' Man in the Moon ' (Harl. MS. 2253, ed. Böddeker, 177). The reeve was the overseer of a farm or manor.

31. There seem to have been some lines omitted between lines 30 and 31. The fox seems to have devoured some of the hens, perhaps two of the four. Cf. 40, 54, 55, oþre 58, 68, 98. Cf. 129 note, 151 note.

43. heddre. Mätzner suggests the insertion of *blod* after *heddre*. He also cites, 'Hwon heo beoð ileten blod on one erm eddre,' *Ancr. Riw.* p. 258. 'Wiðuten eddren capitalen þet bledden,' *ib.*

78. nom þat boket. Cf. the modern uses of the word ' take ' in ' take a high note' in singing, or 'take a fence ' in the sense of ' vault.'

87, 88. The litotes in these lines is effective. The lines have Chaucerian quality.

93. The sense seems to require a negative statement. If so the negative *ne* is carelessly omitted through confusion with the ending *-ne* in *ȝerne*. Cf. *Aquenche*, 112. Or is the line to be understood as meaning, (in general) when he found water, he drank eagerly, but . . ?

96–7, 101–2. Notice the gnomic expressions, which are characteristic of popular lore, from which the present poem has obviously been derived.

106. hiis. The initial *h-* is dialectal ; the vowel length is "poetic license." Cf. Bedier's comment on the carelessness concerning rimes in the French *fabliaux*. (*Les Fabliaux*, pp. 342 ff.)

123-4. The rime seems to indicate Midland dialect, but the rime is obviously imperfect. Cf. 263-4.

128. Sigrim. The distinctively English form of this proper name shows that the story circulated in English popular lore. The same remark applies to *Reneuard*, 133.

135. hedde, Southern form.

140. paradiis. Cf. *Introd.* p. xii.

140-7. This description of the joys of paradise is less concrete than other descriptions in this story. It is expressed in terms appropriate to the listening wolf, but is distinctly reminiscent of the contemporary humorous poem, *The Land of Cokaygne*. For a discussion of the burlesque element in descriptions of an Earthly Paradise, cf. Schofield, *Publ. M. L. A.* xix. 187 ff.

151. There seems to be something omitted at this point, — further evidence (cf. 31 note and 129 note) that this English version is abridged in places.

159. vend for *wend*. See note to vv. 12 and 33.

162. fond. Plainly the rime *fond, goed*, is "poetic license." Cf. Bédier, *op. cit.* 342.

167. beþ, 3 pl. Southern form, cf. 29; 217, etc.

get, a survival of the O. E. mutated plural.

178. to . . . I-take. Cf. Mod. Engl. 'take to drink,' etc.

199. I-faie. The rime shows the manuscript reading to be wrong.

199 ff. The enforced confession of Sigrim finds parallels in the devil's confession in Cynewulf's *Juliana* and in that of Faux-Semblaunt in the *Roman de la Rose*. Analogous literary compositions are the confession of Chaucer's Pardoner and such later satirical compositions as *Colyn Blowbol's Testament*.

207-8. sugge, abugge. A Kentish rime. O. E. *secgan, abycgan*. Cf. 241-2.

224. oþeres kunnes. Cf. *nones kunnes*, 294.

233. bruche. Cf. 21 note.

246. Ich wille oup. Cf. Modern dialect, ' I want out,' etc.

256. Wroggen, 'frogs.' Cf. 12 note, 33, 159 note.

264. Ine, for *inne* (Mätzner), another instance of a word distorted by the scribe for the sake of the rime. Cf. 106, 162. The author of the original was not averse to assonance. Cf. 123-4, 249-50.

265. houssong. Cf. 270, 274. The origin of this interesting word is thus traced by Prof. F. Tupper, Jr.: *houssong* < (*h*)*out-song* < *utsong* < *uhtsong*, 'matins.'

272. curtiler, 'gardener in a monastery.' Cf. the "Curtal Friar" in the Robin Hood ballad.

SIR CLEGES

Since the difference between the two texts is so great that it is impossible to print the variant readings at the bottom of the pages, it seems desirable to illustrate the difference by printing the first stanza of the E. text in full in the notes:—

> WILL ye lystyn, and ye schyll here
> Of Eldyrs that before vs were
> Bothe hardy and wyȝt.
> In the tyme of kynge Vter*e*
> That was Fadyr of kynge A[r]thyr,
> A semely man in siȝt.
> He hade A knyȝt *þ*at hight sir Cleges,
> A dowtyar was non of dedis
> Of the Rovnd tabull Right.
> He was A man of hight statur*e*,
> And therto full fayr of ffetur*e*
> And Also of Gret myȝt.

1, 2. Lystyns, lordynges . . . A conventional minstrel address to his audience. Cf. *Sir Eglamour*, 4, 5, *Sir Isumbras*, 4, 5, *Octavian* (South. vers. 20), etc. The variant forms of this manner of opening a story are illustrated in an interesting manner by Halliwell (*Thornton Romances*, 267-9), who cites the varying opening lines from six texts of *Sir Isumbras*.

3. herdy and wyght. Stereotyped expression. Cf. the *Squyr of Lowe Degre* (ed. Mead), 9, and the parallel passages cited by the editor from *Kyng Alisaunder*, 4892; *Arthour and Merlin*, 4532; *Eglamour*, 8; *Guy of Warwick*, B 1434; *Lancelot*, 2592; *Eger and Grime*, 2573; *Isumbras*, 8. Further instances are not hard to find: *e. g. Sir Degrevant* (ed. Halliwell), 10, 102, and the present poem, 537.

4. Vter and Pendragoun. In the romances of Merlin Vther is represented as being the younger brother of Pendragon. The E. text obviously offers the correct reading here.

6. A sembly man of syght. Cf. 'semely on to see, *Erl of Tolous*, 1217; 'semly were to see,' *Sir Isumbras*, 15. Cf. present poem, 27.

7. Sir Clegys. The name is not a common one. It is used a few times in Malory's *Morte d'Arthur*. The name Syr Clegius (Schir Clegis) also appears in the *Awnturs of Arthur*, 96.

9. ronde-tabull. The connection of this story with the Arthurian cycle, it will be noticed, is the slightest. The story of Sir Cleges, like that of another generous Arthurian knight, Sir Launfal, was originally quite independent.

10–12. For similar conventional descriptions of strength see *Sir Isumbras*, 13–15, etc., *The Grene Knight*, 41, etc.

13. curtas, 15. gentyll and fre. Cf. Chaucer's Knight.

18. gold and fe. A phrase of frequent occurrence. Cf. *Sir Isumbras*, 270, 292, *Sir Amadace*, 849, *Squyr of Lowe Degre*, 481. Cf. present text, 437.

20. buske. Prof. J. M. Hart suggests that the word *buske* here is used transitively in the sense 'hasten' (cf. *N. E. D. buske*, 6) and that its use here is like the modern colloquial transitive use of 'hustle,' an interpretation quite in keeping with the amiable character of the knight. Cf. E. text :

> The pore pepull he wold Releve
> And no man wold he Greve.

25. wyff. Cf. description of a noble wife in *Sir Isumbras*, 25–30.

38. crystynmes. For a contemporary account of Christmas festivities, see *Sir Gawayne and the Grene Knight*, *Sir Perceval*, 1803, stanzas III, xx, xxi, Berners-Froissart, vol. IV, p. 150, Book II, Cap. 28. For contemporary account of entertainment for the poor, see *Clannesse*, 77 ff.

46, 49. Mynstrellus. See note by Halliwell, *Thornton Romances*, p. 270, *Sir Degrevant*, 81 ff., 1157, 1861, *Sir Eglamour*, 1327, *Torrent of Portyngale*, 941–3, *Sir Isumbras*, 19–21, *Libeaus Disconus*, 2116, *Octavian* (South. vers.), 67–72, *Sir Thopas*, 134.

See also *Piers Plowman* (ed. Skeat), B xiii, 225 ff., 437 ff., C viii, 97 ff., C x, 127–136 and notes.

57. dyȝed vpon þe rode. Cf. *Sir Isumbras*, 247, 286.

66. all-myȝht. Note the riming words, *quyte*, *lyte*, showing that the *ȝh* was not pronounced.

73. Hys ryalty he forderyd ay. 'His munificence, he continued ever.' In *N. E. D.* the earliest citation of 'royalty' with this meaning is 1548. E. reads, *This rialte he made than Aye.*

79 ff. At this point this story differs from *Sir Amadace*, of which the beginning is strikingly similar. Sir Amadace is advised to " putte away fulle mony of ȝour men," but prefers to conceal his straitened circumstances, and keeps up appearances by being more liberal than ever, 37–60.

85, 86. Notice the rimes *eue*, *wyfe* (O. E. ī : O. E. ǣ) which indicate a pronunciation of the sound from O. E. ī tending toward the modern pronunciation. Cf. Note to 219, 222, 225, 228.

86. E. has : *The kynge be-thouȝt hym full Evyn.*

87. Cardyff. Caerleon, near Cardiff, is the more usual center in Arthurian story.

89. swownyng. Not unusual for heroes of medieval romance. See *Floris and Blauncheflur*, 246, etc.

92. And he, he had . . . E. offers the better reading, *And howe he hade his maners sold.*

94. Mekyll. Northern dialect. Cf. also 107. In each of these cases E. has the Southern form *mech.*

96. pride, wyde, tyde, syde. These rimes, which are the same in E., are sufficient to indicate a non-Southern dialect.

99. dyuerse mynstralsy. Similar lists of musical instruments are frequent. Cf. *Sir Launfal*, 669, *Pearl*, 91, *Squyr of Lowe Degre* (ed. Mead), 1069 ff., with citations, in the notes, of similar passages, *Rich. Coer de L.* (ed. Weber), 3429, 3430, 4615–4619, *Emare*, 388–390, 867, *Kyng Alisaunder* (ed. Weber), 1041–1046, *Thomas of Erceld.* (Thornton), vv. 257–260, *Libeaus Disconus* (ed. Kaluza), vv. 148–150, *Buke of the Houlate* (ed. Diebler), 755–767. Cf. also *Sir Degrevant* (ed. Halliwell), 35 ff., and note by the editor (p. 289) in which is quoted the following from Lydgate : —

For they koude the practyke
Of al maner mynstralcye,
That any mane kane specifye ;
For ther wer rotys of Almanye
And eke of Arragone and Spayne :
Songes, stampes, and eke daunces,
Dyvers plenté of pleasaunces,
And many unkouth notys newe
Of swich folkys as lovde trewe ;
And instrumentys that dyde excelle,
Many moo thane I kane telle.
Harpys, fythels, and eke rotys,
Wel accordyng with her notys,
Lutys, rubibis, and geterns,
More for estatys than taverns :
Orguys, cytolys, monacordys;
And ther wer founde noo discordys
   Nor variaunce in ther souns,
   Nor lak of noo proporsiouns.

101. notys, *luttys* in E.

106, 107. sore, þer. E. *sore, there*. The apparently imperfect rime seems to be due to scribal writing of *þer* for original *þore*. Cf. the rimes of the sounds concerned, 148, 149, 195, 198, 201, 204, 363, 366, 369, 372, 442, 443, 469, 470, 447–454. For another possible explanation, see 148, 149 note.

112. won to. Cf. *wonte to*, E.

113 ff. Cf. 16 ff., 37 ff. For similar instances of generosity, see *Sir Amadace* (ed. Robson), stanzas IV, V, and XIII, XIV.

119. longes. Northern conjugation.

122 ff. The passage that follows is probably as fine a domestic scene as any in Middle English metrical romance. Dame Clarys challenges comparison with Le Freine, Constance, the faithful wife in *The Pennyworth of Wit*, or even with Griselda. She is the most human of them all. The only scene rivaling the present one, that occurs to me, is the one at the end of *Amis and Amiloun* (ed. Kölbing), 2413–24.

129. stynte. This rime, which occurs in both texts, indicates that in the dialect of the author O. E. *y* sometimes at least appears as *e*. Cf. Morsbach, *Mittelenglische Grammatik*, §§ 127 ff.

148, 149. care, mour. This rime shows the Northern, or Scotch, dialect of this version. The E. version in these lines seems better to preserve the original, ' But neuer-þe-les hys hart was sore.' Cf. 106, 107, note. ' And sche hym Comforttyd more and more.'

151, 152. blyth, blyue. E. has the better reading, *blyth, swyth.*

154. wesche and went to mete. Equivalent expressions are frequent. Cf. *Sir Degrevant* (ed. Halliwell), 662, 1392, and the editor's references to *Emare*, 218, *Sir Gawayne* (ed. Madden), p. 34. Cf. also *P. Plowman*, B xiii, 28, C xvi, 32. ' Thei wesshen and wypeden and wenten to the dyner.'

161. euensong. Vesper services that marked the close of the day (E. *soper*). Cf. *P. Plowman*, C vii, 396, where Gloton and his companions sit in the ale-house ' til euesong rang.'

160, 161. dyde, bede (E. *ded, bede*). Cf. 129 note.

162. serteyn. Cf. *sertayne*, *Ludus Coventriae* (ed. Halliwell) p. 53. I have been unable to make a satisfactory explanation of this word. The reading in E. is clear, *Whan yt was tyme of nyȝt.*

163. rong at þe chyrche. Reference to the bell summoning to matins. In *Piers Plowman*, C x, 227 ff., we read that both *lewede* and *lordes* ought —

> Vp-on Sonedayes to cesse (daily occupations) . godes seruyce to huyre.
> Bothe matyns and messe . and after mete, in churches
> To huyre here euesong . euery man ouhte.
> Thus it by-longeth for lorde, . for lered, and lewede,
> Eche halyday to huyre . hollyche the seruice.

See also *Sir Degrevant* (ed. Halliwell) : —

> Tylle the day wex clere,
> Undurne and mare ;
> Whyle that hurde thei a bell
> Ryng in a chapell ;
> To chyrche the gay dammisel
> Buskede hyr ȝare. (ll. 619–624.)

With an orrelegge one hy3th
To rynge the ours at ny3th
To waken Myldore the bry3th
With bellus to knylle. (ll. **1452–1456.**)

166–8. Not in E.

180. E. has *And put Away penci.*

181–2. Assonance. E. has *cam, than.*

183. stynt, wente. Cf. 129 note, 160 note.

191. pouerte, hert (E. *pouertt, hartt*). The accentuation of *pouerte* varies. That the accentuation indicated by the present rime is not exceptional is shown by the identical rime in *Sir Launfal, herte, povert, scherte, smerte,* ed. Ritson, 195 ff. But see in the present text, *pouerte,* 252, riming with *jorneye, fre, sche.*

194. chery-tre, see Introduction, p. lxvi.

210. Spare wold he nou3ht. Similar verse tags are frequent. Cf. ' for no cost wolde he spare,' Chaucer's *Prologue,* 192. ' For nothyng wolde he spare,' *Sir Eglamour* (ed. Halliwell), 552.

223–5. These lines, so well in keeping with the character of Dame Clarys, are not in E.

219, 222, 225, 228. The rimes, O. E. *-līce,* O. E. *nēah,* O. F. *-té,* seem to indicate a fifteenth-century origin for the poem. The rimes in E. are similar : *sekerly, me, trewly.*

226, 227. mour, þer-fore. (Not in E.) The rimes here indicate a pronunciation different from that indicated in **148, 149.** See also 106, 107 note.

232. dey do spryng. Cf. Chaucer's *Prologue,* 822, *Torrent of Portugal* (ed. Halliwell), 362, etc.

241. dey-lyght. The reference to early rising is not unusual. See *King Horn* (E. E. T. S.), 527, *Sir Eglamour* (ed. Halliwell), 359.

248. so seyth þe boke. A frequent verse tag. Not necessarily a reference to a literary original.

252. E. has the better reading, *As A man in pouerte.*

255. Crystenmes dey. The chronology in this story offers difficulty. The incidents of Christmas eve, 85–162, and of Christmas day, 163–240, have already been narrated. The day of the journey to Cardiff should be the day after Christmas.

258. At none. Since E. has *Anon,* too much weight must

not be laid on the evidence of this passage regarding meal-times. Whether *none* had its earlier reference to 3 P. M., or its later one to 12 M., it can hardly be assumed to have been a time for the principal meal. The fact that this was Christmas day may have some bearing on the subject. Cf. *Piers Plowman* (ed. Skeat), vol. II, p. 112. Cf. *Dame Siriz*, 324 note.

262. portere. There seems to be personal animus in the way the porter is represented. The minstrel was well accustomed to ill treatment from the porters, and the surly porter appears frequently in minstrel story. Cf. *King Horn*, 1155 ff. See note by Creek, *J. G. Phil.* x, 436, and references to *John de Reeue*, 719 ff., *Horne Childe*, 958 ff., etc. For instances where the porter loses his life, see Child, *Engl. and Scot. Pop. Ballads*, no. 119, note III, Part I, p. 95 note.

263. Thow. The distinction between the contemptuous singular and the respectful plural is well illustrated in the language of the servants to Cleges and in his replies.

265. be God. Notice the number of oaths used by the porter and the other servants. Cf. 283, 285, 313, 340, 345.

267. begers route. Cf. *King Horn*, 1159 ff., *Piers Plowman*, B xII, 198 ff., C xv, 138 ff.

"Ich haue mete more than ynough · acnou3t so moche worship
  As tho that seten atte syde-table · or with the souereignes of the
    halle
  But sitte as a begger bordelees · bi my-self on the grounde."

286. thyrd parte. The artificiality of this feature of the present version is apparent. The same applies to v. 317 and v. 346.

293. officers. The French word here has the French nominative ending. E. *vsschere.* Cf. 310.

310, 311. The rimes -*ly* (O. E. *līce*), *sey* (O. E. *seah*), indicate the beginning of the opening in the pronunciation of O. E. *ī*. Cf. 315, 318, and 219–28 note.

319. wone (E. von). Apparently from O. N. *vān.* Cf. *The Erl of Tolous*, 1134. Cited by Emerson, *M. E. Reader*, p. 113, l. 12.

348. oute. E. reads, *Ar forthere gost þu nott*, which affords better rime.

352, 353. gete, mete. The rime, with long vowel, is historically correct. O. E. *mete*, O. N. *geta*.

363 ff. sore, more, be-for. Cf. 106, 107 note, 148, 149 note.

364, 365. rewerd, parte (E. *Reward, part*). Imperfect rime? Cf. 511, 512.

367-9. Not in E.

370. E. has, *Vpe to the desse* (dais) *sir Cleges went*, affording a better idea of the situation in the hall.

376 ff. The pious tone here and elsewhere is hardly in keeping with the nature of the anecdote.

382, 383. Assonance. So in E.

386 ff. The author shows familiarity with the story of the love between Vther and Ygerne, wife of the Duke of Tintagel in Cornwall.

399. hym. E. has the better reading, *nowe*.

406. E. reads, *To the kyng he spake full styll*, which affords better rime and better meaning.

418-20. Not in E.

418, 424. lond our lede. The stanzas are frequently linked together by a form of echo, or of incremental repetition. Cf. 46–49, 59–61, 68–74, 129–133, 188–193, 204–205, 324–325, 333–339, 464–473, etc.

432. Charyte. Charity is personified as a saint. See *Sir Isumbras*, 152, and note by Halliwell in which are cited instances of similar use in Spenser and in Shakespeare (*Hamlet*, IV. 5).

437. had be better : E. *haddyst be better*.

461. sore strokes. Cf. *Sir Eglamour* (ed. Halliwell), 47, ' So sore strokes he them gaue.'

474. ryde ne go, 'ride or walk.' Cf. *Sir Isumbras* (ed. Halliwell), 56, ' I maye bothe ryde and goo.'

479. The minstrel's limited range of expression is evident.

481. parlere. The author of *Piers Plowman* (B x, 93–99) deplores the desertion of the hall for private rooms : —

> Elyng is the halle · vche daye in the wyke,
> There the lord ne the lady · liketh nouȝte to sytte
> Now hath vche riche a reule · to eten bi hym-selue

In a pryue parloure · for pore mennes sake,
Or in a chambre with a chymneye · and leue the chief halle,
That was made for meles · men to eten inne ;

484 ff. The E. text at this point differs in certain important details and seems to preserve better the original story.

> An harpor sange A gest he mowth
> Of a knyght there be sowth ;
>   Hym-selffe werament.
> Than seyd the kynge to þe harpor :
> " Were ys knyȝt Cleges, tell me herre
>   For þu hast wyde I-went.
> Tell me Trewth yf þu Can,
> Knowyste þu of þat man ? "
>   The harpor seyd, " Yee, I-wysse."

> " Sum tyme for soth I hym knewe ;
> He was A knyȝt of youres full trewe.
>   And Comly of Gesture.
> We mynstrellys mysse hym sekyrly,
> Seth he went out of Cuntre :
>   He was fayre of stature."
> The kynge seyd, " be myne hede !
> I trowe þat sir Cleges be dede,
>   That I lovyd peramore :
> Wold god he were A-lyfe !
> I hade hym levere than othyr v.
>   For he was stronge in stowre."

503. had hym leuer. *Had* is used in the sense ' hold,' ' regard.'

524–6. E. reads :

> " Hast þu," he seyd, "thy Reward ? "
> " Be Cryst, he ys to lowe!"
>   The styward seyd with lok Grym.

527, 528. E. is imperfect here. *The dewle hym born on A lowe,* and the lines of the present text seem like awkward impromptu.

544. E. ends with this line, and Weber, not knowing of the existence of the O. manuscript, supplies the following not unsuitable conclusion :

> With many other yeftes moo,
>> Miri to lyue and blyth.
> The knyght rode to dame Clarys his **wyue,**
> Faire[r] ladie was non olyue ;
>> He schewyd his yeftes swyth.
> Now to Mari that hende may,
> For all your sowlys Y her pray
>> That to my talys lythe.

554. coler. " The investiture by a collar and a pair of spurs was the creation of an esquire in the middle ages : "— Fairholt, *Costume in England* (ed. Dillon), II, 127, thus quoted by W. E. Mead in his edition of *The Squyr of Lowe Degre*, p. 47. Cf. Way's exc. note to *Prompt. Parvul. s. v.* Coller, p. 87.

Bibliography

I. DISCUSSION OF FABLIAUX

J. Bédier, *Les Fabliaux*, 2ᵉ ed. Paris, 1895.

J. Bédier, article in the Petit de Julleville, *Histoire de la Langue et de la Littérature française*, vol. II.

J. V. Le Clerc, *Histoire littéraire de la France*, vol. XXIII.

F. Brunetière, *Revue des Deux Mondes*, Sept., 1893.

O. Pilz, *Die Bedeutung des Wortes Fabel*. Stettin, 1889.

B. ten Brink, *Geschichte der englischen Litteratur*, I, 221, 224, 234, 318, 323, II, 130, 136, 153, 159, 167, 170, 179, 621.

J. J. Jusserand, *A Literary History of the English People*, I, 118, 152, 183, 184, 225, 325, 442, 447, 496, 498.

H. Morley, *English Writers*, III, 336, 378.

W. H. Schofield, *English Literature from the Norman Conquest to Chaucer*, 118, 323–326, 338, 348, 479.

Ward and Waller, *Cambridge History of English Literature*, vol. I, ch. XVII.

W. M. Hart, *The Reeve's Tale*. *Publ. M. L. A. America*, XXIII, 1–44.

W. M. Hart, *The Fabliau and Popular Literature*. *Publ. M. L. A. America*, XXIII, 329–374.

H. S. Canby, *The English Fabliau*. *Publ. M. L. A. America*, XXI, pp. 200–214.

C. Fromentin, *Essai sur les Fabliaux Français du XIIᵉ et du XIIIᵉ Siècle*. Saint-Étienne, 1877.

F. Herrmann, *Schilderung und Beurtheilung der Gesellschaftlichen Verhältnisse Frankreichs in der Fabliaudichtung des XII und XIII Jahrhunderts*, diss. Coburg, 1900.

II. COLLECTIONS OF FABLIAUX AND OF STORIES USED IN FABLIAUX

Barbazan, *Fabliaux et Contes . . . des XIIᵉ, XIIIᵉ, XIVᵉ et XVᵉ Siècles . . .* 3 vols. Paris, 1756.

Legrand, *Fabliaux ou Contes du XIIᵉ et du XIIIᵉ Siècle . . .* 4 vols. Paris, 1779.

BARBAZAN-MÉON, *Fabliaux et Contes français des XIe, XIIe, XIIIe, XIVe et XVe Siècles*, nouvelle édition . . . 4 vols. Paris, 1808.

M. MÉON, *Nouveau Recueil de Fabliaux et Contes* . . . 2 vols. Paris, 1823.

JUBINAL, *Nouveau Recueil de Contes, Dits, Fabliaux* . . . 2 vols. Paris, 1839–42

A. DE MONTAIGLON and G. RAYNAUD, *Recueil général et complet des Fabliaux des XIIIe et XIVe Siècles*, 6 vols. Paris, 1872–1890.

F. H. VON DER HAGEN, *Gesammtabenteuer*. 1850.

J. PAULI, *Schimpf und Ernst*, hrgb. v. H. Österley. 1866.

J. ULRICH, *Proben der lateinischen Novellistik des Mittelalters*. Leipzig, 1906.

T. WRIGHT, *Latin Stories* (Percy Soc.). London, 1842.

NICOLE BOZON, *Les Contes Moralisés*, ed. by L. T. Smith and P. Meyer. Paris, 1889.

JACQUES DE VITRY, *Exempla*, ed. by T. F. Crane. London, 1890.

ÉTIENNE DE BOURBON, *Anecdotes historiques, Légendes et Apologues tirés* . . . par A. Lecoy de La Marche (*Soc. de l' Histoire de France*). 1877.

PETRUS ALPHONSUS, *Disciplina Clericalis* (*Soc. des Biblioph. franç. Mélanges*). Paris, 1825.

    Another ed. by F. W. Val Schmidt. Berlin, 1827.

    Cf. V. Chauvin, *Bibliographie des Ouvrages arabes*, IX, pp. 1–44. Liège and Leipzig, 1905.

Le Chastoiement d'un Père à son Fils, publ. by *Soc. des Bibliophiles*, Paris, 1825, and by M. Roesle, Munich, 1899.

    Another shorter French metrical version is published in the Barbazan-Méon collection.

Gesta Romanorum, ed. Keller. Stuttgart, 1842; ed. Österley. Berlin, 1871.

    (English), ed. Herrtage (E. E. T. S.). London, 1879.

Le Violier des Histoires Romaines, ed. M. G. Brunet. Paris, 1858.

K. CAMPBELL, *The Seven Sages* (English). Boston, 1907.

    For bibliography of The Seven Sages see L. Chauvin, *Bibliographie des Ouvrages arabes*, vol. VIII, entire volume. Liège and Leipzig, 1897.

    Cf. also *Catalogue of Romances in British Museum*, vol. III, by J. A. Herbert. London, 1910.

III. DAME SIRIZ

1. Editions of Dame Siriz

I. Wright, *Anecdota Literaria*, pp. 1–13. London, 1844.

E. Mätzner, *Altenglische Sprachproben*, I, pp. 105–13, with an excellent introduction, pp. 103–4. Berlin, 1867.

2. Besides the works containing a general discussion of fabliaux there remain to be mentioned the following works dealing especially with the " Dame Siriz."

W. Elsner, *Untersuchungen zu dem mittelenglischen Fabliau "Dame Siriz,"* diss. Berlin, 1887.

W. Heuser, *Das Interludium 'De Clerico et Puella,'* Anglia, xxx, 306–19.

3. Versions of the Weeping Bitch Story

Kathá Sarit Ságara, transl. by C. H. Tawney, vol. I, pp. 85–91. Calcutta, 1880.

Çukasaptati (textus simplicior), transl. into German by R. Schmidt, pp. 9, 10. Kiel, 1894.

Çukasaptati (textus ornatior), transl. into German by R. Schmidt. Stuttgart, 1899.

The Book of Sindibad (Oriental form of the *Seven Sages*).

Syriac version. *Sindban and the Seven Wise Masters*, transl. by H. Gollancz, *Folk-Lore*, viii, 113 ff.

Greek version. *Syntipas*, critical ed. by Eberhard, *Fabulae romanenses graece conscriptae*, I, 39. Leipzig, 1879. Summarized by Loiseleur-Deslongchamps, *Sur les Fables indiennes*, pp. 106–9. Paris, 1838.

Persian version. *Syndibād Nāma*, analysis by Prof. F. Falconer in Clouston's *Book of Sindibad*, p. 61. London, 1884.

Hebrew version. *Mischle Sindbad*, transl. by P. Cassel, pp. 268–71. Berlin, 1888.

Arabic version. *The Seven Vazīrs*, transl. by J. Scott in Clouston's *Book of Sindibad*, pp. 162 ff.

For reference to other Arabic versions see Elsner, *op. cit.*, p. 8.

Spanish version. Coote's translation of comparative text of the *Libro de los Enganos*.

Disciplina Clericalis, cf. references to editions above, no. XI.

French prose translation (15th cent.) of the *Disciplina Clericalis* (*Soc. des Bibliophiles*). Paris, 1825.

Spanish translation from the *Disciplina Clericalis, El libro de los Enxemplos* (*Bibl. autores españoles*, LI, p. 505).

Icelandic translation from the *Disciplina Clericalis,* ed. by H. Gering, *Islendzk aeventyri,* I, 181. Halle, 1882.

English translation of the *Disciplina Clericalis* in an unpublished manuscript of the Worcester cathedral library. A rotographic copy of this manuscript is in the library of the Western Reserve University.

French metrical versions of the *Disciplina,* see references above to versions of *Le Chastoiement d'un Père à son Fils.*

STEINHÖWEL, *Äsop,* ed. Österly (*Bibl. d. lit. Ver. Stuttg.* 1843), section *Ex Adelfonso,* no. 11.

The story is also included in the Italian fable collection by Tuppo, 1485, the French collection by Machaut, *circa* 1483, the Spanish *Ysopo,* 1496, the Dutch *Esopus,* 1486, and the English edition by Caxton, 1484 (ed. Jacobs, 1889).

Gesta Romanorum, see references above. The *Dame Siriz* story does not appear in the English version.

ALEXANDER DE HALES, *Destructorium vitiorum,* III, X c. Colon, 1485. Ref. from Elsner.

Another edition. Pars tertia, capitulum 10, fol. ci, b. Lutetiæ, 1516.

GOTSCALDUS HOLLEN, *Preceptorium novum et perutile, etc.,* fol. cxcv, c. Colon, 1484.

NICOLAS DE TROYS, *Le Grand Parangon des Nouvelles Nouvelles,* II, fol. XXIX, b. Ref. from Elsner.

P. GRINGOIRE, *Les Fantaisies de Mère Sotte.* (Ms. in Bibl. Nat. at Paris.) Ref. from Elsner.

H. SACHS, *Das wainent Huentlein.* (*Elf Fastnachtspiele aus den Jahren 1553–1554,* hrgb. v. E. Goetze. Halle, 1884.)

IOANNES GOBII, *Scala celi,* 1480.

VINCENTIUS BELLOVACENSIS, *Bibliotheca Mundi,* Section III, *Speculum Morale,* Lib. III, Dist. VI, Pars IX, p. 1325, edition of 1624 (Brit. Mus. Libr.).

Late Latin version publ. by A. Tobler, *Zt. f. rom. Phil.* x, 476–80.

Joh. Herolt, *Discipulus redivivus seu Sermones discipuli*, Section IV, *Promptuarium Exemplorum*, no. 599. Augustæ Vindelicorum, 1728.

Nicole Bozon, *Les Contes moralisés*, ed. by L. T. Smith and P. Meyer (*Soc. des anc. Textes franç.*), 1889, no. 138.

L. Desmoulins, *Catholicon des mal advisez* (ed. J. Petit et M. Le Noir, 1513, fol. Diiij). Ref. from ed. of N. Bozon.

Jacques de Vitry, *Exempla*, ccl. See ref. above.

The same version is included in Wright's *A Selection of Latin Stories from Manuscripts of the Thirteenth and Fourteenth Centuries* (Percy Soc. 8). London, 1842.

Metrical Tales of Adolfus, ed. T. Wright (Percy Soc. 8), Fabula v. London, 1842. (Reprinted from Leyser, *Historia Poetarum Medii Aevi 1721*, p. 2015 ff., cf. Mätzner, *loc. cit.*)

Christiern Hansen, *Komedier*, ed. S. Birket Smith, p. 60. Ref. from Elsner. Kjöbenhavn, 1874.

Prose paraphrase in Le Grand d'Aussy's *Fabliaux ou Contes*, IV, 50–3. Paris, 1829.

IV. THE VOX AND THE WOLF

1. *Discussion of beast tales*

J. Grimm, *Reinhart Fuchs*. Berlin, 1834.

W. J. Thoms, *The History of Reynard the Fox*, reprint of Caxton edition with discussion of the history of the story collection (Percy Soc. 12). London, 1844.

Paulin Paris, *Les Aventures de Maître Renard et d'Ysengrin, son compère, suivies de nouvelles recherches sur le Roman de Renart*. Paris, 1861.

K. Krohn, *Bär (Wolf) und Fuchs*. Helsingfors, 1888.

K. Krohn, *Mann und Fuchs: drei vergleichende Märchenstudien*. Helsingfors, 1891.

Fauriel, *Roman de Renard, Histoire littéraire de la France*, vol. 22.

Potvin, *Le Roman du Renard*, mis en vers, précédé d'une introduction et d'une bibliographie. Paris and Brussels, 1861.

C. Voretzsch, *Der Reinhart Fuchs Heinrichs des Glichezaren und der Roman de Renart*, Zt. f. rom. Phil., xv, 124–182, 344–374, xvi, 1–39. See especially p. 361.

H. Büttner, *Studien zu dem Roman de Renart und dem Reinhart Fuchs.* Strasburg, 1891.

Rothe, *Les Romans du Renard examinés, analysés et comparés.* Paris, 1845.

Jonckbloet, *Étude sur le Roman du Renart.* Groningen, 1863.

Leonard Willems, *Étude sur l'Ysengrinus.* Ghent, 1895.

G. Paris, *Le Roman de Renard.* Paris, 1895.

Reissenberger, *Reinhart Fuchs.* Halle, 1886.

M. de Gubernatis, *La Mythologie zoologique,* vol. ii.

J. Jacobs, *The Fables of Aesop.* Vol. i, History of the Aesopic Fable. Vol. ii, Text and Glossary. London, 1889.

For additional bibliographical references see V. Chauvin, *op. cit.,* ii, pp. 164 ff.

2. *Editions of collections of beast stories*

Méon, *Le Roman du Renard publié d'après les Manuscrits de la Bibliothèque du Roi des xiiie, xive, et xve Siècles,* 4 vols. Paris, 1825.

Chabaille, *Suppléments, Variantes et Corrections.* Paris, 1835.

E. Martin, *Le Roman de Renart,* 3 vols. Paris, 1882–87.

F. Wolf, *Renart le Contrefait,* nach der Handschrift der K. K. Hofbibliothek. Vienna, 1861.

Houdoy, *Renart-le-Nouvel.* Lille, 1874.

Ecbasis cujusdam captivi, Lat. poem of 11th cent. ed. by W. J. Thoms (Percy Soc. 12), 1844; ed. E. Voigt, *Quellen und Forschungen,* no. viii. Strassburg, 1875.

Ysengrimus, ed. by E. Voigt, 1884.

H. der Glichezare, *Reinhart Fuchs,* ed. Grimm. Berlin, 1834.

Reinaert, transl. from Flemish into French by O. Delapierre. Brussels, 1857.

Reineke der Fuchs (Volksbuch). Leipzig, 1840 (?).

Goethe, *Reinecke Fuchs,* xi, vv. 97–131.

English versions of Renard the Fox: 1) ed. Thoms (Percy Soc. 12), 1844; 2) ed. Arber, 1878; 3) ed. Goldsmid, 1884; 4) modernized version by H. Morley (Carisbrooke Library, iv), 1889.

J. Jacobs, see above.

L. Hervieux, *Les Fabulistes Latins depuis le Siècle d'Auguste jusqu'à la Fin du Moyen Âge.* 1st ed. Paris, 1884; 2d ed. 1893.

3. *Editions of Vox and Wolf*

1. Wright and Halliwell, *Rel. Antiquae*, II, 272.
2. Percy Soc. VIII, 1843.
3. W. C. Hazlitt, *Early Popular Poetry*, I, 58 f. 1864.
4. Mätzner, *Altengl. Sprachpr.*, I, 130.

4. *Analogues*

a. *Oriental*

1. Arabic, "Le renard et la hyène," Meidani, *Proverbes* (6), t. II, p. 7. V. Chauvin, *Bibl. des Ouvrages arabes*, III, p. 78, cites Maïdani, *Arabum proverbia*, II, p. 335, no. 64, ed. Freytag. Bonn, 1837.
2. Hebrew, A. Blumenthal, *Rabbi Meir*, p. 100, also 101 ff. Frankfurt, 1888.
3. Hebrew, J. Landsberger, *Die Fabeln des Sophos*, no. 10. Posen, 1859.
4. Indian, *Pantchatantra*, I, 8; *Hitapodesa*, II, 11; Kirchhof's *Wendunmuth*, 7, 26.
5. Indian, *Pantchatantra*, II, 226.
6. Mod. Indian, M. Frere, *Old Deccan Days*. London, 1868.

b. *Versions related directly or indirectly to the "Roman de Renard"*
Reinecke der Fuchs, Volksbuch. Leipzig, 1840.
J. Lassberg, *Lieder Saal*, II, no. 93. Eppishausen, 1820.
Grimm, *Reinhart Fuchs*, pp. 356–8. Berlin, 1834.
John of Sheppey, see Hervieux, *op. cit.*, III, 441.
Odo of Sherington, see Hervieux, *op. cit.*, III, 327.
    Italian fable, publ. by K. McKenzie, *Publ. M. L. A. Amer.*, XXI, 226 ff.
Libro de los Gatos, no. 14 (*Bibl. autores españoles*, LI.).
N. Bozon, *Contes Moralisés*, no. 128.
    For bibliography of the *Disciplina Clericalis* and its translations, see references above.

c. *Versions related to that in the "Disciplina Clericalis"*
G. Wright, *The Principles of Grammar*. London, 1794.
B. Waldis, *Esopus*, ed. by H. Kurz. Leipzig, 1862.

Hans Sachs, *Fabeln*, ed. Goetze. Frankfort, 1888.

R. Henryson, *Poems and Fables*, ed. by D. Laing, pp. 193–202 Edinburgh, 1865. And *Anglia*, ix, p. 470.

La Fontaine, Book xi, Fable 6.

Marie de France, Le Grand d'Aussy, *Fabliaux ou Contes*, iv; p. 396.

F. J. Desbillons, *Fabulae Aesopiae*, 5th ed., Book 8, Fable 24. Paris, 1769.

Gelbhaus, *Ueber Stoffe altdeutscher Poesie*, p. 39. Berlin, 1886.

El libro de los Exemplos, no. cccvii. *Bibl. autores españoles*, li. p. 520.

For editions of this story in fable collections see Steinhöwel in bibliography of *Dame Siriz*.

d. *Other versions*

Verdizotti, *Cento Favole*. Venetia, 1570.

San Bernardino da Siena, *Nouvelette Esempi Morali e Apologhi*, p. 15, *Racconto* vi. Bologna, 1868.

Fable Collection, publ. by J. Baechtold, *Germania*, xxxiii, 257.

G. K. Pfeffel, *Fabeln*, 4, 88.

Jacques Regnier, *Apologi Phaedrii*, Pars i, Fab. 48.

Other fables with beasts, usually fox and wolf, in a well

L. Abstemius, *Hecatomythion secundum*, no. 15.

L. Abstemius, *Hecatomythion*, no. 41.

G. Faerno, *Centum Fabulae*, p. 49. London, 1672.

R. L'Estrange, *Fables of Aesop* . . . Fab. 410. London, 1692.

S. Croxall, *Fables of Aesop and others*, no. 166. Boston, 1863.

Fables Turques, transl. into French by J.-A. Decourdemanche, no. 31.

T. Bewick, *Fables*, 1818.

Lenoble, *Œuvres*, xiv, 515.

Carl Mouton, *Esope-Esopus*, no. 95. Hamburg, 1750.

Fables of Aesop, no. 8. New York, 1862.

e. *Folk-tale versions*

French (Bas-Languedoc). P. Redonnel, *Rev. des trad. pop.* iii, 611, 612.

French (Breton). L. F. Sauvé, *Rev. des trad. pop.* 1, 363, 364.
German (Saxon). J. Haltrich, *Deutsche Volksmärchen*, no. 100. Vienna, 1877.
French (Walloon). A. Gittée et J. Lemoine, *Contes du Pays Wallon*, pp. 159–69. Paris, 1891.
French (La Bresse). P. Sébillot, *Contes du Provinces de France*.
Spanish. Antonio de Trueba, *Narraciones populares*, pp. 91 ff. Leipzig, 1875.
Portuguese. Coelho, *Contos populares portuguezes*, pp. 13–5. Lisbon, 1879.
American Negro. J. C. Harris, *Uncle Remus: his Songs and Sayings*, no. 16.

Additional bibliographical references may be found in Chauvin's *Bibliographie des Ouvrages arabes*, iii, pp. 78, 79, ix, pp. 30, 31.

V. SIR CLEGES

1. Editions

H. Weber, *Metrical Romances*, 1, 329 ff. Edinburgh, 1810.
A. Treichel, *Englische Studien*, xxii, 374 ff.
J. L. Weston, *Modern English rendering in volume with Libeaus Disconus*. London, 19—.

2. Other versions of the story of 'the blows shared'

1. English:
   J. G. Saxe, *The Nobleman, the Fisherman, and the Porter. An Italian legend*.
   Gesta Romanorum (E. E. T. S.), no. 90.
2. French:
   Tallemant des Réaux, *Les Historiettes*. . . .
   L. Moland, *Molière et la Comédie Italienne*, pp. 375, 376.
   Nouveaux Contes à Rire, p. 186. Cologne, 1702.
   Voltaire, *Œuvres Complètes*, t. x, Préface de *Catherine Vadi*, p. 781. Ref. from M. René Basset.
3. German:
   Graesse, *Sagenkreise*, p. 251. Ref. from Liebrecht-Dunlop.

GRIMM, *Kindermärchen*, III, p. 20, no. 7.
PAULI, *Schimpf und Ernst* (ed. Österley), no. 614.
F. BOBERTAG, *Narrenbuch*, pp. 7–86. Berlin, 1885.
F. H. VON DER HAGEN, *Narrenbuch*, pp. 271–352. Halle, 1811.
F. W. EBELING, *Die Kalenberger*. Berlin, 1890.
A. NIEDERHÖFFER, *Mecklenburg's Volks-Sagen*, III, 196–9. Leipzig, 1859.
Lyrum Larum Lyrissimum, no. 184. 1700.

4. Latin :
  J. DE BROMYARD, *Summa Praedicantium*, fol. clxiii, b.
  The same story is told in T. Wright's *Latin Stories* (Percy Soc.), no. 127.
  Facetiarum Henrici Bebelii . . . Libri tres. Tübingen, 1542.

5. Greek :
  E. LEGRAND, *Recueil de Contes Populaires Grecs*. Paris, 1881.
  (This story in its conclusion is unlike that in the *Sir Cleges*.)

6. Spanish :
  Cuentos de Juan Aragones, no. 3 in *Tunoneda, El Sobremesa*, etc. Ref. from Liebrecht-Dunlop.
  Margerita Facetiarum Alfonsi Aragon, p. 4 b. Argent. 1508.

7. Swedish :
  BÄCKSTROM, *Svenske Volksböcker*, 2. Oefvers., p. 78, n. 30.

8. Italian :
  STRAPAROLA, *Piacevole Notte*, n. 7, Fav. 3.
  MARC. MONNIER, *Les Contes Populaires en Italie, La Nouvelle du Sommeil*, pp. 236, 237.
  Nerucci, *Sessanta novelle populari montalesi*, n. 27, *La novella di sonno*, pp. 233–7. Florence, 1880.

9. Turkish :
  FLÖGEL, *Geschichte der Hofnarren*, 176–8.

10. Arabic :
  R. BASSET. *Contes et Légendes arabes*, no. 57. *Rev. des trad. pop.*, XIII, 675–7.
  R. BASSET, *Nouveaux Contes berbères*, Paris, 1897. Other Arabic versions cited by M. Basset are :
  Kitab Nexhat el Djallas, p. 23.

Mas'oudi, *Prairies d'or*, t. viii, ch. cvxiii, p. 163. Reproduced by Ben Sedira, *Cours de Littérature arabe*, 348, p. 32 ff. Found also in *Les Mille et une Nuits*, ed. Beyrout, t. iii, p. 176 ; ed. Quaire, t. ii, p. 206.

3. Related stories

Les Quatre Souhaits Saint-Martin. The different versions are discussed by Bédier, *op. cit.*, pp. 212-28.

Lucky they are not Peaches. W. A. Clouston, *Popular Tales and Fictions*, vol. ii, 467 ff. This tale is closely associated with the one in *Sir Cleges*.

Fable of Avaricious and Envious. See notes by Jacobs in his edition of Aesop's Fables.

Du Vilain au Buffet, Montaiglon-Reynaud, iii, Fab. 80.

4. Other stories having points of resemblance to that in " Sir Cleges "

The ballad of *Hind Etin.* Child, Ballads.

N. Bozon, *Contes Moralisés*, no. 112.

Adventures of Owleglass, no. 39.

P. Sébillot, *Contes des Provinces de France. Les Jacqueus à la Cour.*

Del Convoiteus et de l'Envieus (Montaiglon-Raynaud, v, 211-4).

Latin *Gesta Romanorum*, ed. Österley, cap. 73.

Glossary

Glossary

A, interj.: S 365, V 172, C 109. O.E. a.

a, prep., *in*: V 36. O.E. an, on.

abide, v. tr., *wait for*: imper. 2 sg., abid, S 293. O.E. abīdan.

abite, v. tr., *to bite* : pret. part., abiten: *bitten, tasted*, V 203. O.E. abītan.

aboue, adv., *above*: S 413. O.E. ābufan on bufan.

aboute, adv., *about* : S 80, C 277 ; abouten, V 15. O.E. ā-butan.

abugge, v. tr., *atone for*: inf., V 208. O.E. abycgan.

ac, conj., *but* : V 59, 84, 106. O.E. ac.

acorde, v., *to agree with* : pret. part., a-corde, C 368. O.F. acorder.

acoursed, pret. part., *ac-cursed*: V 55. O.E. cursian + prefix a.

a-do, n., *to do, affair, business*: C 527. M.E. at do, a Northern form.

adoun, adv., *down* : V 38, 57, etc., C 188 ; doun, V 247 ; done, C 97; doune, C 452. O.E. of dūne.

aduersarys, n. pl., *adversaries* : C 431. O. F. aversaire (aversier, adversier).

afalle, v., *to fall down*: pret. part., afalle, V 18. O.E. afeallan.

a-ferd, adj., *afraid*: C 220. O.E. afǣred.

afingret (see **hofþurst**), pret. part., *ahungered*: V 2, 4, 110, 190, 258, etc. O.E. ofhyngrod, ofhingrod, p. p.

after, prep., *after*, *for*:
V 61, C 161, 246, 448,
523; affter, S 197, 412;
concerning, V 52; *according to*, S 53, C 240. O.E.
æfter.

after, adv., *afterward* : C
151, 211, 383, 389, 454.
O.E. æfter.

after-werd, adv. : C 270,
463, 548; aftyr-werd, C
472. O.E. æfterweard.

ageyn, adv., *again*, *back*:
C 175, 318; aʒein, S 296.
O.E. ongēan.

a-ʒene, prep., *against*, *on
account of*: C. 135. O.E.
ongēan.

ago, pret. part., *gone*: V 49;
ago, V 153. O. E. agān.

agrise, v. intr., infin., *be
alarmed*, *frightened* : V
240. O.E. agrīsan.

Ailmer, pr. n.: V 271.

al, adj., *all* : S 49, 134,
153, etc., V 111, 200,
etc.; all, C 11, 14, 29,
110, 276, 430, etc.; alle,
V 63, 147, 156. O.E.
eall.

al, adv.: S 151, V 17; all,
C 68, etc.

al, pron.: S 63, 146; all,
C 56, etc.

alas, interj.: S 333. O.F.
a las, ha las.

al-hone, adv., cf. *a-lone*.

aliue, adj., *alive*: V 183.
O.E. on līfe.

allegate, adv., *in every
way*: S 398. Cf. O.N.
alla götu. Not cited earlier
than 1200. See *N. E.D.*

all-thyng, n., *everything* :
C 305. O. E. ealle þing
(pl.).

all-wey, adv., *in any case*:
C 228.

almes, n., *alms*, *charity* :
gen. sg. almes, V 44.
O.E. ælmysse.

almes-dede, n., *almsdeed,
almsgiving*: S 207.

almiʒtten, adj., *Almighty*:
n. sg., S 25, 322, 371;
all-myʒht, C 66 ; all-
myʒht, C 539. O.E. æl-
miht, adj.; ælmeahtig,
adj.

almus-folke, n., *almsgiv-
ers*: C 31. Earliest in-
stance of this sense cited
by *N.E.D.* is 1709.

alon, adv., *belonging*(?): S
10. O.E. [andlang] ge-
lang.

a-lone, adv., *alone*: C 186;
al-hone, V 275.

alpi, adj., *single*: V 132. O. E. ānlīpig, ænlīpig, etc.

als, also, al so: see **as**.

also, conj., *also*: C 477; all-so, C 414. O. E. eal-swā.

amend, v. tr., *amend*: imper. 2 sg., S 113. O. F. amender.

amidde, prep., 'in middle of,' 'half way down': V 241. O. E. on middan.

amidward, adv., *in the middle of*: V 274.

among, adv., *among*: V 266. O. E. onmang.

among, prep.: C 326, 446, 515. O. E. onmang.

and, conj., *and*: S 3, 5, etc., V 18, 19, etc., C 1, 3, etc.; *if*, S 164, 363, C 300, 350, 524; and if = *if*, S 168, 392, 394; a, scribal error for and, S 361; an, S 140, 145; on = 'and,' S 240, see Notes; and = 'by' in the phrase, on and on, V 197, 269. O. E. and, ond. In conditional sense, possibly from O. N. enda. See *N. E. D.*

angry, adj., *angry*: C 303;

angary, C 442; fr. anger, n. [O. N. angr] + y, adj. ending.

ani, adj., *any*: S 15, 41, etc.; eni, S 363, 373, etc.; any, C 117, 119, 205, etc. O. E. ænig.

anon, adv., *at once*: S 155, C 320, 401, 404; *presently*, C 398. O. E. on ān.

anon-ryght, adv., *right away*: C 531, 541.

anouȝ, see **I nou**.

anoundred (an + hundred), V 8.

ansine, n., *longing, desire, want*: S 306. O. E. sīn, sȳn, f. sight + prefix an-, see *N. E. D.*

ansuerd, v., pret. 3 sg., *answered*: C 433. O. E. andswarian.

ansytourres, n., *ancestors*: C 2. O. F. ancestre.

any, see **ani**.

apayd, pret. part., *pleased*: C 485. O. F. a payer, apaier.

aperseiuede, v., pret. 1 sg., *perceived, observed*: V 213. O. F. aperceveir.

aquenche, v., inf. transf., *appease*: V 13, 112. O. E. acwencan.

ar, prep., *ere, before*: S
108; conj., *before*, S 381.
See er.

aray, n., *array, dress*: C
261. O.F. aret, arroi, ar-
roy, etc.

a-ray, v., infin., *array,
dress*: C 543. O. F. ar-
(r)eier, areer, arreer, ar-
(r)oier, etc.

arise, arisen, v., *arise*: infin., V 239, 264; imper.
3 pl., ariseþ, V 269. O.E.
arīsan.

arme, n., *arm*: C 477 ; pl.,
armys, C 123. O.E. earm.

(Kyng) Artour, pr. n., gen.
sg., C 5.

as, conj.: S 1, C 21, 97,
137, etc.; al so, S 267;
al-so, V 217; als, C 121;
als . . . as, C 141, 206,
339 ; also . . . as, S 95.
O.E. ealswā.

ascape, v., infin., *escape*:
S 370. O.F. escaper.

aske, v., pres. 1 sg., *ask,
request*: C 428. O.E. āc-
sian. See axe.

askyng, n., *asking, request,
boon*: C 344, 357, 362,
506. O.E. acsung.

assent, v., pres. 1 sg.,
agree, consent : C 145,

sente, C 289. O.F. as-
(s)enter.

assunder, adv., *asunder* :
S 360. O.E. on sundran.

at, prep.: S 141, etc., V
21, *etc.*, C 8, etc.; *by*,
C 284. O.E. æt.

aþurst, adj., *thirsty*: V 66;
hofþurst, V 274. O. E.
ofþyrst, p. p. of 'ofþyr-
stan.' Cf. afingret, p. p.

a-two, adv., *in two*: C 476.
O.E. on tū, on twā.

a-vayle, v., infin., *avail,
help*: C 396. Not in O.
Fr.; first quoted from
Cursor Mundi.

auenture, n., *adventure* :
V 70. O.F. aventure.

awai, adv., *away*: S 149,
437; wei, V 53; away,
S 17; a-way, C 68; a-wey,
C 74, 80, 150, etc. O.E.
onweg.

awarie, v., subj. 3 sg., *curse*:
S 332. O.E. awergian.

awecche, v., infin., *awak-
en*: V 267. O.E. awec-
c(e)an.

awne, adj., *own*: C 389,
440, 534. O.E. āgen.

awreke, pret. part.,
avenged: V 64. O. E.
awrecan.

axe, v., pres. 1 sg., *ask*:
V 52. See **aske**.

ay, adv., *ever*: S 304, C
73. O.N. ei, ey.

bad, bade, v., pret. 3 sg.,
bade, see **bidde**.

bake, n., *back*: C 245, 359.
O.E. bæc.

bare, adj.: C 17. O.E. bær.

be, ben, v., infin., be, S
46, C 26, 44, 136, 202,
etc.; ben, S 99, 247, 295,
V 105, 118, 162, etc.;
pres. 1 sg., am, S 162,
etc., V 103; ame, C 220,
408; be, C 423; pres. 2
sg., art, S 117, 167, V
130, etc.; arte, C 535;
hertou (art + thou), V
120; bes. *art*, S 444;
pres. 3 sg., is, S 33,
etc., V 127, etc., C 217;
his, S 28, 142; hiis,
V 106; pres. 3 pl., beþ,
V 49, 153, 166, etc.;
be, C 309; is, C 48;
pres. subj., 1 sg., be, C
308; 2 sg., be, S 296; 3
sg., be, S 25, 226, C
288; 2 pl., be, C 134;
pret. 1 sg., was, C 112;
2 sg., were, V 60, 219,
C 330; 3 sg., wes (usual

in S & V); was, S 76,
C 49, 68, etc.; ves, S 79,
V 258; wes him (reflex-
ive), V 31, 261; pret.
1 pl., weren, V 64, 3 pl.,
weren, V 28, 40, 289;
were, C 2, 31, 168, 453;
wer, C 17, 35, 51, etc.;
pret. subj., 3 sg., were, S
246, 336, V 43, 218;
wer, C 502; 1 pl., weren,
V 64; 3 pl., weren, V 204;
were, C 70; pret. part.,
ben, S 68, V 185, 200,
etc.; iben, V 87, I-ben,
V 100; be, C 437. O.E.
bēon, wesan.

be, prep., *by*: C 58, 133,
171, 265, etc.; *according
to*, C 525. See **bi, by**.

be-cause, conj., C 221.
M.E. hybrid compound.
O.E. be + O.F. cause.

bedde, n., *bed*: S 102, V
214, 216, etc.; *bede*, C
161. O.E. bedd.

bede, v. tr., *offer, announce*:
infin., bede, S 40; pres. 1
sg., bede, S 129, 130; 3
sg., bedeþ, S 374; pres.
subj. 3 sg., bede, S 363;
pret. 3 sg., beed, S 349;
bed, S 367. O.E. bēo-
dan.

befel, v., pret. 3 sg., befell, happened : S 16.
O.E. befeallan.
be-for, prep. : C 183, 403;
be-fore, C 2, 372; be-
forne, C 399. O.E. befor-
an, bifora, befora (hind),
etc.
began, see biginne.
begers, n., beggars: poss.
pl.,C 267. O.F. begard.
be-hold, v., see, behold: infin., C 279; pres. imper.
2 sg., C 276; biheld,
pret. 3 sg., V 15. O.E.
bihaldan; W. S. beheal-
dan.
be-hynd, adv., behind: C
46. O.E. behindan.
belle, n., belly (in oath =
O.F. ventre bleu (dieu)
quoted by Mätzner)
scarcely as in Wright =
tunic or = bell (?): S 390,
421.
be-lyue, adv., quickly, at
once: C 139; blyue, C
152; bliue, V 109. M.E.
comp. bi-life, etc. See
bliue.
benedicite, n., blessing :
benedicite be herinne =
'God save us,' S 193.
Lat. benedicite.

bere, v., bear: infin., C
551; imper. 2 sg., C 245;
bore, p. p., V 116; born,
p. p., C 387. O. E.
beran.
beryes, n., berries : pl., C
201, 203. O.E. berie.
bes, v., pres. 2 sg. = O.E.
bis, bist (Orrm. best,
etc.) : thou art, S 444.
See be, ben.
best, adj.: C 142, 159, 212.
O.E. bet(e)st.
be-syde, adv., beside: C
187; by . . . syde, C 87.
O.E. be sidan.
bete, v., remedy : infin., V
276. O.E. bētan.
bete, v., beat : infin., V
290, C 20, 298. O.E.
bēatan.
beter, adj., better : S 274,
C 236; betere, S 389;
better, C 26, 147. O.E.
betera, bet.
be-thought, v., reflex.,
seemed : pret. 3 sg., C 90;
reflected, pret. 3 sg., C
349. O.E. biþencan.
bey, v., pret. 3 sg., bowed:
V 194. O. E. būgan,
beah, bugon, bogen.
bi, prep., along: S 1, 74; in
oaths, S 31, 89; concern-

ing, S 143, V 210; *according to*, S 253, 405, V 50; *beside*, S 383. O. E. bī. See **be**.

bicharde, v., pret. 3 sg., *deceived, beguiled*: V 293. O.E. becerran.

biche, n., *bitch*: S 354; bicche, S 372. O. E. bicce.

bicom, v., *become*: S 376. O.E. becuman.

bidde, v., *pray, bid, command, invite*: infin., V 179; pres. 1 sg., bidde, S 209; pret. 1 sg., bad, S 399; 3 sg., bade, C 398; pret. part., I-bede, V 135, 255; bede, C 330. Results from confusion of two distinct words, O.E. *biddan*, 'pray,' and *béodan*, 'offer,' 'command.'

biden, v., *bide, live to*: S 116; pres. 1 sg., bide, S 26, 133, 433. O.E. bīdan. See **abide**.

biginne, v., *begin*: pres. 3 sg., biginneþ, V 80; pret. 3 sg., bigon, S 7, 24, 302, 353; bigan, V 107; bigon to = 'did' (?), S 297, 417, 420; pret. 3

pl., be-gan, C 58; pret. part., bigunne, S 384. O. E. beginnan.

bi-go, v., pres. subj. 3 sg., *encompass, take possession of*: V 53. O.E. begān.

bi-ȝende, prep., *beyond*: S 105. O.E. begeondan.

biȝete, n., *getting, earnings, spoil* (Mätzner): V 248. Not cited in O.E. Formed from O.E. verb, begitan. See *N.E.D.*

biheld, pret., see **be-hold**.

bihete, v., *promise*: pres. 1 sg., S 428. O.E. behātan.

bileue, v., *leave, remain*: pres. subj. 3 sg., bileue, V 198; imper. 2 sg., bilef, *leave*, S 217. O.E. belǣfan.

bimelde, v., pres. subj. 2 sg., *betray*: S 38. M.E. compound from O.E. bi, prep. + meldian.

bind, v., *bind*: pres. 3 pl., V 254; pret. part. (harde), I-bonden = 'hard pressed,' S 204. O.E. bindan. See **hounbinde**.

bineþe, adv., *beneath*: V 253. O.E. biniþan, beneoþan.

binomen, binome, pret.

part., *taken away*: S 295, V 173. O.E. beniman.

bireued, v. tr., pret. part., *taken from*: S 336. O.E. bereafian.

biset, v., *invested*: pret. part., S 274. O.E. besettan.

bi-þenche, v. reflex., *bethink oneself, reflect*: infin., V 83; pret. 3 sg., biþoute, S 13; pret. part., biþout, V 81. O. E. biþencan.

bitide, v., *happen, betide*: infin., S 124. M.E. compound, bi, prep. + O.E. tīdan.

bi-wonne, pret. part., *won*: S 381. M.E. compound, bi, prep. + O. E. winnan.

blame, n., *charge, blame*: S 198, 393, C 529. O.F. blâme.

blame, v., *blame*: infin., S 56. O. F. blâmer, blasmer.

bled, v., *bleed*: infin., C 336. O.E. blēdan.

blesse, v., *bless*: infin., S 258; opt. 2 sg., blesse (þe), '*God bless you*,' S 201; opt. 3 sg., I-blessi, S 161. O.E. blētsian.

bleþeli, adv., *gladly*: S 35; bleþeliche, V 171. Derived from O. N. bleaþ, 'weak,' 'gentle,' 'kind,' but influenced in meaning by O.E. blīþe. See *N. E. D.*

blisse, n., *bliss*: V 140, 144, 294. O.E. blīðs.

bliþ, adj., *glad*: S 259; bliþe, V 249; blythe, C 140; blyth, C 151. O.E. blīþe.

bliue, cf. be-lyue, adv.

blod, n., *blood*: V 40, 51; dat., blode, C 60. O.E. blōd.

bloke, n., *block*: C 452. O.F. bloc.

blome, n., *bloom*: S 294. O.N. blōm.

body, n., *body*: C 299. O. E. bodig.

boinard, n., *fool, knave*: S 288. O.F. buinard.

boke, n., *book*: C 248. O. E. bōc.

boket, n., *bucket*: V 78, 80, 88, 232; boketes, V 73. O.F. buket (?).

bold, adj., *assured, certain*: S 54; bolde, C 331. O. E. beald.

boldly, adv., C 328. O.E.
bealdlīce.

bond, adj., *bond, enslaved*:
C 114. O.E. bonda, n.

bone, n., *request, boon*: S
375. O.N. bōn, corr. to
O.E. bēn.

bone, n., *bone*: C 476;
pl. bones, V 63. O.E.
bān.

bore, p. p., see bere, v.

bote, prep., *but, besides*: S
137, V 39, 164, 254;
bot, C 69, 75, 83, 428.
O.E. būtan.

bote, conj., *but*: S 38, 41;
bot, C 251, 320; bote,
unless, S 234, V 43, 193;
bot, C 286, 316; bote if,
unless, S 181; bot if, C
344, 353; bote þat, *unless*,
S 400. O.E. būtan.

bote, n., *remedy*: C 361.
O.E. bōt.

both, adv., C 32, 51, 65,
114, 140; bothe, C 3,
31; boþe, S 121, 150, V
167; boþ, S 86; boþen,
V 26. O.N. bāðar.

boþe, pron., *both*: C 31.
O.N. bāðar, m., bāðir,
f., bæði, bāði, n.

Botolfston, pr. n., *Boston*:
S 77.

boue, prep., *above*: S 90.
O.E. bufan.

bowȝe, n., *bough*: C 196,
199; bow, C 214. O.E.
bōg.

bred, n., *bread*: S 327. O.
E. brēad.

breke, v., *break*: infin., C
266; pret. 3 sg., breke,
S 356; brake, C 476.
O.E. brecan.

brest, n., *breast*: V 194.
O.E. brēost.

bringen, v., *bring*: infin.,
S 189, 404; bringe, V
126; pres. subj., 2 sg.,
bringe, S 400; pres. im-
per. 2 sg., bryng, C 399;
pret. 3 sg., broute, S 92,
V 104, 259; brohute, V
70; browȝt, C 274; brouȝt,
C 304, 334, 400, 403;
brouȝht, C 216; pret. part.,
I-brout, S 244, 424, V 82,
122. O.E. bringan.

broþer, n., *brother*: S 135.
O.E. brōðor.

brouke, v., *use, enjoy*: pres.
1 sg., S 273. O.E. brū-
can.

bryght, adj., *bright*: C 388.
O.E. beorht.

bruche, n., *breach, opening*:
V 21, 233. O.E. bryce.

buggen, v., *buy*: S 272;
pret. part.,bouȝht, C 283,
335. O.E. bycgan.

burste, v., *burst*: pret. subj.
3 sg., S 360. O.E. ber-
stan.

burþ, v. impers., *behooves*:
pres. 3 sg., S 82. O.E.
bȳrian.

buske,v.,*to thrash,hustle*(?)
box(?): infin., C 20. Du.
boxen ; L. G. baksen,
baaksen.

by, see bi, prep.

callyd, v., *called* : pret. 3
pl., C 494, 533. O.E.
ceallian.

can, see con.

cardyff, pr. n. : C 87, 233,
239, 544 ; cardyfe, C
254.

care, n., *care, anxiety*: C
148. O.E. cearu.

carrals, n., *carols*: pl., C
103. O.F. carole.

castell, n., *castle*: C 544.
Late O.E. castel, fr. O.N.
F. castel.

castell-ȝate, n., *castle gate*:
C 256.

cellerer, n., *cellarer*: V 59.
Anglo-Fr. celerer; O.F.
celerier.

certes, adv., *certainly*: S
61, 139. O.F. certes.

chapitre, n., *chapter, ec-
clesiastical court*: S 244.
O.F. chapitre.

charyte, n., *charity* : C
432. O.F. charitet.

chauntecler, pr. n.: V 37,
46.

cheken, n., *cheeks*: pl., S
358. O.E. ceāce.

chere, n., *cheer, look, expression*: C 30, 124, 147,
156, etc. O.F. chere.

cherle, n., *churl*: C 331;
chorle, C 296. O.E.
ceorl.

chery, n., *cherry*: C 211;
pl., cherys, C 279, 311,
374, etc. O.N.F. cherise.

cheryd, v.,*cheered*: pret. 3
pl., C 33. From chere,
n.; O.F. chere, chiere.

chery-tre, n., *cherry tree*:
C 194. M.E. compound,
but cf. O.E. cyrstreow.
Cf. *N.E.D.*

ches, v., *choose*: infin., C
427. O.E. cēosan.

chesyn, n., *cause*: be che-
syn of = *because of,*C 171.
O.F. acheson, acheison;
Lat. occāsiōnem.

childe, n., *child*: dat., V

228; pl., children, V 116, 155; chylder, C 83, 160, 167, 173, etc. O.E. cild.

chorle, see **cherle**.

chyrche, n., *church* : dat., C 163. O.E. cyrice.

clarc, n., *clerk*: S 348, 366, 380, 387; clerc, S 353, 363, 373; pl., clarkes, S 248. O.F. clerc.

(dame) **Clarys**, pr. n.: C 28, 551, 557.

(sir) **Clegys**, pr. n.: C 7, 37; sir cleges, C 259, 271, 295, 301, 322, 328, 382, 439, 533; cleges, C 145, 403, 494; syr clegys, C 238, 247; syr cleges, C 86, 89, 169, 253, 289, 319, 349, 361, 373, 445, 478, 483, 505; syr ——, C 466.

clene, adj., *pure*: V 227, 250, C 211; klene, V 178. O.E. clæne.

clere, adj., *clear, bright*: C 374, 557, 575. O.F. cler.

cloþed, v., *clothed*: pret. part., S 6; I-cloþed, S 319. O.E. cláðian.

clothes, n., *clothes*: C 332. O.E. cláðas.

clothyng, v. n., *clothing*: C 260.

cloute, v., *clout, beat*: infin., C 270. O.E.* clūtian, of which only the pret. part., geclūtod, survives.

cnowe, v., *know*: infin., S 122. O.E. cnáwan.

cnul, n., *knell* : V 251. See **soule-cnul**.

cold, n., *cold*: S 312; adj., V 254; colde, V 255. O.E. ceald, adj.

coler, n., *collar*: C 554. O.F. colier.

comandyd, v., *commanded*: pret. 3 sg., C 382. O.E. comander.

come, n., *coming*: S 108, V 134. O.E. cyme.

comen, v., *come*: infin., comen, V 136, 180, 230, 235, etc.; kome, V 174; com, C 23, 511; come, C 330; cum, C 343; pres. 2 sg., commys, C 284; comyst, C 314, 318; pres. imper. 2 sg., com, S 22, 28, V 37; 3 pl., komeþ, V 270; pres. part., comyng, C 224; pret. 1 sg., com, S 1, 64, 180; 2 sg., come, S 262; 3 sg., com, S

22, etc., C 122, 181, 295; come, V 17; come hire, S 299; pret. 3 pl., comen, V 287; com, C 115, 256; pret. part., I-com, S 162; I-comen, V 59; comen, S 296. O.E. cuman.

comener, n., *commoner*: C 65. M.E. formation from O.F. comun.

comforth, v., *comfort*: pres. 3 sg., C 149. O.F. cunfort, confort.

commyng, v. n., *coming*: C 280.

con, v., *know, know how, can*: pres. 1 sg., con, S 47, 65, 206, 450; cone, S 168; 2 sg., const, S 285; can, C 490; 3 sg., can, V 97; pret. 2 sg., couþest, S 188, 220; pret. 3 sg., couþe, C 208; pret. subj. 3 sg., kouþe, V 184. O.E. can, con, cūðe.

conseyle, n., *advice*: C 393. O.F. conseil.

content, adj., *contented, satisfied, glad*: C 395, 564. O.F. content.

contre, n., *country*: C 43. O.F. contree.

coppe, n., *cup*: S 329; cowpe, C 550. O.E. cuppe.

Corne-weyle, pr. n.: C 387.

cost, n., *cost*: C 120. O.F. cost.

couenant, n., *covenant*: C 480; couenand, C 435. O.F. co(n)venant.

couþe, couþest, see **con**.

crafftes, n., *crafts*: pl., S 190. O.E. cræft.

craue, v., *ask*: infin., S 352. O.E. crafian.

crede, n., *creed*: S 209. O.E. crēda.

Crist, pr. n., *Christ*: S 332, etc.; cryst, C 522; gen., crystes, C 133.

Cristine, adj., *Christian*: V 120. Anglo-Fr. Cristien.

croune, n., *tonsure*: S 348. Anglo-Fr. coroune.

Crystenmes, pr. n.: C 85, 255; crystyn-mes, C 38. Late O.E. crystes mæsse.

cunne, n., *kind*: nom. sg., kun, V 123; kunne, V 54; kynne, C 569; gen. sg., kunnes, V 146, 224, 294; cunnes, S 15; nom.

pl. (?), cunne, V 166. O. E. cynn.

cursede, v., pret. 3 sg., *cursed* : V 259. O. E. cursian.

curtasly, adv., *courteously*: C 507.

curteis, adj., *well-man-nered, courteous*: S 119, 341 ; curtas, C 13, 570. O. F. corteis.

curteisi, n., *courtesy, man-ners*: S 110; curtasse, C 455. O. F. cortesie.

curtiler, n., *gardener*: V 272. O. F. cortiller.

dai, n., *day*: S. 150, 208, 345 ; day, S 16 ; dey, C 30, 39, 135, 158, 232 ; pl., daies, V 48, 152 ; dayes, V 49; daus, S 324; lif-daie, V 200. O. E. dæg, dagas.

dame, n., *lady*: S 37, 61, etc., C 217; dame clarys, C 28, 557 ; dam clarys, 551. O. F. dame.

dansyng, v. n., *dancing*: C 104.

dar, v., = þar, etc., pres. 2 sg., *needest*: S 260. O. E. þearf.

ded, adj., *dead*: S 309, V

149, 191 ; dede, C 500. O. E. dēad.

dede, n., *deed, thing*: S 41, V 223. O. E. dǣd.

dede, v., see do.

del, n., *lament, grief*: S 344, 356. O. F. doel.

dele, v., *divide, give* : in-fin., C 515. O. E. dǣlan.

deley, n., *delay* : C 264. O. F. delei.

deleyd, v., *delayed*: pret. part., C 441. O. F. de-layer.

depe, adj., *deep*: V 109. O. E. dēop.

dere, adj., *dear*: C 202. O. E. dēore.

dere, adv., *dearly*: C 283, 335. O. E. dēore.

derne, adj., *secret*: S 130. O. E. derne, dierne.

dernelike, adv., *secretly*: S 86.

desesyd, v., *troubled, af-flicted*: pret. part., C 191. O. F. desaaisier.

dettys, n., *debts*: pl., C 562. O. F. dette.

deuel, n., *devil*: V 104, 282. O. E. dēofol.

dey, see dai.

dey-lyght, n., *daylight*: C 241.

deyntes, n., *dainties*: pl.,
C 413. O.F. deyntee.

do, don, done, v., *do, cause
to, give, put*: infin., do,
cause, S 126, *cause to*,
V 251; don, *do*, S 32, 35,
53 ; done, *do*, V 236;
pres. 1 sg., do, *cause to*,
V 51; 2 sg., dest, *dost*,
V 33, 35, 152; dost, S
377 ; 3 sg., do, C 232 ;
3 pl., doþ, *do*, V 217 ;
pres. subj. 2 sg., do, *give*,
V 192 ; 3 sg., do, *grant*,
S 322, 330 ; pret. 3 sg.,
dede, *caused*, V 67 ;
dyde, *did*, C 573 ; pret.
3 pl., dyd, *did*, C 574;
dyde, *did*, C 160 ; pret.
subj. 1 sg., dude, S 172 ;
pret. part., I-don, V 106,
put, S 323 ; don, *done*,
S 226, V 39, C 49, *com-
pleted*, C 178 ; do, *done*,
V 68, *made*, C 411; I-do,
done, V 222. O.E. dōn.

done, adv., *down*: C 97.
See **adown.**

dore, n., *door*: S 301, V 27,
C 293. O.E. duru.

dou, n., *dough*; V 256.
O.E. dāh.

douȝtyer, adj., *more dough-
ty*: compar., C 8. Late

O.E. dohtig, for earlier,
dyhtig, dihtig.

doun, n., *down*: V 247 ;
doune, C 452. See **adoun.**

doute, n., *doubt, fear*: C
273. O.F. doute.

douter, n., *daughter* : S
339, etc. O.E. dohtor.

draw, v., *draw*: pres. subj.
2 sg., draw, C 268 ; pret.
3 sg., drew, C 88 ; drou,
V 277. O.E. dragan.

dred, adj., *afraid*: S 409.
Aphetic form from M.E.
adrad, O.E. of dræd(d).

drede, n., *dread, fear*:
dat., V 89. M.E. noun
from O.E. verb drædan.

dreri-mod, adj., *sad in
heart*: S 149. M.E. com-
pound, O. E. drēorig +
mōd.

driȝtte, n., *Lord*: S 408.
O.E. dryhten.

drinke, v., *drink*: infin.,
V 79; pret. 3 sg., dronk,
V 93. O.E. drincan.

drinke, n., *drink*: S 133,
V 143 ; drunche, V 14 ;
pl., drynkes, C 118. O.E.
drinc, str. m., drinca, w. m.

driuen, pret. part., *driven*:
S 247. O.E. drīfan.

drou, see **draw.**

drunche, see drinke.

drofe, v., *drove*: pret. 3
pl., C 158. O.E. drīfan.

dude, see do.

duell, v., *dwell*: infin., C
82 ; pret. 3 pl., duellyd,
C 87. O.E. dwellan.

duntes, n., *blows, strokes*:
pl., V 295 ; dyntes, C
444. O.E. dynt.

dyde, v., see do.

dyght, pret. part., *made
ready* : C 242, 257 ;
dyȝht, C 168, 540. O.E.
dihtan.

dyȝed, dyed, v., *died*: pret.
3 sg., C 57, 306. Early
M.E. deȝen. O.N. deyja.

dyntes, see duntes.

dyuerse, adj., *divers, different kinds of* : C 99.
O.F. divers(e).

eddre, n., *vein* : V 45,
heddre, V 43. O.E. ǣdre.

ede, v., *went*: pret. 3 sg.,
V 69; hede, S 347, 380,
V 275. O.E. ēode, see go,
gon.

efft-sones, adv., *again*: S
384. O.E. eft sōna.

egre, adj., *eager*: V 289.
O.F. egre, aigre.

eien, n., *eyes*: pl., S 281;

heien, S 357; heie-ren-
ning, S 283. O.E. ēage.

eilleþ, v., *aileth*: pres. 3 sg.,
S 337. O.E. eglan.

eke, conj., *also*: S 159,327.
O.E. ēac.

eldyst, adj., *eldest*: superl.,
C 243. O.E. ieldest.

elles-wer, adv., *elsewhere*:
V 208. O.E. elles hwǣr.

els, conj., *else*: C 265, 348.
O.E. elles.

ende, n., *end*: S 62, C 576.
O.E. ende.

enderdai, n., *a day re-
cently past (N. E. D.),
other day*: S 366. M.E.
compound, O.N. endr +
O.E. dæg.

enes, adv., *once*: S 383.
Early M.E. ænes; O.E.
ǣne.

eni, see ani.

entente, n., *intent, plan,
purpose*: C 240, 486, 561.
O.F. entente.

ernde, n., *errand, business*:
S 347; hernde, S 40, 97,
214, 226, 410. O. E.
ǣrende.

erne, v., *run*: infin., V 16.
O.E. iernan.

erour, adv., *before*: V 4.
O.E. ǣror.

eroust, adv., *first*: V 16, 124. O.E. ǣrest.

erþe, n., *earth*: S 107, 325, 416; erth, C 378. O.E. eorðe.

esyly, adv., *easily*: C 245. O.F. aisié, p. p.

eten, v., *eat*: infin., S 279; pret. 3 pl., hete, V 156; pret. part., I-ete, V 98, 169; ete, C 157. O.E. etan.

eþe, adv., *easily*: S 338. O. E. ēaþe.

euch, euche, adj., *each, every*: V 101, 224, 285. O.E. ǣlc.

eue, n., *eve*: C 85. O.E. ǣfen.

euele, adv., *evil, ill*: S 173, etc. O.E. yfel.

euensong, n., *vespers*: C 161. O.E. ǣfen-sang.

euer, euere, adv., *ever*: S 26 etc., V 141, C 115, 141, 149, 190, etc. O.E. ǣfre.

euer-lastyng, adj., *everlasting*: C 177, etc.

euer-more, adv., *evermore*: S 385.

euery, adj., *every*: C 22, 37, 80, 104, 105, etc. O.E. ǣfre, ǣlc.

euerychon, pron., *every* one: C 185; heuereuchon, V 270.

euyn, adv., *even*: C 468. O.E. efne.

fader, *father*: C 5, 246. O.E. fæder.

faille, n., *fail*: S 187. O.F. faillir.

fain, adv., *gladly*: S 309, 393. O.E. fægen, adj.

fair, adj., *fair*: S 6; feir, S 339; feyr, C 19, 371; feyre, C 11, 381; compar., feiror, S 340; superl., feyrest, C 311. O.E. fæger.

faire, adv., *fair*: S 160; feyre, C 234, 371. O.E. fægre.

fallen, v., *fall*: pres. 3 sg., falleþ, S 306; pret. 3 sg., fell, C 89, 148, *befell, happened*, C 85; pret. part., fallyn, C 17; fallyd, C 96. O.E. feallan.

fals, adj., *false*: C 308. O. F. fals.

falsdom, n., *falsehood*: S 65. M. E. compound. Earliest citation in *N.E. D.*, 1297.

falsete, n., *falseness*: S 101. O.F. falseté.

fare, v., *fare, go*: infin.,
S 152, V 141, C 236;
pres. 1 sg., fare, S 173,
V 202. O.E. faran.

fast, adv., *quickly*: C 325,
563. O.E. fæste, adv.

faste, v., pret. 3 sg., *fasted*:
S 324. O.E. fæsten.

fe, n., *money, property*: S
382, C 18, 437. O.E.
feoh.

fecche, v., *fetch*: infin., S
314; pret. subj. 2 sg.,
feche, S 386. O.E. fec-
can.

fede, v., *feed, nourish, sus-*
tain: pres. 1 sg., S 208,
321; pret. 1 sg., fede; C
114. O.E. fēdan.

feire, n., *fair*: S 77. O.F.
feire.

fele, adj., *many*: V 166;
felle, C 406 (?). O.E.
fela.

fere, n., *companion, friend*:
V 120, C 125; I-fere, V
172, 185. O.E. gefēra,
m.

fere, n., *companionship*: in
the phrase, in fere, *to-*
gether, C 201. O.E.
gefēr, n.

ferli, adj., *wonderful*: S
277. O.E. fǣrlīc.

ferre, adv., *far*: C 207, 489.
O.E. feor.

fest, n., *feast*: C 38, 44,
49; feste, C 71, 412; ac.
pl., festes, C 55, 59; feste,
C 61. O.F. feste.

festyd, v., *feasted*: pret.
3 sg., C 64. O.F. fes-
ter.

fete, n., *feet*: pl., C 314.
O.E. fēt.

fetour, n., *feature*: C 11.
O.F. faīture.

feyle, n., *fail, doubt*: C
390. O.F. faile, faille.

feylyng, v. n., *fail*: C 384.

feyre, adj., adv.; see
fair(e).

finden, v., *find*: infin., S 34;
finde, S 316; fonde, S
342; pret. 1 sg., foud
(scribal error ?), V 162;
pret. 3 sg., fond, V 21,
93, 294, C 200; founde,
S 407, V 73, 92; found,
C 219; pret. part., founde,
S 422; founden, *invented*
(Mätzner), S 203. O.E.
findan.

fiue, num., *five*: V 29. O.
E. fīf.

fle, v., *fly*: imper. 2 sg., V
38; pret. part., flowen, V
31. O.E. flēogan.

fles, n., *meat*: S 327. O.E. flæsc.

flet, n., *floor*: S 273. O.E. flet(t).

flok, n., *flock*: V 29. O.E. flocc.

flore, n., *floor*: S 102. O.E. flōr.

flowen, see **fle.**

fode, n., *food*: C 119. O. E. fōda.

fol, n., *fool*: S 115. O.F. fol.

fol, adv., see **ful.**

folewe, v., *follow*: infin., S 350. O.E. folgian.

fomen, n., *foes*: pl., V 288. O.E. fāhman.

fond, fonde, v., see **finden.**

fonde, v., *try*: infin., S 241, 393. O.E. fandian.

for, prep., *for*: S 35, etc., C 57, 113, 119, 455, etc.; *because of*, C 34. O.E. for, fore.

for, conj., *for*: S 79, C 96, 304, 450, 506.

forderen, v., *to promote, advance*: pret. 3 sg., forderyd, C 73. O.E. fyrðr(i)an.

foreward, n., *agreement, covenant*, S 256. O.E. foreweard.

forȝelde, v., pres. subj.

3 sg., *pay, requite*: S 37, 326, 415, V 226. O.E. forȝi(e)ldan.

for-ȝeue, v., *forgive*: infin., V 175; forgiue, S 334; pres. 1 sg., forȝeue, V 225; imper. 2 sg., forȝef, V 209. O.E. forgi(e)fan.

forȝeuenesse, n., *relenting*: V 295. O.E. forgifnes, forgyfenes, etc.

forhelen, v., *conceal*: p.p. forholen, S 237. O.E. forhelan.

forsake, v., *forsake*: pret. part. forsake, V 177. O.E. forsacan.

forsape, v., *transform*: infin., S 369. O.E. forsceppan.

fort, conj., *until*: V 17 (for + to), see **for to.**

forþ, adv., *forth*: S 397; forth, C 337. O.E. forþ.

for-þi, conj., *therefore*: S 171, 180, 344, etc.; forþen, S 185. O.E. for þȳ.

for þider, S 411; = forth + þider.

forþinken, v., *repent*: pres. 3 sg., forþinkeþ, S 139. O.E. forðencan.

for to, introducing an infinitive: S 151, 152, 239;

forto, C 164, 424, 482;
for-to, C 150. Earliest
citation in *N.E.D.*, 1200.

fortone, n., *fortune*: C
497. O.F. fortune.

foud, found, founden, see
finden.

foure, num., *four*: C 470.
O.E. fēower.

fourti, num., *forty*: S 324.
O.E. fēowertig.

fre, adj., *free, noble*: S 34,
339, C 114, 246, 536;
compar., freour, S 342.
O.E. frēo.

fre-borne, adj., *free born*:
C 408.

frely, adv., *freely*: C 429.
O.E. frēolīce.

frend, n., *friend*: S 152,
185, V 133; pl., frend,
V 160. O.E. frēond.

frere, n., *friar*: V 266, 271,
279, C 32; pl., freren, V
262. O.F. frere.

fressch, adj., *fresh*: C 379.
O.E. fersc.

fro, prep., *from*: S 380, C
176, 305, 335. O.N. frā.

frute, n., *fruit*: C 231;
fruyt, C 206, 307. O.F.
fruit.

frythe, n., *wood*: C 549.
O.E. fyrð, fyrhð.

ful, adj., *full*: S 158; full,
C 24. O.E. ful.

ful, adv., *full, entirely,
quite, very*: S 3, 34, V
215; fol, S 35, etc.; full,
C 108, 234, 256, etc.;
ful wel, S 257, 278, 450,
V 238; full wele, C 485.
O.E. ful.

fullen, v., *fulfil*: infin., S
239; fyll, *fill*, C 230.
O.E. fyllan.

fulþe, n., *filth*: V 165. O.E.
fȳlð.

furmeste, adj., *first*: V 21.
O.E. fyrmest.

fyll, see fullen.

fynd, v., *find*: infin., C 47.
O.E. findan.

gabbe, v., *jest, lie*: imper.
2 sg., V 121. O.F. gab-
(b)er, O.N. gabba.

gan, v., *did*: pret. 3 sg., C
59, 146, 214, etc.; gon,
V 1, 83, 195, 240; pret.
3 pl., gounnen, V 283.
Aphetic form of began.
In this sense from 1200.

gange, v., *go, walk*: S 262,
308, 437. O.E. gangan.

gar, garen, v., *make, cause*:
infin., S 281, 290, 449.
O.N. ger(o)a.

gare-mersy, n., *great thanks, gramercy*: C 421. O.F. grand merci.

garthyn, n., *garden*: C 187, 218. O.N.F. gardin.

gent, gente, adj., *gentle, noble*: C 253, 386. O.F. gent.

gentyll, adj., *gentle, noble*: C 15, 25, 309, 536, etc., O.F. gentil.

gentyll-men, n., *gentlemen*: pl., C 65. M. E. compound. *N. E. D.* 1275.

get, n., *goats*: pl., V 167. O.E. gāt, gēt.

gete, v., *get*: infin., S 14, C 155, 352; geten, S 447; subj. 1 sg., gete, S 234; O.E. gietan, gitan; O.N. geta.

geue, v., *give*: infin., S 223, 388; ȝeue, S 191; gyff, C 287, 513; pres. 2 sg., ȝeuest, S 287; pres. subj. 3 sg., ȝeue, S 442, V 34; pret. 3 sg., ȝaue, C 290; ȝaffe, C 461; gafe, C 451, 550, 554; gaff, C 18, 454; gaffe, C 541; pret. part., I-giuen. O.E. gifan.

geyst, n., *geste, tale*: C 484. O.F. geste.

gift, n., *gift*: S 223; gyft, C 405; gyfte, C 346, 467, 479; pl., giftes, S 388; gyftes, C 50, 282. O.E. gift.

gin, ginne, n., *trick, cleverness, contrivance, trap*: S 289, V 72, 77, 82, 86, 103, 125. O.F. engin.

gistninge, n., dat., *feast, banquet* (Mätzner): V 255. Scand. Cf. O. Sw. gästning.

glad, adj.: S 328, 402, V 249, C 30, 124, 136, 397, etc. O.E. glæd.

gladly, adv.: C 244. O.E. glædlīce.

go, gon, v., *go, walk*: infin., go, S 185, 297, 319, V 1, etc., C 146, 239, 259, 272, etc.; go = *walk*, C 474; gon, S 135, 156, 417, V 108, 283, C 50, 184; pres. subj. 3 sg., go, C 420; 1 pl., go, C 139; pres. imper. 2 sg., go, C 296; pret. 3 sg., went, C 292, 324, etc.; wente, C 186, 277, 290; pret. 3 pl., went, C 154, 161, 167, etc.; wente, C 178;

pret. part., gon, S 76;
gon = *ago*, C 500; I-
gon, S 80, etc. See also
ede, hede. O.E. gān,
wendan.

God, pr. n., *God*: S 25,
315, etc., C 176, 179,
etc.; goed, S 210, 314,
317, 322, 330; gen. sg.,
godes, S 197, V 56, 57,
C 164; dat. Gode, V
158. O.E. God.

gode, adj., *good*: S 300, V
172, C 51, 118, 229,
etc.; god, S 285; goed, V
173. O.E. gōd.

gode, n., *goods, wealth*: V
147, C 58, 68, 419, 425;
goed, V 161; god, C 70,
155; godes, C 137. O.E.
gōd.

Goder-hele, in phr. to
goder hele, *to (your) good
fortune*: S 261; used like
a nom. sg., goder-hele,
S 269. Laʒ. to godere
þire hæle = O.E. to gōdre
hæle.

gode sir, n., like A. F.
beau sir, *dear sir*: C 271.

godlec, n., *goodness, bene-
fit*: S 227. O. N. gōð-
leik-r.

godnedai, phr., *good day*:

accus. sg., S 145; goddai,
S 397.

godnes, n., *goodness*: C 29;
good, C 574; *good for-
tune*, C 224. O.E. gōd-
nes.

goed, n., *good*: S 252, V 39,
46; god, S 285. O.E. gōd.

gold, n., *gold*: C 18, 53,
288. O.E. gold.

gome, n., *sport*: V 24. O.
E. gamen.

gon, v., pret. 3 sg., see **gan.**

gore, n., *front section of a
skirt, wider at bottom than
at top*, by synecdoche,
skirt, petticoat, gown:
under gore = under one's
clothes (*N.E.D.*): S 5.
O.E. gāra.

gossip, n., *sponsor in bap-
tism*: V 116, 208, etc.
O.E. godsibb.

gounnen, see **gan.**

gouþlich, adj., *goodly of appearance, handsome*: S 5.
O.E. gōdlīc.

grace, n., *grace*: C 497.
O.F. grace.

gradde, v., *cried out*: pret.
3 sg., V 282.

grante, v., *grant*: infin.,
C 362; pres. subj. 2 sg.,
grante, S 375, C 344;

graunte, C 286, 316; 3 sg., grante, S 362; pres. imper. 2 sg., grante, C 357; pret. 3 sg., grantyd, C 320; pret. part., grantyd, C 238, 506. O. F. graunter.

grantise, n., *grant, concession*: S 414. O. F. grantise.

grantyng, n., *granting, boon*: C 434; granteyng, C 440.

grasyos, adj., *gracious*: C 172. O. F. gracious.

gref, n., *reluctance*: S 36. O. F. grief, gref.

gren, adj., *green*: C 200. O. E. grēne.

gret, adj., *great*: sing., V 168; pl., grete, V 155, 290; sg. and pl., grete, C 5, 31, 104, 221, 282, 292, etc. O. E. grēat.

grete, v., *greeted*: pret. 3 sg., C 465; grette, S 160. O. E. grētan.

greten, v., pres. 3 pl., *weep*: S 357. O. E. grǣtan.

grette, v., see grete.

greuans, n., *ill fortune*: C 222. O. F. grevance.

greue, v., *grieve*: infin., S 59; pret. 3 sg., greuyd, C 442; pret. part., greuyd, refl., C 450. O. F. grever.

grew, v., see grow.

griþ, n., *peace*: S 267; grythe, C 299, 546. O. E. griðð, O. N. griðð.

grome, n., *anger, wrath*: S 197. O. E. grama.

ground, n., *ground*: C 375; dat., grounde = *bottom*, V 74, 91. O. E. grund.

grow, v., *grow*: pres. 3 pl., C 204; pres. part., growyng, C 378; pret. 3 sg., grew, C 307. O. E. grōwan.

grym, adv., *grimly*: C 526. O. E. grim.

grymly, adv., *grimly*: C 465. O. E. grimlīce.

grythe, n., see griþ.

gyft, n., see gift.

gytherners, n., *player on the gittern*: C 101. O. F. guitern.

ȝare, adv., *for a long time*: V 169. O. E. gēara.

ȝare, adv., *readily, quickly*: C 469. O. E. gearo.

ȝat, n., *gate*: V 20; ȝate, C 284. O. E. geat.

ȝe, pers. pron., *ye, you*: C 1, 233, 235, 365, 429; dat.,

ou, V 215; ȝou, C 377,
etc.; accus., ou, V 214,
216; ȝou, C 272, etc.;
gen., ȝour, C 303, 407,
408, etc.; of ȝoure, *of
yours*, C 495. O.E. ȝē,
ēower, ēow.

ȝe, affirm. part., *yea*: S 232,
V 176, 207, C 538. O.
E. gēa.

ȝef, ȝif, conj., *if*: ȝif, S
59; ȝef, V 98, 204; if,
S 32, 52, etc., C 490;
yff, C 208, 268; if þat,
S 52; ȝif þat, S 59; ȝeif
þat, S 443. O. E. gif.
See if.

ȝelpe, v., *boast*: infin., S
227. O.E. gielpan.

ȝenge, adj., see ȝong.

ȝer, n., *year*: pl. ȝer, S 67;
sing. & pl. ȝere, C 37,
55, 64, 204, 205, 571.
O.E. gēar.

ȝerne, adv., *earnestly, eagerly*: S 13, V 15, 93. O.E.
georne, adv.

ȝet, adv., *yet*: S 111, 404,
V 153. O.E. giet.

ȝeue, v., see geue.

ȝif, conj., see ȝef.

ȝirne, v., *desire*: pres. subj.
2 sg., ȝirne, S 45. O.E.
giernan.

ȝol, n., *Yule, Christmas*: S
116. O.E. gēol, geohol.

ȝong, adj., *young*: sing.,
S 361; pl., ȝong, C 566;
pl., ȝenge, C 517. O.E.
geong.

ȝonge, v., *go*: infin., V 61.
See gonge.

ȝurstendai, n., *yesterday*:
S 73. O.E. geostran +
dæg.

ȝus, adv., *yes*: S 294. O.E.
gise, gese.

ha, pers. pron., see hoe.

haiward, n., *hedge war-
den, hayward*: V 26. M.
E. compound. O.E. hege
+ O.E. weard.

hakney, n., *hackney*: C
251. O.F. haquenée.

half so, adv., *half so*: V 4.
O.E. healf swā.

halle, n., *hall*: S 22, C
314, 326; hall, C 324,
325. O.E. heall.

halp, see helpe.

han, see haue.

hang, v., *hung*: pret. 3
pl., C 153. O.E. hōn,
hēng.

harde, adv., *hard, strongly*:
S 204, V 195. O. E.
hearde.

harper, n., *harper*: C 484;
herper, C 487; pl., her-
pers, C 101. O.E. hear-
pere.

haue, v., *have*: infin., haue,
S 164, C 36, 225, 282;
hauen, S 196; han, V 87;
hafe, C 235; pres. 1 sg.,
haue, S 58, 424, C 143,
205, 207, etc.; habbe,
S 67, V 200, 201, 203,
210; habe, S 91; have,
V 40; pres. 2 sg., hauest,
S 194, 256, 268, V 47,
54, 173, 185, 244; hast,
C 411, 412; has þou?, C
355; pres. 3 sg., haueþ,
S 112, 214, 216, etc., V
122, 168; hath, C 231;
pres. 3 pl., haueþ, S 310;
pres. subj. 2 sg., haue,
S 51, 145; pres. subj. 1
pl., haue, C 226; im-
per. 2 sg., haue, S 270;
pret. 1 sg., heuede, S
339, V 134; 3 sg.,
heuede, S 9, 422, V 68,
etc.; hedde, V 285; hede,
V 288; had, C 7, 25,
29, etc.; *held, regard-
ed,* C 503; pret. 3 pl.,
had, C 137, 157; pret.
subj. 1 sg., hedde, V
135; 2 sg., hade, *wouldst*

have, C 438; heuedest, S
250, V 177. O.E. habban,
hæfde.

haui, haue + I.

he, pers. pron.: nom., he, S
4, 7, etc., V 3, 5, etc.,
C 7, 10, etc.; dat., him,
S 142, V 2, etc.; hym,
C 36, 56, 75, etc.; ac-
cus., him, S 13, 94, V
114, 259, etc.; hym, C
23, 123, 124, etc.; hine,
V 123. O.E. hē, his,
him, hine.

heddre, see eddre.

hede, v., see ede.

hede, n., see heued.

hedlyng, adv., *headlong*:
C 360. M.E. formation
from O.E. hēafod + O.E.
-ling. Cf. O.E. bæcling.

heie, heien, see eien.

heie-renning, n., *running
at the eyes*: S 283. Not
cited in *N.E.D.*

heiȝtte, v., *is named*: pret.
3 sg., S 177; heyte, V
271; pret. 3 sg., hyght,
C 28; pret. part., hyȝt,
C 7. O.E. hātan, hēt.

held, see holden.

hele, see goder-hele.

helen, v., *conceal*: infin., S
241, 253. O.E. helan.

help, n., *help*: S 164, 236, 371. O.E. help.

helpe, v., *help*: infin., S 188,210,228; pres. 3 sg., helpys, C 127; pres. 3 pl., helpen, S 211; imper. 2 sg., help, S 221; pret. 3 sg., halp, V 84. O.E. helpan.

hem, pers. pron., see **hy.**

hen, n., *hen*: accus. sg., V 7; nom. pl., hennen, V 28, 32, 35; gen. pl., hennen, V 40. O.E. henn, hen.

hende, adj., *gracious, courteous*: S 119, 154; hend, C 570. O.E. gehende.

hende, adv., *graciously*: S 61. O.E. gehende.

hente, v., *took*: pret. 3 sg., C 123, 278. O.E. hentan.

her, adv., *here*: S 68, 194, 252, etc., V 140; here, C 217, 488, etc. O.E. hēr.

her-bifore, adv., *heretofore*: V 222. O.E. hēr + beforan.

herdy, adj., *hardy, brave*: C 3, 329, 537. O.F. hardi.

here, pers. pron., see **hy.**

here, v., *hear*: infin., C 1,

482, 488, etc.; pres. 1 sg., here, V 128; pret. 1 sg., herde, S 2, 73; herd, C 126; pret. 3 sg., herde, V 170; herd, C 98, 104; inf., I-here, S 368, V 186; pres. 1 sg., I-here, V 119; pret. 3 sg., I-herde, V 113. O.E. (ge)hīeran.

her-inne, adv., *herein*: S 25, V 104; her-in, S 321. O. E. hērinne.

herknen, v., *listen*: infin., S 50. O.E. hercnian.

herlot, n., *rascal*: C 355. O. F. herlot, (h)arlot, *vagabond*.

hernde, n., see **ernde.**

hernest, n., *real meaning*: S 230. O.E. eornust.

herpers, see **harper.**

herte, n., *heart*: S 10, 356, 360; hert, C 190. O.E. heorte.

hertely, adv., *heartily*: C 409. In *N.E.D.* first qu. fr. Cursor Mundi.

Hertou, *art thou*, see **be, ben.**

hete, see **eten.**

heþen, adv., *hence*: S 295. O.N. heðan.

heþer, see **hider.**

heued, n., *head*: S 335; hede, C 266, 299. O.E. hēafod.

heuede, v., see **haue.**

heuene, n., *heaven*: S 325, 416; heuen, C 575. O. E. heofon.

heuene-blisse, n., *bliss of Heaven*: V 233.

heuene-king, n., *Heaven's King*: S 31, 89; heuen-kyng, C 109. O.E. heofoncyning.

heuereuchon, pron., see **euerychon.**

heui, adj., *heavy, sad, depressed*: V 278; heuy, C 322. O.E. hefig.

hey, adv. phrase, on hey, *on high, to a height*: V 31. O.E. hēah, see **hy.**

hic, see **I.**

hider, adv., *hither*: S 180, 261; heþer, C 330. O.E. hider.

hiderward, adv., *here*: S 255. O.E. hiderweard.

hile, see **goder-hele.**

hine, pers. pron., see **he.**

hire, pers. pron., see **hoe.**

hire, poss. pron., *her*: S 412, etc.; hyr, C 243. O.E. hiere, hire. See **hoe.**

his, hiis, v., see **be.**

his, poss. pron., *his*: S 10, etc., C 58, 312; hys (sing. & pl.), C 61, 62, 74, 152, etc. O.E. his.

hit, pron., *it*: S 28, 45, 60, etc., V 46, 60, etc.; it, C 88, 165; yt, C 321, 441, etc. O.E. hit.

hoe, pers. pron., *she*: nom., hoe, S 20, 23, 179, etc.; ha, S 362; dat., hire, S 10; hyr, C 146; accus., hire, S 14, 151, etc. O. E. hēo, hire, hire, hīe. See **sche.**

hoe, pl., see **hy.**

hoeld, v., see **held.**

hof, prep., see **of.**

hofþurst, adj., (of+þurst), *thirsty*: V 274. See aþurst, V 66; see afingret, p. p. O.E. ofþyrsted, ofþyrst, p. p.

holde, adj., see **olde.**

holden, v., *hold*: infin., S 71; hold, C 38, 61, 91, 546; pres. 1 sg., hold, *regard, consider,* C 142; 2 sg., oldest, S 115; pret. 3 sg., hoeld, V 5; 3 pl., held, C 55; p.p., hold, *regarded, considered,* C 565. O.E. healdan.

holi, adj., *holy*: S 205, 254;
holy, C 135. O.E. hālig.

hom, n., *home*: S 97, etc.,
V 34, C 178; home, C
180, 556. O.E. hām.

hom-come, n., *homecoming*:
S 293. O.E. hamcyme.

hon, prep., see on.

hond, n., *hand*: dat., C 196,
198; honde, S 240, V
102; pl., hondes, C 95,
106. O.E. hand, hond.

hondred, num., *hundred*:
S 104; hundryth, C 555.
O. E. hundred, North.
hundraðˍ, hundreðˍ, n.

hongi, v. intr., *hang*: infin.,
V 88, 232; pret. 3 pl.,
hang, C 153. O.E. han-
gian; hōn, hēng.

honour, n., *honor*: C 377.
O.F. honur.

honouren, v., *honor*: p. p.
honouryd, C 412. O.F.
(h)onorer.

hope, v., *hope*: pres. 1 sg.,
C 144; pret. 3 sg., hopyd,
C 72; hopede, V 79. O.
E. hopian.

hore, poss. pron., *their*: S
210. O.E. hiera; hiora,
heora. See hy.

hore, n., *whore*: S 99. O.
N. hóra. O.H.G. huora.

hors, n., *horse*: C 248; pl.,
C 52. O.E. hors.

hote, v., *command*: pres.
1 sg., V 36. O.E. hā-
tan.

hou, conj., *how*: S 14, 292,
etc.; ou, V 230. O.E.
hū.

hounbinde, v., *unbind*:
pres. subj. 3 sg., S 315.
O.E. un + bindan.

houncurteis, adj., *uncour-
teous*: S 46. O.E. un +
O.F. corteis.

houndes, n., *dogs*: V 290,
O.E. hund.

hounderstonde, v., *understand*: infin., S 263; pret.
3 sg., hounderstod, V 77.
O.E. understandan.

houne, adj., see ouene.

hounger, n., *hunger*: S 310,
312; V 13, 68, 168, etc.;
honger, V 112. O.E. hun-
gor.

hounlawe, n., *wrong*: S
60. M.E. word, O.E.
un + O.E. lagu.

hounsele, n., *unhappi-
ness*: S 175. O.E. unsǣl,
m.

houp, adv., see oup.

houre, poss. pron., *our*: S
31, 89, 236, 408, etc.,

V 35, 59. See oure. O.E.
ūre.

hous, n.; *house*: S 273, V 11,
27; house, S 92, V 261.
O.E. hūs.

hous, 1 pers. pron., see ous.

houssebonde, hosse-
bande, n., *husband*: S
137; hossebande, S 341.
l. O. E. hūsbōnda. O.N.
husbondi.

houssewif, n., *housewife*:
S 361. M.E. compound:
first qu. fr. Ancren
Riwle.

houssong, n., *matins*: V
265, 270; houssonge, V
274. O.E. ūhtsong.

houte, adv., see oute.

how-þat-euer, adv., *how-
ever*: C 420. Not cited in
N.E.D.

hundryth, see hondred.

hy, pers. pron., 3 pl., *they*:
V 41, 42, 204, 283; hoe,
V 264, 268; gen., here,
V 43, 265, 267, 274;
hoere, V 272; hore, S
210; dat., hem, S 210,
212, V 45; accus., hem,
V 162, 267; Ime (?), V
264. O. E. hīe (hȳ),
hiera (hiora, heora), him.
See þei, and þer.

hy, hye, adj., *high*: C 10,
422, 498. O.E. hēah.
See hey.

hye, pers. pron., see hoe.

hyȝht, v., *promised*: pret.
3 sg., C 468; pret. 3 pl.,
hyght, *owed*, C 562. O.E.
hātan, he(h)t.

hyght, hyȝt, *was named*,
see heiȝtte.

hym-selue, pron., *himself,
he*: nom., C 63.

I, pron., 1 pers., I: S 32,
47, 50, etc., C 112,
142, etc.; ich, S 2, 26,
etc., V 36, 103, 119,
128, 132, 133, 162; ihc,
S 148, V 159; hic, S
237; Y, C 111, 114,
219, 220, 298, 315,
etc.; dat. sing., me, S
42, V 38, C 286; accus.
sing., me, S 29, C 272,
etc. O.E. ic, mīn, mē,
me(c).

I-bede, p. p., see bidde.

I-ben, p. p., see be.

I-blessi, see blesse.

I-boen, part. adj., *ready*: S
434. Prefix i + O. Dan.
bōin.

I-bonden, part. adj., *bound*:
harde ibonden, 'hard

pressed,' 'in straits.' S 204. See bind.

I-brout, see bringen.

ich, see I.

iche, see ilke.

I-cloþed, see cloþed.

I-crope, v., *crept*: pret. part., V 28. O. E. crēopan.

I-do, i-don, p. p., see do.

I-ete, see eten.

if, see ȝef.

I-faie, adv., *gladly*: V 199. O. E. gefægen.

I-fere, see fere.

I-gon, see go(n).

i-here, see here.

I-kaut, v., *caught*: p. p., V 86, 103. O. F. cachier.

I-knede, p. p., *kneaded*: V 256. O. E. cnedan.

I-kneu, see knowen.

I-knowe, p. p., *confessed*: V 182. M. E. cnawenn, qu. fr. Orm. etc. in the sense of *acknowledge, confess*; cf. M. E. a-knowe, O. E. oncnāwan.

ilke, adj., *each, every*: S 208, 307; *same, very*, S 289, V 47, 99, 271, etc.; Iche, *each*, C 512. O. E. ælc.

I-loke, p. p., *locked*: V 20. O. E. lūcan.

I-loued, see loue.

I-maked, see make.

Ime (?), V 264, refl. pron. accus. constr. after arisen. Cf. hy; or = inne (*Maetzner*), prep., *in*.

I-munt, p. p., *meant, intended*: V 244. O. E. myntan.

in, prep., *in*: S 6, 15, etc., V 25, 82, etc., C 105, etc.; yn, C 4, 14, 104, etc.; ine, V 138, 162, 163, C 134; ime (?), V 264. O. E. in.

in, inne, adv., *in, inside*: S 20, 300, V 22, 23, 25, etc. O. E. in.

in-dede, adv., *indeed*: C 499.

inne, n., *house*: S 19, 299, 406. O. E. inn, in.

I-nou, adj., *enough*: S 93, V 24, 147; I-nowe, V 288. O. E. genōh.

I-nou, adv., *enough*: V 79, 83, 259, 278; I-nowȝe, C 519. O. E. genōh.

in-to, prep.: S 22, C 324; yn-to, C 177, 187. O. E. into.

in-werd, adv., *inward*: C 268, 511. O. E. inweard.

ioies, pl. see Ioy.

I-seie,I-sey,I-siist,see se.
I-shend, see shend.
I-shoed, part. adj., *shod*:
S 320.
I-sriue, see sriue.
I-stounge,v.,p.p.,*pierced,
thrust* : V 292. O. E.
stingan.
I-swonge,v.,p.p.,*swinged,
beaten*: V 291.
it, pers. pron., see hit.
I-take, see take.
I-wend, see wene.
I-wis, adv., *certainly*: S 43,
143; mid I-wisse, V 234,
293. O.E. gewis.
I-wreken,v.,p.p.,*avenged*:
S 215. O.E. wrecan.
I-writen, v., p. p., *writ-
ten*: V 204. O.E. wrītan.

jentyll, adj., *gentle, noble*:
C 60. O.F. gentil.
Ihesu, pr. n.: C 109, 376,
380; Ihesu cryst, C 170.
jorneye, n., *journey*: C 249.
O.F. jornee.
Ioy, n., *joy*: C 552, 572,
576; pl., ioies, V 166.
O.F. ioye.
iugement, n., *judgment*:
S 246. F. jugement.
iuperti, n., *venture*: S 276.
O.F. iu parti.

kare, n., *care*: S 153, 442,
V 34,142,164, etc. O.E.
cearu, caru.
kenne, v., *teach*: infin., S
264. O.E. cennan.
kepe,v.,*keep*: subj. 2 sg., C
174; 3 sg., C 176. O.E.
cēpan.
king, n., *king*: S 31, 89,
426; kyng, C 274, 281,
287, 343, etc.; gen.,
kynges, C 346. O. E.
cyning.
klene, see clene.
knaue, n., *young man*: S
201. l.O.E. cnafa, O.E.
cnapa.
kne, n., *knee*: C 169, 191.
O.E. cnēo.
knelen, v.,*kneel*: pret. 3 sg.,
knelyd, C 169, 188, 191;
pres. part., knelyng, C
372,375.O.E.cnēowlian.
knyȝht, n., *knight*: C 7,
13; knyght, C 25, 60;
pl., knyghtes, C 503.
O.E. cniht.
knowen, v., *know*: pres.
2 sg., knowyst, C 491;
pret. 3 sg., kneu, V 114;
I-kneu, V 123; pret. 3 pl.,
knew, C 566; p.p., knaw,
C 528. O.E. cnāwan; see
also I-knowe, p.p.

kok, n., *cock*: V 30, 31, etc. O.E. cocc.

kors, n., *curse*: V 201. O.E. curs.

kun, kunne, see **cunne**.

kyssen, v., *kiss*: pret. 3 sg., kyssed, C 124. O.E. cyssan.

lady, n., *lady*: C 28, 175, 229. O.E. hlæfdige.

lame, adj., *lame*: S 199. O.E. lama.

landes, see **lond**.

(at þe) **last**, n., *at last*: C 67; laste, S 141. O.E. latost.

late, v., see **let**.

late, adv., *late*: V 81. O.E. læt.

law, n., *law*: C 525. O.E. lagu.

lawe, v., *laugh*: infin., lawe, S 401; pret. 3 sg., lou, V 23, 148; pret. 3 pl., lewȝe, C 517, 520. O.E. hlehhan, &c.

lede, v., *lead*: infin., lede, S 211; pres. 1 sg., lede, S 174, 175; 3 pl., ledeþ, S 304. O.E. lædan.

lede, n., *people*: C 418, 424. O.E. lēode.

lef, adj., see **leue**.

lefmon, n., see **leuemon**.

left, v. intr., *remained*: pret. 3 sg., C 81, 82. O.E. læfde.

left, v. tr., *left*: p. p., C 75. O.E. læfan.

lege, adj., *liege*: C. 407, 421, 493, etc. O.F. lige, liege.

leien, v. *lay, place*: pret. 3 sg., leyd, C 475. O.E. lecgan.

leng, lengour, adj., compar., *longer*: S 148, V 42; lenger, C 196. O.E. leng.

lepen, v., *leap*: imper. 2 sg., lep, V 234; pret. 3 sg., lep, V 22, 78, etc. O.E. hlēapan.

lere, v., *teach*: infin., V 231. O.E. læran.

lerne, v., *learn*: infin., S 48; pret. 1 sg., lernede, S 98. O.E. leornian.

les, adj., *less, smaller*: C 226, 569. O.E. læssa.

les, n., *falsehood*: C 493. O.E. lēas.

lese, v., *lose*: pres. 2 sg., lesest, S 134; 3 sg., leseþ, S 141; p. p., leste, C 70; lore, C 34; lorn, C 405. O.E. lēosan.

lesing, n., *falsehood*: S 203, 283. O.E. lēasung.

leste, conj., *that —not*: S 202. O.E. *þȳ lǣs þe*.

leste, adj., *least, smallest*: pl., C 413. O.E. lǣst.

leste, v., see lese.

lete, v., *let, permit*: infin., *let blood*, V 51; pres. 1 pl., late, C 230; pres. subj. 3 sg., lete, S 196, 364; imper. 2 sg., let, S 29; late, C 272; p. p., leten, V 40, 45. O.E. lǣtan.

lete, v., *leave off, cease*; infin., C 61. O.E. lettan.

lette, n., *hindrance* : C 459. M.E. first qu. from 1175.

lettyng, v. n., *hindering*: C 291, 297. O.E. lettan. O.E. letting.

leue, n., *leave, permission*: S 58, V 25, C 290. O.E. lēaf.

leue, adj., *dear, beloved*: S 135, 171; lef, S 33; compar. leuere, *liefer, preferable*, S 382, V 7; leuer, C 503; cf. compounds: leuelif, leuemon. O.E. lēof.

leue, v., *grant*: pres. subj. 3 sg., S 147, 212, 215. O.E. lĩfan, lȳfan.

leuelif, n., *sweetheart*: S 30.

leuemon, n., *sweetheart, leman*: S 418, 447; leumon, S 127; lefmon, S 376. O.E. lēof+mann. Early M.E. compound.

leuen, v., *leave, abandon*: infin., S 153. O.E. lǣfan.

leute, n., *loyalty, fidelity*: S 229. O.F. leute, lewté.

leuys, n., pl. *leaves*: C 200. O.E. lēaf.

lewȝe, see lawe.

leyd, see leien.

libe, v., *live*: infin., V 42; lyfe, C 78; liuie, V 165; pres. 1 sg., liue, S 333; pret. 3 pl., lyued, C 571. O.E. lifian, libban.

lie, v., *lie, prevaricate*: infin., V 132, imper. 2 sg., liȝ, S 229. O.E. lēogan.

lif, n., *life*: S 82, V 178, etc.; lyfe, C 26, lyffe, C 177; liif, V 188; dat., liue, V 211, 227, 250; pl., liues, S 304. O.E. līf.

lif-dayes, n. pl., *life days*; V 49; lif-daie, V 200. O.E. līfdagas.

liȝt, adj., *easy*: V 236. O.E. liht.

liken, v., *please*: infin., S
82; like, S 257. O.E.
līcian.

lim, n., *limb*: pl. limes, S
311. O.E. lim.

Lincolne-shire, pr. n.: S
78.

liuie, see libe.

lo, interj., C 217. O.E.
lā.

loke, v., *look, see to it that*:
pres. imper. 2 sg., S 357,
398, 440, C 276; pret.
3 sg., lukyd, *looked, appeared*, C 526. O.E.
lōcian.

lond, n., *land*: C 16, 117,
418, 424, 549; londe
(dat.), S 266, V 101;
pl., landes, C 94; lon-
dys, C 548. O.E. land,
lond.

longe, adv., (time), *long*:
V 280; long, C 356.
O.E. lang.

longen, v., *belong*: pres. 3
sg., longes, C 119, 542.
M.E. longen (first certain
qu. fr. Cursor Mundi).
cf. O.E. gelang, adj.

lord, n., *lord*: C 172, 176,
etc., louerd, S 17, 31,
etc.; pl., lordes, C 326,
446, etc. O.E. hlāford.

lordynges, n., *sirs*: pl., C 1.
M.E. first qu. fr. Orrm
(laferrdinngess, pl.), etc.

lore, v., see lese.

lore, n., *lore, learning, lesson*: S 4, 264. O.E. lār.

lorn, see lese.

loþ, adj., *loath, unpleasant,
hateful*: S 42, V 6, 219.
O.E. lāþ.

lou, louȝ, see lawe.

loue, n., *love*: S 12, etc.,
C 302. O.E. lufu.

loue, v., *love*: infin., S 87,
144; louien, S 7, 265;
pres. 1 sg., loue, S 233; 2
sg., louest, S 231; 3 sg.,
loueþ, S 94, 362; pret. 1
sg., louyd, C 501; pret. 3
sg., louede, S 343; p. p.,
I-loued, S 67, 178. O.E.
lufian.

louerd, n., see lord.

loue-uerc, n., *love-work*:
S 374.

luitel, adv., *little*: S 362, V
260. O.E. lȳtel.

lukyd, see loke.

lust, n., *desire*: V 96, 100.
O.E. lust.

lyde, n., *lid*: C 278, 310.
O.E. hlid.

lyfe, v., see libe.

lyfe, lyffe, n., see lif.

lyften, v., *lift*: pret. 3 sg.,
lyfte, C 310. Icel. lypta.

lyke, conj., *like*: C 452.
O. E. ge-līc.

lyne, v., *cease*: infin., C
133. O. E. linnan.

lyre, n., *cheek*: C 153.
O. E. hleor.

lysten, v., *listen*: imper. 2
pl., lystyns, C 1. O. E.
hlystan.

lyte, n., *little*: C 69. O. E.
lӯt.

lytell, adj., *little* : C 76.
O. E. lytel.

lythe, n., *limb* : C 298.
O. E. liþ.

lyued, see libe.

mai, v., *can, may*: pres. 1
sg., mai, S 32, etc., V
141; may, V 230, C 141,
496; 2 sg., mait, S 49;
miȝt, S 135, 227; miȝtt,
S 34; maiȝt, S 258, 259,
389, etc.; maut, S 221;
may, C 488; mai, S 122;
may, C 203, etc.; 2 pl.,
may, C 235; 3 pl., may,
C 47; pres. subj. 1 sg.,
moue, S 370; pret. 1 sg.,
myght, C 511; pret. 3
sg., miȝtte, S 83, 237, V
112; miȝte, V 87; myȝht,

C 26, 78; mouȝht, C 339;
3 pl., myȝht, C 155, 159;
myȝt, C 520; pret. subj.
3 sg., moute, S 14.
O. E. mugan, mæg.

maiden, n., *maiden*: S 92.
O. E. mægden.

main, n., *strength*: dat.,
maine, V 279. O. E. mæ-
gen.

maister, n., *master*: V.
206, 272. O. F. maistre.

maistri, n., *artifice, trick*:
S 277. O. F. maistrie.

make, v., *mate*: S 107.
O. E. gemaca.

make, v., *make*: infin., S
39, 222, C 59, 112;
maken, S 142, 263; pres.
3 pl., makeþ, V 29; pres.
subj. 2 sg., make, C 300;
1 pl., make, C 140; pres.
imper. 2 sg., make, S 240,
328; pres. part., makyng,
C 195; pret. 2 sg., mad-
yst, C 110; 3 sg., made,
C 71, 84, 94, etc.; 1 pl.,
made, C 480; 3 pl., made,
C 156; p. p., maked, S
200, 256; I-maked, V 72.
O. E. macian.

maki, make + I: S 344.

man, n., *man*: C 6, 8, etc.;
mon, S 3, 71, 122, 219,

etc., V 285; gen. manus,
C 119; pl., men, V 6, C
79, 350; gen. pl., men,
S 207. O.E. mann.

maner, n., *mansion*: pl.,
maners, C 62, 74, 92.
O.F. manoir.

manere, n., *manner, way,
kind of*: S 367; maner, C
203, 252, 556; pl. (?),
maner, C 559. O.F.
manere.

many, adj., *many*: C 103,
571, etc.; many a, C 33,
64, 463, 472; moni, S
67, 178, V 173; moni
a, S 224. O.E. manig,
monig.

marchaundise, n., *mer-
chandise*. O.F. marchan-
dise.

Margeri, pr. n.: S 177,
231.

marke, n., *mark*: S 224.
O.E. mearc.

Mary, pr. n.: C 313, 340;
seynt Mary, C 265.

masse, n., *mass*: V 252.

may, see mai.

me, indef. pron., *one*: S 76,
V 75. See mon.

me, pers. pron. See I.

mede, n., *reward*: S 166,
191 etc. O.E. mēd.

meding, n., *reward*: S 271.
O.E. mēd.

meke, adj., *meek*: C 21.
M.E. meoc, mec, first
qu. fr. Orrm.

mekyll, adj., see muchel.

mel, n., *meal*: V 173; wiþ
þi meel, ' toward thy
meal,' V 247; gen., melys,
C 353. O.E. mǣl.

mend, v., *mend, improve*:
infin., C 54. O.F.
amender.

menen, v., I. *complain,
lament* : pret. 3 sg.,
ment, C 126. II. *mean,
intend*: p. p., mente, C
458. O.E. mǣnan.

menis, n., *laments*: S 142.
O.E. mene.

menske, n., *honor* : S 93.
O.N. menniska, *human*.

merci, n., *mercy!*: S 127;
mersy, *thanks*, C 421.
O.F. mercit, merci.

merueilen, v., *marvel*:
pret. 3 sg., meruylled, C
312. O.F. merveillier.

mery, adj., *merry*: C 136;
merry, C 140, etc.; merye,
C 397. O.E. myrige.

mes-auenter, n., *misfor-
tune*: S. 202. O.F. mes-
aventure.

mete, n., *food*: S 133, 280, 316, V 14, 170, etc., C 22, 139, 143, etc.; pl., metys, C 118. O.E. mete.

mete, v., *meet, encounter*: infin., S 394, V 6; meten, V 7; pres. 3 pl., meten, S 358; pret. 3 sg., mette, S 157, V 242; 3 pl., mette, C 462. O.E. mētan.

meþ, n., *moderation*: V 97. O.E. mǣþ.

meyd, n., *maid*: C 21. O. E. mægeþ.

mi, poss. pron., *my*: S 30, 91, etc., V 187, 193, etc.; my, C 125, 173; mine, S 311, 405, V 100, 160, 182; before vowels or h-, min, S 40, 293, etc., V 185; myn, C 344, 357, 431. O.E. mīn.

mid, prep., *with*: S 93, 159, V 14, 30, 55, 62, 72; mit, S 289. O.E. mid.

miȝt, n., *might*: dat., miȝtte, S 253, 405; myȝht, C 12. O.E. miht.

mikel, adj. & adv., see **muchel.**

milde, adj., *mild*: S. 159. O.E. milde.

mile, n., *mile*: pl., an hon-dred mile, S 104. O.E. mīl.

mis, v., *miss, lose*: infin., S 144. O.E. missan.

misdede, n., *misdeeds*: pl., V 182. O.E. misdǣd.

mi-selue, reflex. pron., *my-self*: S 183; miself, S 184; my-selue, *I, myself*, C 351, 427. Originally mē-self.

misferen, v., *to go astray, transgress, do wrong*: pret. 2 sg., misferdest, V 212. O.E. misfēran.

mo, adj. & adv., *more, greater*: V 145, 204, C 82, 458; more, S 103, 265, V 206, C 366, 369; mour, C 13, 149, 222, 224, 225, 226, etc. O. E. mā, māra.

mod, n., *mood, heart, frame of mind*: S 109, 113, 181, etc.; mode, C 54, 303, 312. O.E. mōd.

modi, adj., *proud*: S 3, 348, 417. O.E. mōdig.

mold, n., *earth*: C 285. O.E. molde.

mon, indef. pron., *one*: S 131. O.E. man. See **me.**

mon, n., see **man.**

mon, v., *must*: pres. 1 sg.,

S 182. O.N. monn, 1st
& 3rd sing., mon, mun.

mon, n., *moan*: acc., mon,
C 107; acc., mone, C
84. Cf. O.E. mænan, v.

moni, see **many**.

more, adv., see **mo**.

morne, n., *morn, morning*:
C 241. O.E. morgen.

most, adj. & adv., *most,
greatest*: C 48; moste, C
413. O.E. mæst.

mote, v., *may, must*: pres.
1 sg., mote, C 538; 2 sg.,
most, S 437, V 207, 208;
3 sg., mot, S 233; mote,
C 362; pres. subj. 1 sg.,
mote, S 116; 3 sg., mote,
S 212. O.E. mōt.

moue, v., see **mai**.

mouȝht, see **mai**.

mour, see **mo**.

mourne, v., *care, worry,
mourn*: infin., S 148. O.
E. murnan.

mournyng, v. n., *mourn-
ing*: C 121.

moute, see **mai**.

mouþe, n., *mouth*: V 100;
mouthe, C 209. O.E.
mūþ.

much, adv., see **mikel**.

muchel, adj. & adv., *much,
great*: S 140, 175, 227,

305, 443, V 98; muchele,
S 153, 163; mikel, S
194, 265, 312; mych, C
79; myche, C 426;
mekyll, C 12, 84, 94,
107, etc.; mykyll, C
488. O.E. mycel, micel.

mustart, n., *mustard*: S
280; mustard, S 287. O.
F. mostarde.

myche, see **muchel**.

myȝht, v., see **mai**.

myght, n., see **miȝtte**.

mykyll, see **muchel**.

mynstralsy, n., *minstrelsy*:
C 99. O.F. menestral-
sie.

mynstrellus, n. pl., *minstrels*: C 46, 49. O.F.
menestrel.

myrth, n., *mirth, pleasure,
joy*: C 91, 112, 158, etc.;
myrthe, C 552; pl. myr-
thys, C 47. O.E. myrgð,
mirhð.

my-selue, see **mi-selue**.

nabbe (ne + habbe), v.,
S 68, V 39.

nai, adv., *nay*: S 43, 179;
nay, V 188, C 45. O.N.
nei.

nakerner, n., *kettle-drum
player*: pl. nakerners, C

100. O. F. nacre, na-
quere, etc. + -er, ending.

name, n., *name*: C 66, 115,
530; nome, S 195, V 36,
57. O. E. nama.

namore (na + more), adv.,
no more: S 260, V 65.
O. E. nā mōre.

nay, see nai.

ne, adv., *not*: S 46, etc.,
V 42, etc.; ni, S 157. O.
E. ne.

ne, conj., *nor*: S 39, 48,
etc., V 5, 146, etc., C
20, 27, etc. O. E. ne.

nedde (ne+hadde): V 100,
169, 286; neddi (ne +
hadde + I), V 99.

nede, n., *need*: S 163, 210,
V 225, 276, C 438; at
nedys, C 8. O. E. nīed.

ne-hond, adv., *almost,
nearly*: C 70. M. E. neih
hond, Ancr. Riwle, etc.;
nerehond, nerhond, Cur-
sor Mundi, etc.

nei, ney, adv., *nigh*: S 310,
V 32, etc.; ny, C 222.
O. E. nēah.

neiȝebore, n., *neighbor*: V
115. O. E. nēahgebūr.

nelde, n., *old woman*: S
173, 217, 232, 249, 371,
385, 415, 436 See Notes.

nelle (ne + wille): S 48, V
188; neltou (ne + wilt
+ þou), V 189; nul (ne
+ wil), S 314; nulli
(ne + will + I), S 295;
nolde (ne + wolde), V
161.

ner, adv., *near*: V 38. O.
E. nēar.

nere, adv., *nearer*: C 343.
O. E. nēarra.

neren (ne + weren), S 274.

nes (ne + wes), V 2.

nesten, v., *build a nest*:
pres. 2 sg., nestes, V 48.
O. E. nist(i)an.

neþer ... ne, conj., *neither
... nor*: C 250, 474.

neuede (ne + heuede), v.:
S 11, V 98.

neuere, adv., *never*: S 100,
V 3, 48; neuer, C 341,
V 145, 198; newer, S
118. O. E. næfre.

neuer-þe-les, conj., *nevertheless*: C 443.

new, adj., *new*: pl., C 379.
O. E. nīwe.

newyng, n., *novelty*: C
381.

niȝt, n., *night*: S 150; niȝte,
V 111; nyȝht, C 30;
nyght, C 162, 307. O.
E. niht.

nimen, v., *take*: pret. 3
sg., nom, V 78; p. p.,
nomen, V 250. O. E.
niman.

nis (ne + is), V 145, 164.

nist (ne + wist), see **wot**.

no, adj. & adv., *no*: S 71,
122, 148, 196, 305, C
20, 34, 45, 82, etc.; non,
S 65, 136, V 42, 146, C
319, 321, 361; none, S
245, V 3, 84; nones, V
294. O. E. nān.

nobull, adj., *noble*: C 521.
O. F. noble.

noen, see **none**.

nolde, v., see **nelle**.

nom, see **nimen**.

nome, see **name**.

nomon (no + man), n.: S
342. O. E. nān mon.

non, pron., *none*: S 11, 66,
129, 324 (?), V 160, C
8, 14, 26, 27, etc. O.E.
nān.

none, n., *noon*: C 88, 258;
noen, S 433; to non, S
324 = 'until noon.'
O.E. nōn.

nones-kunnes, adj., *no
kind of*: V 294.

not (ne + wot), v., *knows
not*: pres. 3 sg., S 305,
V 160. O.E. ne + wāt.

not, adv., *not*: C 46, 50,
etc., see **nout, nouiȝt**.

noþer . . . ne, conj., *neither
. . . nor*: C 116, see
**neþer . . . ne, nouþer
. . . ne**.

no-þing, n., *nothing*: S 44,
352, V 183, 253; no-
thyng, C 428.

notys, n., (?): C 101. See
Notes.

nou, adv., *now*: S 145,
279, 285, 424, V 106,
152; now, C 136, 145.
O.E. nū.

nou, conj., *now that*: S 58.
O.E. nū.

nouiȝt, *not at all*: S 56;
nouȝht, C 127, 210, 284,
401. O.E. nā + wiht. See
nout.

nout, adv., *not*: S 38, 68,
229, 243; nohut, V 220.
O. E. nā-wiht. See
nouiȝt.

nout, indef., *naught, nothing*: S 47, 48, 206, V
39, 77; nouȝht, C 110;
nouȝt, C 275; nowȝht,
C 305; noȝht, C 514.
O.E. nā + wiht.

nouþe, adv., *now*: V 55,
99. O.E. nū + þā.

nouþer . . . ne, conj., *nei-*

ther ... *nor*: S 308, 372,
V 5; noþer ... ne, C
116. See neþer ... ne.
O.E. ne + ægþer. See
neþer, noþer.
now, see nou.
nowylte, n., *novelty*: C 217.
O.F. novelté.
nu, see nou.
nul, nulli, see nelle.
ny, see nei.
nyght, see niȝt.

of, prep., *of*, *from*: S 4,
77, etc., V 26, etc., C
4, 9, 56, 60, 66, 102,
etc.; hof, S 2, V 295;
off, C 2, 29, 99, 100, 101,
102, 110, etc.; *from*, S
189, V 56, 267, C 134;
for, C 111, 191, 410;
of me I-don hit hiis = 'it
is all up with me,' V 106.
O.E. of.
of, adv., *off*: S 335. O.E.
of.
offycers, n., *officer*: sing.,
C 293. O.F. officier.
ofseen, v., *see*, *observe*:
pret. 3 sg., ofsei, V 10.
O.E. ofsēon.
of-slyfe, v., *slice off*, *slive*
(see Jos. Wright): infin.,
C 214. O.E. (to) slīfan.

ofte, adv., *often*: V 35, 185,
210, etc. O.E. oft.
ofte-tyme, adv., *often*: C
488.
of-þinken, v. impers., *cause
regret, repent*: pres. 3 sg.,
of-þinkeþ, V 205. O.E.
ofþyncan.
old, adj., *old*: S 199, C 517;
olde, C 332; holde, S
302, 331; hold, C 566.
O.E. eald.
oldest, v., see holden.
omnipotent, adj.: C 179.
O.F. omnipotent.
on, prep., *on*: S 16, 47,
102, etc., C 85, 153,
169, etc.; onne, C 80,
193, 372, 378; hon, S 18,
on þat, *on condition that*,
S 38; on ende, *to an end*,
S 362; on hey, *above*, V
31. O.E. on.
on, indef. art., see a.
on, pron., *one*: S 2; one,
C 13, 423. O.E. ān.
one, num., *one*: V 7, C 75,
81, 209, etc.; on, V 198
O.E. ān.
oneth, adv., *not easily*: C
78. O.E. unēaðe.
onwis, adj., *unwise*: S 218,
445; ounwis, S 117.
O.E. unwīs.

on-wold, v., *wield, control*: infin., S 311. O.E. anweald, anwald, n.

opdrowe, v., *draw up*: pret. 3 pl., V 287. O.E. dragan, drōg, drōh, drōgon, dragen.

ope, adv., *open*: V 27. O.E. open.

oppon, prep., *upon*: S 204, 345. O.E. uppon.

opward, adv., *on the way up*: V 242. O.E. upweard.

opwinde, v., *wind up*: infin., V 75. O.E. windan.

or, conj., *or*: C 35, 348, 358, etc.; our (most frequent form in C), 55, 226, etc. See oþer.

ore, n., *grace, favor*: V 189. O.E. ār.

oþer, conj., *or*: S 133, 183, 395, V 52, 120, 208, etc.; oþer . . . oþer, *either . . . or*, V 14. O.E. āhwæþer, āwþer. See or.

oþer, adj., *other, second*: S 136, V 76, C 53, 319, 321; pl., oþre, V 217. O.E. ōþer.

oþer-weys, adv., *otherwise*: C 321.

ou, pron., see ȝe.

ou, adv., *how*: V 230. See hou.

ouene, adj., *own*: S 421; houne, S 390. O.E. āgen.

ouer, prep., *over*: V 22. O.E. ofer.

ouer, poss. pron., *our*: C 218, 221, 376. O.E. ūre. See oure.

ouer-al, adv., *everywhere*: V 9, 19, 69, etc. O.E. ofer eall. Cf. Mod. Germ. *überall*.

ouer-gon, v., *pass*: p. p., ouer-gon, C 182; pret. 3 sg., ouer-hede, V 90. O.E. ofergān, ofereode.

ouer-hede, see ouer-gon.

ouȝht, n., *aught, anything*: C 34. O.E. āht, āwiht.

ounder, prep., *under*: V 41, 47, 51. O.E. under.

ounderfonge, v., *receive*: infin., V 196; pres. 2 sg., ounderfost, S 378. O.E. underfōn.

ounseli, adj., *unhappy, miserable, wicked*: S 98. O.E. unsælig.

ounwis, see onwis.

oup, adv., *up*: V 246; houp, V 126. O.E. ūp, upp.

our, conj., see or.

oure, poss. pron., *our*:

S 75, etc., V 54; houre,
S 31, 89, 236, 408,
V 35, 59. O.E. ūre. See
ouer.

ous, pers. pron., *us*: S 90;
vs, C 140; hous, S 220.
O.E. ūs. See **wē.**

out, adv., *out*: S 345, 441,
C 360; oute, C 348;
houte, S 79. O.E. ūt.

oute, v., *ought* (?): pret.
3 sg., C 63. O.E. āhte.

out of, prep., *out of*: S 347,
V 1, 109, C 174, 295,
457. O.E. ūt of.

palferey, n., *palfrey*: C
250. O.F. palefrei.

palle, n., *a costly cloth*: S
23. O.E. pæll.

palys, n., *palace*: C 181.
F. palais.

pannyer, n., *pannier, bread
basket*: C 242, 244, 323,
373; panyer, C 230. F.
panier.

paradiis, n., *paradise*: V
140. O.F. paradis.

paramour, adv., *fervently*:
C 501. O.E. par amour.

parlere, n., *room for conversation, parlor*: C 481.
O.F. parloir.

par ma fai, French form of

asseveration, *by my faith*:
S 436.

parte, n., *part*: C 286, 317.
F. part.

parte, v., *divide*: infin., C
350. F. partir.

pas, n., *step, gait*: C 292
O.F. pas.

pater-noster, n., *Lord's
Prayer*: S 209. Lat.

pay, n., *pleasure, taste,
satisfaction*: C 48, 144.
O.F. paie.

pay, v., *pay*: infin., C 430,
449; pret. 3 sg., payd,
C 509; pret. 3 pl., payd,
C 563. O.F. paier.

Pendragoun, pr. n.: C 4.

penes, n. pl., *pence*: S 274.
O.E. penning, pening.

pepir, n., *pepper*: S 279.
O.E. pipor.

pes, n., *peace*: C 546. O.F.
pais.

peyn, n., *pain*: C 176.
O.F. peine.

pikes, n., *pikes*: pl., V 62,
284. O.E. pīc.

pilche, n., *fur garments*: S
225. O.E. pilece, pylce.

pine, n., *pain, trouble*: S.
305, V 142. O.E. pīn.

place, n., *place*: C 105. F.
place.

plaie, v., *play*: infin., S 438; pley, C 160. O.E. plegian.

plente, n., *plenty*: C 24, 225. O.F. plente.

plenyng, v. n., *lamentation*: C. 221. O.F. plaign-.

pley, see **play**.

pliȝtte, v., *plight*: S 252. O.E. pliht, *pledge*. O.E. plihtan.

plukken, v., *pluck, pull*: pret. 3 sg., plukyd, C 338. O.E. pluccian.

pore, adj., *poor*: C 32, 35, 260, etc. O.F. povre.

porter, n., *doorkeeper*: C 262; pourter, C 277. O.F. portier.

pouerte, n., *poverty* : S 304, C 17, 191, 252, 540. O.F. poverte.

pound, n., *pound*: S 224; pl., pownd, C 555. O.E. pund, pl., pund.

pourtenans, n., *appurtenances*: n. pl., C 545. O.F. apartenance, etc.; aphetic, partenance, see Godefroy.

praere, n., *prayer*: C 195. O.F. preiere.

pray, v., *pray*: pres. 1 sg., C 138, 272; pret. 3 sg.,

prayd, C 170, 175, 189; *asked, inquired*, C 508. O.F. preïer.

present, n., *gift*: C 274, 281, 394; presante, C 304; presant, C 334; presente, C 371, 385. O.F. present.

presente, v., *present, offer*: infin., C 234; pret. 3 sg., presente, C 492. O.F. presenter.

presentyng, v. n., *present making*: C 410.

prest, n., *priest*: V 52, 193; pl. prestes, S 248. O.E. prēost.

presyng, v. n., *pressing, urging*: C 300. M.E. verbal noun. In *N.E.D.* from 1400 on.

pride, n., see **prude**.

pris, n., *high esteem, worth, price, value*: S 120, 446. O.F. pris.

priuite, n., *privacy*: S 84. O.F. privité.

profer(en), v., *proffer*: pret. 3 sg., proferd, C 371. A.F. profre.

proud, adj., *proud* : S 3. O.E. prūt.

prude, n., *pride*: S 125; pride, C 79, 96. O.E. prȳte.

putte, n., *pit, well*: V 71,
113, 117, 119, 241,
etc.; put, V 261. O.E.
pyt.
pypers, n., *pipers*: C 100.
O.E. pipere.
pytewysly, adv., *piteously*:
C 108. O.F. pitos, pi-
teus.

qued, n., *evil*: V 210;
quede, V 224. Early
M.E. cwead, cwed, cwad.
qued, adj., *evil*: V 200.
quelle, v., infin., *kill*: S
183. O.E. cwellan.
quen, n., *queen*: C 389.
O.E. cwēn.
quod, v., *quoth, said*: pret.
3 sg., S 27, V 33, 53, 118,
127, 199, 207, 221, etc.;
quaþ, V 37, 96; quoþ,
C 145. O.E. cwæþ.
quyte, v., *free, release*:
infin., C 72; refl., *to
acquit oneself well, do
one's part*, C 63. O.F.
quiter.

radde, v., see **rede**.
ragges, n. pl., *rags*: C
359. Cf. O.E. raggig,
adj., *shaggy*.
raþe, adv., *soon*: S 226;

compar. raþer, *sooner,
before*, V 68. O.E. hraþe.
rawȝht, see **recche**.
recche, v., *reck, care*: pres.
1 sg., recche, V 228;
pret. 3 sg., route, V 260.
O.E. rēcan.
recche, v., *reach, come*:
infin., V 268; pret.
3 sg., rawȝht, *reached,
caught*, C 196. O.E. rǣ-
can.
recche, v., *expound, preach*:
infin., V 268. O.E. rec-
can.
red, n., *counsel, advice*: S
328, 350, 378; rede, V
50; reed, V 192. O.E.
rǣd.
rede, v., *counsel, advise*:
pres. 1 sg., rede, S 375,
C 129, 133, etc.; pres.
subj. 3 sg., rede, V 130,
149, 246; pret. 3 sg.,
radde, S 152, 185. O.E.
rǣdan.
redi, adj., *ready*: S 434;
redy, C 22, 168. Cf.
O.E. rǣde, or gerǣde.
rehete, v., *cheer, comfort*:
infin., C 19. O.F. re-
heter.
relesen, v., *relish*: pret.
3 sg., relesyd, C 211.

See reles, n., *haste, aftertaste, impression,* in *N.E.D.*

rene, v., *run*: infin., S 281. O.E. rinnan.

Reneuard, pr. n.: V 133.

renning, n., *running*: S 283. O.E. ærninge.

renoune, n., *renown*: C 5. O.F. renon.

rente, n., *rent, income*: C 555. O.F. rente.

repent, v., *repent*: pres. 1 sg., C 434. F. repentir.

rerde, n., *speech*: V 114. O.E. reord.

reste, n., *rest*: S 11, 291. O.E. rest.

reue, n., *reeve*: V 26. O.E. gerēfa.

reuell, n., *revel*: C 482. O.F. revel.

reuliche, adv., *sadly, piteously*: S 302, V 107. O. E. hrēowlīc.

reuþe, n., *pity*: S 318. O. E. hrēow, adj.

rew, v., *rue, pity*: infin., C 269; imper. 2 sg., rew, S 114; impers. reflex. pres. 3 sg., reweþ, S 235. O.E. hrēowan.

rewerd, v., *reward*: pres. subj. 3 sg., C 364. O.N.

F. rewarder. O.F. reguarder, regarder.

rewerd, n., *reward*: C 449, 524. O. N. F. reward. O.F. reguard, regard.

ribe, n., *rib*: V 41. O.E. ribb.

riche, adj., *rich*: S 21, etc.; ryche, C 35, 43, 327; rych, C 51, 52, 61, 118. O.E. rīce.

riȝt, adv., *right, straight, exactly*: V 274; ryȝht, C 9, 36, 477; ryght, C 165, 254, 468. O.E. riht.

ringe, v., *ring*: infin., V 251. O.E. hringan.

ro, n., *rest, quiet*: S 291. O.E. rōw.

robys, n., *robes*: pl., C 52. O.F. robe.

rode, n., *rood, cross*: S 323; C 57, 306, 336; roed, S 254. O.E. rōd.

Rome, pr. n.: S 105.

ronde, adj., *round*: C 9, 201. O.F. roönde.

rong, v., *rung*: pret. 3 sg., C 163. O.E. hringan.

ros, v., see **ryse**.

roune, n., *colloquy, counsel*: S 71. O.E. rūn.

route, n., *throng, company*: C 267. O.F. route.

route, v., see recche.

ryall, adj., *royal*: C 392.
O.F. real, roïal.

ryalty, n., *royalty, munifi-cence*: C 73. O.F. realté.

rych, ryche, see riche.

ryches, n., *riches*: C 568.
F. richesse.

ryde, v., *ride*: infin., C 249,
474. O.E. rīdan.

ryfe, adj., *speedily, quickly*
(See *N.E.D.*, B. 4) : C
180. O.E. rīf.

ryght, ryȝht, see riȝt.

ryse, v., *arise*: infin., C
197; pret. 3 pl., ros, C
167. O.E. rīsan.

saie, v., *say*: infin., S 2, 55;
saien, S 49; sugge, V
207; suggen, V 265; sey,
C 45, 67, etc.; pres. 1
sg., saie, S 143; pres.
2 sg., seist, S 61; pres. 3
sg., seiȝ, S 179; seiþ, S
303; seyth, C 248; pres.
subj. 2 sg., saie, S 435;
imper. 2 sg., sei, V 229;
say, V 121; pret. 3 sg.,
saide, S 187; sede, V
129, 150; seide, V 226,
269; seyd, C 125, 176,
etc.; pret. 3 pl., seide,
V 211; seyd, C 521;

p. p., said, S 268; sehid,
V 210; I-seyd, C 484;
pres. 2 sg., seist on,
attributest, S 198. O.E.
secgan.

sake, n., *sake*: V 44, C
416. O.E. sacu.

same, n., *shame, dishonor*:
S 55, 128; scham, S 126;
shame, S 251; shome, S
196, 216, 247; V 35, 58,
99. O.E. sceamu.

saue, v., *save*: pres. subj.
3 sg., C 416. O.F. sau-ver.

saulys, see soule.

saute, v., *reconcile, bring
to terms*: infin., S 220;
p. p. (as adjective), saut,
S 222. O.E. sahtlian.

sautrey, n., *psaltery*: C
102. O.F. psalterie.

sauyoure, n., *Savior*: C
376. O.F. sauveour.

sawe, n., *saying, words*:
S 57. O.E. sagu.

scaþe, n., *harm*: S 235. O.
E. sceaða.

schake, v., *slip away*;
infin., C 58. O.E. scacan.

schall, schuld, etc., see
shal.

scham, see same.

sche, pers. pron., *she*: C 29,

123, 124, 149, etc.;
dat., hyr, C 146; gen.
(poss.), hyr, C 243. See
hoe.

schen, adj., *bright*: C 388.
O.E. scīr.

schewe, see schowe.

schofe, v., *shove*: infin., C
360. O.E. scūfan.

schowe, v., *show, reveal*:
infin., S 69 ; schew, C
215; pret. 3 sg., schewyd,
C 374. O.E. scēawian.

schulder, n., *shoulder*: C
476. O.E. sculdor.

sclepen, v., *sleep*: pret. 3
pl., sclepyd, C 163. O.
E. slǣpan.

scorne, n., *scorn*: C 402.
O.F. escorne.

se, v., *see*: infin., se, S 165,
340; sen, S 278; pres. 1
sg., se, S 319; 2 sg., I-
siist, V 232; 2 pl., se, C
127; pret. 1 sg., I-seie,
V 218; sey (MS. ley), V
216; 3 sg., I-sey, V 280;
saw, C 341, 361, 379;
sei, V 281; sey, C 311,
319; p. p., se, C 205;
sene, C 212. O.E. sēon,
gesēon.

secc, adj., see selk.

sechen, v., *seek*: pret. 3

sg., souȝht, C 448; p. p.,
sought, C 206; sout, S
423. O.E. sēcean.

sehid, v., see saie.

seke, adj., *sick*: V 41; sek,
S 199. O.E. sēoc.

seknesse, n., *sickness*: S
200. O.E. sēocnes.

seli (wif), adj., *good woman*: S 315, 337. O.E.
(ge) sǣlig.

selk, adj., *such*: S 101;
secca, S 83; silk, S 198;
sulke a, S 264; selke
a, S 313; sych, C 55,
59, etc., sych a, C 235;
451. O.E. swilc, swelc.

sellen, v., *sell*: p. p. sold(e),
C 74, 93. O.E. sellan.

sembly, adj., *seemly*: C 6;
compar. semblyer, 27.
O.N. sœmiligr.

send, v., *send*: infin., C
573; pres. subj. 3 sg.,
sende, S 236; pret. 3 sg.,
send, C 386, 523; sente,
C 192, 377; p. p., send,
S 214, 412; sente, C
231. O.E. sendan.

senne, see sunne.

sente, v., *assent*: pres. 1
sg., sente, C 289. Cf. assent.

sep, see shep.

serewe, n., *sorrow, care, grief*: S 182; sereue, S 186; sorrow, C 94, 128, etc. O.E. sorh, sorg, dat., sorge.

serteyn (?): C 162.

serue, v., *serve*: pres. 2 sg., seruest (affter), *earnest*, S 197; pret. 3 sg., siruyd, C 535; p. p., serued, C 391. O.F. servir.

seruys, n., *service*: C 164, 178. O.F. service.

sese, v., *cease*: imper. 2 sg., C 303. O.F. cesser.

seth, conj., *since*: C 213, 342; seth þat, C 427. O.E. siððan

setten, v., *set, put*: infin., S 62; pret. 3 sg., sete, C 62; p. p., sett, *seated*: C 481. O.E. settan.

sey, see saie.

seynt, n., *saint*: C 265, 432. O.F. seint.

shal, v., *shall, ought*: pres. 1 sg., S 50, etc.; schall, C 266, 270, etc.; 2 sg., shalt, S 118, 165, etc., V 235; schall, C 263, 269, etc.; 3 sg., shal, S 111, etc.; 1 pl., schall, C 225, 236; 2 pl., schall, C 1, 233; 3 pl., shulen, S 275,

438; pret. 1 sg., schuld, C 350, 351, etc.; 3 sg., schuld, C 136, 282; 3 pl., shulden, V 264, 268; schuld, C 36, 44, etc.; pret. subj. 1 sg., schulde, S 59, V 138; 2 sg., shuldest, S 432; scholdest, V 136, 180; shuldich (schulde + ich), V 163, 181; shuldi (schuld + I) S 106. O.E. sceal, scealt, sculon, sceolde, etc.

shame, see shome.

shenden, v., *disgrace, confound*: p. p., shend, S 346; I-shend, S 213. O.E. scendan.

shep, n., *sheep*: pl., V 167, 203; sep, S 272. O.E. scēap, scēp.

sheppen, v., *create*: pret. 3 sg., shop, S 354. O.E. scieppan, scippan.

shiling, n., *shillings*: pl., S 270. O.E. scilling.

shome, see same.

shon, n., *shoes*: S 225. O.E. scēo, scōh; pl., scēos, scōs.

shop, see sheppen.

shuldi, see shal.

Sigrim, pr. n.: V 128.

sike, v., *sigh, groan*: infin.,

S 260; siken, V 195; pres. part., sy3eng, C 98, 108, 354. O. E. sīcan.

siker, adj., *certain, secure:* S 240, V 58; sykerly, adv., C 219, 315. O. E. sicor.

silk, see **such.**

singe, v., *sing:* infin., S 401, V 252; syng, C 104. O. E. singan.

sinke, v., *sink:* infin., V 80, 239. O. E. sincan.

sire, n., *lord, husband, sir:* S 75, V 37; sir, C 127. O. F. sires, sire.

Siriz, pr. n.: S 154, 161, 418, 420; Siriþ, S 221, 268, 297.

siþ, n., *time:* S 258. O. E. siþ.

sitten, v., *sit:* infin., S 50; site, S 308; sitte, V 281; sytte, C 520; imper. 2 sg., site, S 28; pret. 3 sg., sat, V 30, 117; pret. 3 pl., seten, V 32. O. E. sittan.

skil, n., *right:* S 52; skyll, C 165. Icel. skil.

sleie, adj., *sly, shrewd:* S 159; sley, V 262. O. N. slægr.

slep, n., *sleep:* V 267. O. E. slæp.

slete, v., *slit, bait:* infin., V 289. O. E. slītan.

slo, v., *slay, kill:* infin., slo, S 184; p. p., slain, S 310. O. E. slēan.

smal, adj., *small:* V 248; pl., smale, V 155. O. E. smæl.

smere, adv., *scornfully:* V 23. Cf. Bradl.-Stratm. Dict.

smertly, adv., *quickly:* C 263, 266, 310. O. E. smeart, adj.

smite, v., *smite:* pret. subj. 3 sg., S 335. O. E. smītan.

so, adv., *so:* S 12, etc., V 2, etc., C 15, 77, etc. O. E. swā.

so, conj., *so that, until:* C 67, V 10; in asseverations, S 26, 116, 133, 273, 433, V 149, C 416, 419, 425; correlative, *as . . . as*, S 156. O. E. swā.

sohute, see **souȝht, sechen.**

solas, n., *solace:* C 519. O. F. solaz.

sold, see **sellen.**

solen, adj., (?) *alone* (?) (so expl. by Maetzn.): S 238. O. F. solain.

som, adj., *some, some kind of:* V 18; soum, V 104;

somme, V 192; soumme, V 125. O.E. sum.

somer, n., *summer*: S 294. O.E. sumor.

somer, adv., *sumpter horse* (?): S 247. See Notes.

som-tyme, adv., *a certain time, once*: C 494, 533.

som-what, adv., *somewhat*: C 147, 561. O.E. sum+hwæt.

sonde, n., *message*: C 111. O.E. sand, sond.

sone, adv., *at once*: S 246, 262, 376, V 52, 61, 235, C 89, 238, 278, 337. O.E. sōna.

sone, n., *son*: S 167, 194, V 199; son, C 243, 253, 323. O.E. sunne.

sore, adv., *much, very, greatly*: V 66, 190, 205, 240, C 95, 98, 106, etc. O.E. sār.

sori, adj., *sorrowful*: S 338, 344. O.E. sārig.

sorow, see serewe.

soþ, n., *truth*: V 121, 129, 157, etc.; soth, C 67, 157, 258. O.E. sōþ.

soþliche, adv., *truly*: S 391. O.E. sōþlīce.

souȝht, see sechen.

soule, n., *soul*: S 213, 314, V 252; gen., soul, V 252; pl., saulys, C 575. O.E. sāwel, etc.

soule-cnul, n., *soul-knell*: V 251.

sout, see sechen.

sowne, n., *sound*: C 98. F. son.

spare, v., *spare*: infin., C 210; pres. subj. 2 sg., spare, S 443. O.E. sparian.

speche, n., *speech*: V 223. O.E. spæc, spræc.

sped, n., *success*: S 141. O.E. spēd.

spede, v., *prosper, succeed*: infin., S 131, 212, 449; pres. subj. 3 sg., spede, C 419, 425; p. p., sped, S 410. O.E. spēdan.

speken, v., *speak*: infin., S 81, etc., V 170; speke, C 383; pres. 1 sg., speke, S 355; pret. 3 sg., spac, S 331; spake, C 406; spak, V 65; p. p., speken, S 216. O.E. sprecan.

spel, n., *story*: S 62. O.E. spel.

spendyd, v., *spent*: p. p., C 68. O.E. spendan.

speres, n., *spears*: pl., V 292. O.E. spere.

spesyally, adv., *especially*:
C 508. O.F. especial.

spille, v., *ruin*: S 233,
432. O.E. spillan.

splen, n., *spleen*: V 47.
Lat. splēn.

spouse, n., *spouse, wife*:
S 91. O.F. espouse.

spryng, v., *spring*: infin.,
C 232. O.E. springan.

spytously, adv., *angrily*:
C 262. O.F. despit.

squyre, n., *squire*: C 398,
553, 560; pl., squyres,
C 16. O.F. esquire.

srift, n., *shrift*: V 186, 196.
O.E. scrift.

sriue, v., *shrive*: infin.,
V 184; p. p., I-sriue,
V 176. O.E. scrīfan.

sroud, n., *dress*: S 6. O.E.
scrūd.

srud, v., *clad*: p. p., S 23.
O.E. scrȳdan.

staff, n., *staff*: C 247,
251, 294; pl., staues, V
62, 284, 292. O.E. stæf.

standyng, see stond.

stark, adj., *strong, large*:
S 223. O.E. stearc.

statour, n., *stature*: C
10; stature, C 498. F.
stature.

staues, see staff.

sted, n., *steed, horse*: C
250. O.E. stēda.

stel, n., *steel*: S 95. O.E.
stȳle.

stere, v., *control, steer*: infin., C 150. O.E. stēo-
ran.

sterten, v., *start*: pret. 3
sg., sterte, C 325, 337.
O.N. sterta.

steruen, v., *die*: pret. 2 sg.,
storue, V 151. O.E. steor-
fan.

stewerd, n., *steward*: C
325, 337, 367, 448, 451,
523, etc.; stuerd, C 547.
O.E. stīward.

stinken, v., *stink*: pret. 3
sg., stank, V 94. O.E.
stincan.

stond, v., *stand*: infin., C
267; pres. 3 sg., stondes
to, *inclines toward*, C
417; pres. part., stand-
yng, C 294; pret. 3 sg.,
stode, C 121, 349; stod,
V 257. O.E. standan,
stōd.

stones, n., *stones*: pl., V 62;
ston, V 284. O.E. stān.

stonk, see stinken.

storue, see steruen.

stounde, n., *time*: S 419,
V 213. O.E. stund.

stoure, n., *conflict*: C 504.
O. F. estour.

strek, v., *stretch*: infin., S
441. O. E. streccean.

strengþen, v. refl., *try (to
do something)*: infin., S
170. O. E. strengðu, n.

strete, n., *street*: S 395, V
5. O. E. strǣt.

strok, see stryke.

stroke, n., *stroke*: C 451;
pl., strokes, C 454;
strokys, C 515. O. E.
strīcan.

strong, adj., *strong*: S 12,
C 537; pl., stronge, V
62; stronge, adv., *strongly*: V 195, 273. O. E.
strong.

stryffe, n., *strife*: C 174.
O. F. estrif.

stryke, v., *strike, go*: pres.
imper. 2 sg., C 456;
pret. 3 sg., strok, V 9.
O. E. strīcan, *go, move,
run*.

sugge, suggen, v., see saie.

sulke, see selke.

sumdel, adv., *somewhat*:
V 237. O. E. sum +
dǣl.

stynt, v., *restrain*: infin.,
C 183; stynte, C 129.
O. E. styntan.

suete, see swete.

sueting, n., *darling*: S
222. O. E. swēte + M. E.
-ing.

sunne, n., *sin*: S 334, V
165; senne, S 194; pl.,
sunnen, V 177, 197. O.
E. synn.

sweren, v., *swear*: pret.
3 sg., S 421. O. E.
swerian.

swete, adj., *sweet*: S 127,
etc.; suete, S 176, 195,
C 313. O. E. swēte.

swiche, see selke.

swikele, adj., *deceiving*:
V 86, 103. O. E. swicol.

swin, n., *swine*: S 272. O.
E. swīn.

swinke, n., *labor*: S 134,
330, V 144. O. E. ge-
swinc.

swinken, v., *labor, work*:
pres. 3 sg., swinkeþ, S
140. O. E. swincan.

swiþe, adv., *soon*: S 411;
suiþe, S 156; *very*, S
302, V 12, 168, 190,
262, 273; *much*, V 4,
110. O. E. swīþe.

swor, v., see sweren.

swownyng, n., *swoon*: C
89. Cf. O. E. swōgan, ge-
swōgung, geswōwung.

sych, syche, see selk.

syde, n., *side*: C 80, 104. O.E. sīde.

syght, n., *sight*: C 6, 27, 296. O.E. gesiht.

syȝeng, see sike.

syȝhyng, n., *sighing*: C. 363. O.E. sīcan.

sykerly, see siker.

syluer, n., *silver*: C 53, 288. O.E. seolfor.

symple, adj., *simple, plain*: C 261. F. simple.

syng, see singe.

syre, see Cleges.

sytall, n., *citole*: C 102. O.F. citole.

sytte, see sitten.

tabull, n., *table*: C 9. O. F. table.

take, v., *take*: infin., S 106, C 128, 437; pres. imper. 2 sg., take, C 244; pret. 3 sg., toke, C 247, 323; p. p., I-take, V 43, *taken to*, V 178. O.N. taka.

tame, adj., *tame*: S 200, C 116. O.E. tam.

tary, v., *tarry, delay*: pres. imper. 2 sg., C 356; pret. 3 sg., taryd, C 401. O.E. tergan, influ-

enced in meaning by O. F. targer.

taute, see teken.

tayst, v., *taste*: infin., C 208. O.F. taster.

teken, v., *teach, show, direct*: pres. 2 sg., tekest, S 230; pret. 3 sg., taute, S 219. O.E. tǣcan.

telle, v., *tell*: infin., S 186, V 131, 187; tellen, S 242, V 206; pres. 1 sg., telle, S 387; tell, C 237, 315; 2 sg., tellest, S 52; 3 sg., tellys, C 532; pres. imper. 2 sg., tel, S 171, V 197; tell, C 530; pret. 3 sg., tolde, S 76; p. p., told, S 51. O.E. tellan.

ten, v., *draw, tug*: pret. 3 sg., tey, V 279. O.E. tēon.

tenandrys, n., *tenancies*: pl., C 93. O.F. tenance, tenanche.

tenant, n., *tenant*: pl., tenantes, C 19. O.F. tenant.

tene, n., *vexation*: S 158, 174. O.E. tēona.

tere, n., *tear*: pl., teres, S 358; terys, C 152. O.E. tēar.

tey, see **ten.**

þa, scribal error for þat (?):
S 140, 218.

þan, dem. pron., see **þat.**

thanke, v., *thank*: pres.
1 sg., C 111; pres. subj.
1 pl., thanke, C 227;
pret. 3 sg., thankyd, C
190, 507; 3 pl., than-
kyd, C 179. O.E. þan-
cian.

þarfore, see **þer-fore.**

þar-þoru, conj., *thereby*:
S 346.

þat, dem. pron., *that*: S
139, etc., V 118, etc.,
C 28, 39, 43, 335, etc.;
dat., þan, V 55, 108;
instr., þe, S 389, V 202;
þat = *of that*, S 51. O.
E. þæt.

þat, conj., *that* : S 11, 147,
etc., V 42, 136, etc.,
C 206, etc.; that a, C
236; *until that*, S 51,
299; *so that*, V 42, 75,
C 75, 77; þa, scribal
error (?), S 218. O.E.
þæt.

þat, rel. pron., *that, who*:
S 21, etc., V 119, etc.,
C 2, 16, 23, 48, etc.;
that which, S 165, V 285,
C 287, 513; þa, scribal

error (?), S 140; wam,
whom, S 387. O.E. þæt,
hwām.

þat, def. art., see **þe.**

þau, conj., *though*: S 45,
55, 97, 104, etc.; thoff,
C 70. O.E. þēah.

þe, pers. pron., see **þou.**

þe, def. art., *the*: nom., þe,
S 12, etc., V 16, 19, 31,
etc., C 49, 157, etc.;
the, C 25, 60, 112, 175,
etc.; þat, S 331, V 74,
76, 94; dat., þe, S 74,
141, V 1, 11, 41, 74,
etc., C 9, 39, etc.; ac-
cus. or dat. (?), þen, S 19,
22, 299; accus., þene, V
113, 126, 242, 280, 281,
287; þat, V 75, 78. O.E.
sē, sēo, þæt, etc.

the, v., *prosper*: infin., C
538. O.E. þēon.

theder, see **þider.**

þef, n., *thief*: V 102. O.E.
þēof.

þei, pers. pron., *they*: nom.,
C 31, 35, 36, etc.; they,
33, 87, 116, etc.; the,
C 163, 179; dat., þem,
C 209, 563; þeym, C
515; accus., þem, C 430.
See **hy.**

þen, conj., *than*: S 123,

266, 275, 426, V 8. O.E.
þonne.

þene, adv. & conj., *then*:
V 64; þenne, S 331, 365,
etc.; than, C 23. O.E.
þonne. See þo.

þer, adv., *there*: V 92, 262,
etc., C 82, 94, 107, 187;
þer, V 73; þere, V 94, 127,
152, 232, 233; þare, V
33, 171; thore, C 443;
thare, C 470; ther, C
453, 568, 576, etc. O.
E. þǽr.

þer, conj., *where*: S 21, 23,
etc., V 162. O.E. þær.

þer, poss. pron., *their*: C
48, 54, 167, etc.; ther,
C 575. O.N. þeirra. See
her.

þer-by, adv., *thereby*: C
197.

þer-fore, adv. + conj.,
therefore: S 196, V 202,
C 227; þarfore, C 580;
therfor, C 129; þer-for,
C 385.

þerinne, adv., *therein*: V
28, 78, 85, 126, 234.
O.E. þærinne.

þer-of, adv., *thereof*: S 9,
V 18, 24, 249.

þer-on, adv., *thereon*: C
200; þer-one, C 78.

þer-to, adv. + conj., *there-
to*: C 11, 238, 289, 438.

þes, n., *thighs*: pl., S 441.
O.E. þēoh.

þeþer, see þider.

þewe, n., *propriety*: dat.,
S 72. O.E. þēaw.

þi, poss. pron., *thy*: S 29,
147, V 247, C 113, 115,
246; þine, S 49, 190,
429, V 40, 134, 155,
211; þin, S 283, V 189,
C 417; thy, C 111, etc.
O.E. þīn.

þider, adv., *thither*: S 155,
262, V 13, 259; þidere,
V 268; þeþer, C 166;
theder, C 483. O. E.
þider.

þilke (þe + ilke): S 124,
258, 326, 419, V 148.
O.E. þilc.

þing, n., *thing*: S 32; swete
þing, *darling*, S 425; pl.,
thinge, C 275; thyng,
C 111; thynges, C 52,
53. O.E. þing.

thinke, v., *think, intend,
remember*: infin., C 496;
pres. 1 sg., thynke, C
527; pret. 3 sg., thouȝt,
C 63, 182, 208; þoute, V
125; þohute, V 13. O.E.
þencan.

þinkeþ, see þunche.

þis, dem. pron. & adj., *this*: S 27, 217, 289, C 14, 113, 135, etc.; thys, C 273, 307, 341, 422; pl., þes, S 275; þis, C 203. O.E. ðes, ðeos, ðis.

þo, conj., *when, then*: S 301, V 16, 23, 82, 170, 290, etc. O.E. þā. See þen.

thoff, see þau.

þohut, n., see þout.

þonk, n., *thanks*: V 158. O.E. þanc, þonc.

thore, see þer.

þoru, prep., *through*: S 125, 190; þar þoru, 346; throuȝhe, C 391. O.E. þurh.

þou, pers. pron., *thou*: nom., S 34, 38, etc., V 35, 38, etc., C 110, 268, 284, 411; þo, S 287; thow, C 263, 269, 412, 436; dat., þe, S 33, 34, 37, 40, 130, etc., C 287; accus., þe, S 39, V 51, 122, C 111, 263, 270, 348; the, C 436. O.E. þū, þē. See þi and ȝe.

thouȝt, v., see thinke.

thouȝt, n., see þout.

þousent, n., *thousand*: V 203. O.E. þūsend.

þout, n., *thought*: S 118, 147, 430; thouȝt, C 128, 148; þohut, V 223. O.E. þōht.

þre, num., *three*: V 153; thre, C 350. O.E. þrēo.

throuȝhe, see þoru.

thryfte, n., *thrift*: C 347, 466, 478. O.N. þrift.

þunche, v. impers., *seem*: infin., S 238; pres. 3 sg., þinkeþ, S 218, 286; pret. 3 sg., þoute, V 94; thouȝt, C 516. O.E. þyncan.

þurst, n., *thirst*: S 310, 312, V 67. O.E. þurst.

þus, adv., *thus*: S 24, V 158; thus, C 64, 354. O.E. þus.

thy, see þi.

thyng, see þing.

þynke, see thinke.

thyrd, num., *third*: C 286, etc. O.E. þridda.

thys, see þis.

til, prep., *until*: S 292, 293; tyll, C 573; to, S 354. O.N. til.

tille, v., *till*: pres. subj. 2 sg., S 440. O.E. ti-lian.

time, n., *time*: S 124, V 263;
tyme, C 4, 113, etc. O. E.
tima.

to, prep., *to*: S 40, etc., V
17, etc., C 16, etc.; *until*,
C 74, 163, 512, 564;
sign of the infin., S 7,
etc., V 6, etc., C 54, etc.
O. E. to.

to, adv., *too*: S 343, V 81,
98, etc., C 331, 426.
O. E. to.

to-breke, v., *break down*,
break to pieces: infin.,
V 63; pret. part., to-
broke, V 19. O. E. tobre-
can.

to-dai, n., *to-day*: S 316,
404.

togedere, adv., *together*: V
156, 214, 216; togeþer,
C 167; to-geder, C 462.
O. E. tō-gædere.

to-ʒeines, prep., *against*:
V 95. O. E. to-gēanes.

tokenyng, *token, sign*: C
220, 223, 552. O. E. tāc-
nung.

to-morow, adv., *to-morrow*:
C 232; to-morowe, C 239.

tong, n., *tongue*: C 355.
O. E. tunge.

to niʒt, adv., *to-night*: V
191.

torn, see **tourne.**

toune, n., *town*: S 70, 347.
O. E. tūn.

tourne, v., *turn*: pres. subj.
3 sg., S 147; imper. 2 sg.
torn, S 109, 113; pret.
part., turnd, S 430. O. E.
tyrnan, turnian.

to-werd, prep., *toward*: C
88. O. E. tōweard.

traueyled, v., *travelled*:
pret. 3 sg., C 16. O. F.
travailer.

traueyll, n., *labor, journey*: C 352. O. F. travail.

tre, n., *tree*: C 218, pl.,
treys, C 206. O. E. trēow.

treie, n., *affliction, grief*:
S 158. O. E. trega.

treuly, adv., *truly*: C 29,
105, 143; trewly, C 142;
treulye, C 228; trew, C
490. O. E. trēowlīce.

trewe, adj., *true*: S 95,
121; trew, C 77, 125,
308; compar., trewer, S
122. O. E. trēowe, trȳwe.

trinyte, n., *Trinity*: C 202.
O. F. trinite.

trouþe, n., *truth*: S 252.
O. E. trēowð.

trouue, v., *believe*: pres. 1
sg., S 369; 2 sg., troustu,
S 370. O. E. trūwian.

trumper, n., *trumpeter*: pl.,
trumpers, C 100. O.F.
trompeor, trompere, &c.
truse, v., *pack*: C 348.
O.F. trosser, trouser.
twake, v., *thwack*: infin.,
C 358. O.N. þjökka.
twenti, num., *twenty*: S
270. O.E. twentig.
two, num., *two*: V 32, C 83,
173; tuo, V 73. O.E.
twā.
tyde, n., *time*: C 90, 188.
O.E. tīd.
tyll, see til.
tyne, see time.

uaile, v., *avail, assist*: infin., S 188. O.F. valoir.
valew, n., *value*: C 76.
O.F. value.
vansyd, v., *advanced*: pret.
3 sg., C 569. O.E. avan-
cer.
vend, v., see wende.
verament, adv., *verily,
truly*: C 189, 237. O.F.
verablement.
vif, n., *woman*: S 83. O.E.
wīf.
vilani, n., *baseness, shame*,
the opposite to curteisi:
S 128; uilani, S 250. O.F.
vilainie.

vilte, n., *meanness, shame*:
S 47. O.F. vilté.
vind, v., *find*: pres. 3 sg.,
V 253. O.E. findan.
vn-couered, v., *uncovered*:
pret. 3 sg., C 373. O.F.
cuvrir, covrir.
vnder, prep., *under*: S 5.
O.E. under.
vnderneth, prep., *under-
neath*: C 194.
vnto, prep., *unto*: C 144,
386.
volf, vuolf, see wolf.
vow, n., *vow*: C 522. O.F.
veu, vou.
vox, n., *fox*: V 1, 16, 81,
96, 107, 113, 123, 127,
131, 139, 157, 176, 188,
196, 221, 231, 238, 239,
242, 245, 260; wox, V
12, 33, 37, 293. O.E.
fox.
vp, adv., *up*: C 166, 244,
278, 310; vppe, C 97.
O.E. ūp, upp.
vpon, prep., *upon*: C 57,
218, etc. O.E. uppon.
vpstond, v., *stand up*: infin., C 197.
vs, see we.
vsscher, n., *door-keeper*: C
310, 313, 460. O.F. us-
sier.

Vter, pr. n.: C 4.

vyset, v., *visit*: infin., C23.
O. F. visiter.

waie, n., *way*: S 1; wei, S
395; wey, V 5, C 159,
254. O.E. weg.

wakese, v., *grow, wax*:
infin., S 182; wex, C
151. O.E. weaxan.

wal, n., *wall*: V 10,
19; walle, V 11. O.E.
weall.

walken, v., *walk*: pret. 3
sg. walkyd, C 97. O.E.
wealcan.

wane, see þat.

wanten, v., *want, lack*:
pret. 3 pl., wantyd, C 116.
O.N. vanta.

war, inter. adv., *where*: V
137. O.E. hwǣr.

warm, adj., *warm*: pl.,
warme, S 225. O.E.
wearm.

warryng, n., *denying*: C
439.

war-to, inter. adv., *why*:
S 313.

waschen, v., *wash*: pret. 3
pl., wesch, C 154. O.E.
wæscan, waxsan, etc.

wat, inter. pron., *what*: S
29, 64, etc., V 33, 152,
etc.; what, S 172, C 91.
O.E. hwæt.

wat, rel. pron., *that which*:
C 126. O.E. hwæt.

wat, indef. pron., *what*:
V 89. O.E. hwæt.

wat, adv., *why*: V 163.
O. E. hwæt.

wat, interj.: S 235, 285.
O.E. hwæt.

water, n., *water*: V 92,
93, 94. O.E. wæter.

way, see **weien.**

we, interj., *alas*: S 115.
O.E. wā, O.N. vei.

we, pers. pron., *we*: C 139,
141, etc.; ouer, C 139,
218, 221; owre, C 143;
vs, C 57, 140, 174, etc.
O.E. wē, ūre, ūs.

wedded, part. adj., *wedded*: S 8; wedde, S 137;
wedyd, C 125. O.E.
weddian.

wede, n., *garments*: pl., C
327. O.E. wǣd.

wede, n., *pledge, mortgage*:
C 62. O.E. wedd.

weder, adv., *whither*: V
244, 245. O.E. hwider,
hwæder.

weien, v., *weigh*: pret. 3
sg., way, V 237. O.E.
wegan.

wel, adv., *very much* : S 13, 82, 94; *very*, V 16, 66, 248, C 337; *well*, S 212, 226, C 126, 127, 141, 280. O.E. wēl.

welcome, adj., *welcome*: S 26, 255, 425 ; welcomen, S 167; compar., welcomore, S 426. O.E. wilcuma, *n.*

welde, v., *wield, rule*: infin., S 83, 146, 325; pres. 3 sg., weld, C 56. O.E. wealdan.

welpe, n., *whelp*: S 287; welp, S 372. O.E. hwelp.

wen, conj., *when*: S 198, V 75, 268; wenne, interrog., S 284, V 151; when, C 49, 88, etc.; when þat, C 496. O.E. hwænne, hwonne.

wende, v. tr., *turn*: S 118, 151, 181. O.E. wendan.

wende, v. inter. & reflex., *turn, wend, go* : pret. 3 sg., wend, S 17; wente, S 149; wente him, S 19, 155; wente hire, S 406; pret. 3 pl., wente, C 80; pret. part., wend, S 345; wende, *gone*, V 74; vend, *come*, V 159. O.E. wendan.

wene, v., *ween, believe*: pres. 1 sg., V 128; pret. 1 sg., wende, V 217; pret. 3 sg., wende, V 275; wend, C 405; pret. part., I-wend, V 134. O.E. wēnan.

wenne, n., *joy, bliss*: S 26. O.E. wynn.

wepen, n., *weep*: pret. 3 sg., wep, V 107; wepyd, C 95, 106. O.E. wēpan, wēop.

wepne, n., *weapon*: V 286. O.E. wǣpen.

wer, conj., *where*: S 284, C 47; wer þat, C 567. O.E. hwǣr.

were, v., *wear*: infin., C 554; pret. 3 pl., weryd, C 327. O.E. werian.

werk, n., *work*: pl., werkes, S 245. O.E. weorc.

werld, see **world**.

wer-mide, adv., *wherewith*: V 112.

wern, v. *deny, refuse*: inf., C 464, 473. O.E. wiernan.

wernyng, v. n., *refusal*: C 316.

werre, n., *war*: C 16. O.F. werre.

wes, was, ves, were, weren, v., see **be**.

werþ, v., see worþe.

wesch, see waschen.

weste, v., see wite.

wex, v., see wakese.

wey, see waie.

what, see wat.

what þat euer, pron., *whatever*: C 364, 415.

when, see wen.

where-for, conj.: C 510.

wheþer, conj., *whether*: C 35, 288, 308. O.E. hwæðer.

who, inter. pron., *who*: C 329. O.E. hwā.

wi, conj., *why*: S 64, 315; why, C 510. O.E. hwȳ.

wicchecrafft, n., *witch-craft*: S 206. O.E. wicce-cræft.

wiche, v., *use witchcraft*: infin., S 353. O.E. wiccian.

widewene, n., *widow*: gen. pl., widewene, V 201. O.E. widwe, widuwe.

wif, n., *woman, wife*: S 27, 121, 315, V 154; wiue, V 212, 228; wyfe, C 77, 83, 122, etc.; wyff, C 25; pl., wiues, S 303. O.E. wīf.

wiis, see wis.

wiit, n., *wit, intelligence*: V 70, 124. O.E. wit [t].

wile, conj., *while*: S 70, 438. O.E. hwīlum.

wile, n., *time*: S 103, 444. O.E. hwīl.

Wilekin, pr. n.: S 43, 229, 236, 255, 386, 400, 409, 423, 425, 427; Wile-kinne, S 407.

wille, v., *will*: pres. 1 sg., S 87, etc., V 131, 146, 231; wile, S 191, 241; wote, V 175; wyll, C 239, 397; 2 sg., wolt, S 241; woltoce, V 196; wyll, C 415; 3 sg., wolle, S 369; wyll, C 287; pret. 1 sg., wolde, S 334, 431, V 179; wold, C 120, 528; 3 sg., wolde, S 238, V 46, 171; wold, C 19, 20, 23, etc.; 2 pl., wold, C 513; 3 pl., wold, C 46; pret. subj. 1 sg., wolde, S 64, V 179; 2 sg., woldest, S 172; 3 sg., wolde, S 131, 238. O.E. willan.

wille, n., *will*: S 29, etc., V 95, 96; wil, S 53; wylle, C 407. O.E. willa.

willi (wille + I), S 35, 41, etc.

wimmon, n., *woman* : S
8; womon, S 122; wi-
mon, S 205; pl., wim-
men, V 8; O.E. wīfman.

winde, v. intr., *wind,
turn, go* : infin., V 76;
pret. 3 sg., wond, V 22.
O.E. windan.

winne, n., see **wenne**.

wis, adj., *wise* : S 4; wiis,
V 105. O.E. wīs.

wise, n., *wise, manner* : S
15, V 3. O.E. wīse.

wite, v., *know* : infin., S
29, 307; pres. 1 sg., wot,
S 284, V 191; pret. 1 sg.,
weste, S 79, 237; pret.
3 sg., weste, S 220, V 59,
238; wyst, C 280. O.E.
witan.

witerli, adv., *certainly* : S
232. O.N. vitrliga.

wiþ, prep., *with* : S 23,
174, etc.; wiz, S 162;
wīth, C 54, 81, 82;
wyth, C 502, 578; *by
means of*, S 207; wiþ þat,
provided that, S 192,
226, 386; *toward*, V
247. O.E. wiþ.

with-draw, v. : infin., C
263; imper. 2 sg., C 332.

wiþ-houten, prep., *with-
out* : S 36, 96; wiþ-

houte, S 392; wiþouten,
V 25, 142; with-outen,
C 273, 390; with-oute,
C 264; with-outyn, C
50, 299; with-out, C 297,
316; with-owtyn, C 459.
O.E. wiþūtan.

wiþinne, adv., *within* :
V 11. O.E. wiþinnan.

wiz, prep., see **wiþ**.

wo, inter. pron., *who* : V
122, 127. O.E. hwā.

wo, n., *woe* : S 303, V 2,
53, etc., C 90. O.E. wā.

wo, adj., *woeful* : S 298,
379. þat me is wo = 'I am
sorry,' S 379. O.E. wā.

wod, adj., *mad* : S 182,
286, V 258. O.E. wōd.

wode, n., *wood, forest* : V
1, 109. O.E. wudu.

wold, v., see **wille**.

woldi (wold+i), S 88, 243,
etc.

wolf, n., *wolf* : V 108,
118, 129, 137, 150, etc.;
volf, V 148; vuolf, V
221; wolfe, V 181. O.E.
wulf.

woltou (wolt + þou), V
186, 196.

won, n., *dwelling* : S 21.
Cf. O.E. (ge)wuna, wu-
nian, wunung.

won, n., *quantity, store*: S 132.

won, adj., see **wonte**.

wond, v., see **winde**.

wonde, v., *turn aside, hesitate*: S 138, C 120. O. E. wändian.

wonder, n., *wonder*: S 359. O.E. wundor.

wone, n., *hope, thought*: C 319. O.N. vān.

wone, n. v., *dwell*: pret. 3 sg., wonede, S 20; pret. 3 pl., woneden, V 262; pret. part., woned, *accustomed, used, wont*, V 105. O.E. wunian. See **wonte**.

wonne, v., *won*: pret. part., S 58. O.E. winnan.

wonte, adj., *wont*: C 91; won, C 112. O.E. wunod.

word, n., *word*: S 240, V 132, C 367; pl., word, S 159; wordes, V 148, C 406. O.E. word.

world, n., *world*: S 243; worlde, V 162, 163; werld, C 14; gen. sg., worldes, V 161. O.E. weorold.

worschype, n., *worship, honor*: C 39, 56; wyr-schyp, C 79. O.E. weorþscipe.

worschypped, p. p. a., *honored*: C 414.

worse, **wors**, adj., *worse*, S 378, V 202. O.E. wyrs.

worþe, v., *become*: pres. 1 sg., worþe, V 191; pres. 3 sg., worþ, V 298; pres. subj. 3 sg., worþe, S 213, V 96; pret. 3 sg., werþ, V 66. O.E. weorþan.

wose, pron., *whoso*: S 445; wose-euer, S 361. Cf. O.E. swāhwāswā.

wot, v., see **wite**.

wou, n., *wrong*: S 96. O. E. wōh.

wouing, v., *plying*: n., *wooing*: S 125. O.E. wōgian.

wous, adj., *ready*: V 12. O.E. fūs.

wox, see **vox**.

wraþþen, v., *make angry*: infin., S 41. O.E. (ge)-wrāþian.

wrecche, n., *wretch*: S 298, 313, V 253; wrecke, V 288. O.E. wrecca.

wrenche, n., *trick, artifice*: dat., V 84. O.E. wrenc.

wringen, v., *wing*: pret. 3

sg., wrong, C 95, 106.
O.E. wringan.

wrogge, n., *frog*: pl.,
wroggen, V 256. O.E.
frogga.

wroþ, adj., *angry*: V 220.

wroþe, adv., *angrily*: V
291. O.E. wrāð.

wrong, n., *wrong*: S 10.
O.E. wrang.

wroug, see **wringen**.

wrout, p.p., see **wy, che.**

wyde, adj., *wide*: C 93.
O.E. wīd.

wyfe, wyfe, see **wīf.**

wyght, adj., *nimble, strong*:
C 3, 295, 537; wyȝht,
C 33. O.N. vīgr, m.,
vīgt, n.

wylde, adj., *wild*: pl., C
116. O.E. wilde.

wylle, n., see **will.**

wyneng, v. n., *winning,
gain*: C 317.

wyped, v., *wiped.* pret. 3
sg., C 152. O. E. wīpian.

wyrche, v., *work, perform*:
inf., C 164; p. p., wrout,
S 112; wrought, C 213; i-
wrought, C 342. O.E.
wycran.

wyst, see **wite.**

wytte, n., *wight, man*: C
521. O.E. wiht.

Y, see **wite.**

ybe, ybouȝt, ydiȝt, ydon,
etc., see **be, bie, diȝt,
don,** etc.

ye, demonstr. pron., instru-
mental case: C 236.
O.E. þē, þӯ.

yȝoue, v., pret. part., see
ȝeue.

y-nouȝ, see **nou.**

y-slawe, v., pret. part., see
slo.

ywis, adv., see **wis.**